the tantric curse

Anupama Garg was born in Kanpur, Uttar Pradesh. She has studied chemistry, business management and law. She has been training under her guru, Baba Batuk Nath ji, a renowned Tantric and head of the Bhoot Nath Charitable Trust, for the last twenty-two years. Presently, she conducts experiential workshops for corporates, hospitals, college and schools under the name 'Life by Choice'. She also devotes time at the ashram of her guru, the Bhoot Nath Ashram.

Anupama is married and lives with her husband and son.

the tantric
curse

. . . .

ANUPAMA GARG

RUPA

Published by
Rupa Publications India Pvt. Ltd 2015
7/16, Ansari Road, Daryaganj
New Delhi 110002

Sales Centres:

Allahabad Bengaluru Chennai
Hyderabad Jaipur Kathmandu
Kolkata Mumbai

ISBN: 978-81-291-3752-4

First impression 2015

10 9 8 7 6 5 4 3 2 1

The moral right of the author has been asserted.

Dedicated to my guru
BABA BATUK NATH JI.
Faith is the ability to surrender completely,
that has to be lived to be understood.

1

1980

AMAVASYA IS A night without the moon; all is dark and appears strangely mysterious. The following night marks the new phase of the moon. On one such amavasya night, an eight-year-old girl walked into Shaktidham, a sadhanasthal. The Goddess of Tantra, Kamakhya, was the deity of Shaktidham.

Concealed in the wooded outskirts of Varanasi, Shaktidham had no boundaries as the place was feared. Rumours claimed that human beings were sacrificed to attain power, by the sadhak of Shaktidham, who possessed the power to change anyone's fate. People said that he had the power to kill and perform miracles, but a power that one should stay away from. Stories were being whispered that he was powerful enough to change the mind of God when things were going wrong, and could make everything go wrong when things were going right.

Tonight, Shaktidham was reverberating with intense chants. The girl moved towards the source of the chants, as if in a trance. In her mind's eye, she could see a triangular havan vedi, where the age-old sacred fire ritual (havan) is offered to the deity. Vedi is the structure constructed to perform the havan. In her mind's eye, she could see the sadhak making offerings to the glowing sacred fire and the two statues of Goddess Kali. The sadhak suddenly stopped, as in his mind's eye, he could see dainty feet moving towards the sadhanasthal. Every step was bringing an unknown but potent force closer. The fire burned brilliantly, as if in welcome.

Inside the ashram, Satya picked up the sacred bell. It began to oscillate in a rhythm, without him moving his hand. He stood up, startled. 'What was this force, which had changed the entire vibrations in the temple?' he thought, puzzled. He had never encountered a situation like this before and didn't know what to expect or do.

As the girl walked in the direction towards the sadhanasthal, a hand came out of nowhere and caught her wrist firmly. The girl looked like a doll, in a white dress with frills, and her curly brown hair tied with a white ribbon fell to her waist. Her skin was milky white, with a soft pink glow. She had large almond-shaped brown eyes, which feared only one thing—the dreams they saw when they were closed. She looked at the hand which pulled her; it was strong with long fingers that still held her wrist tight. It had pulled her into a room that she was walking past, without her even noticing. She looked up and saw a boy with thick black hair falling on his forehead. He was looking at her, with his naughty twinkling eyes and a smile that would set any heart fluttering in a few years. He was a boy with chiselled features, clear wheat complexion and long curled eyelashes. He was wearing a white kurta and pyjama. He was tall, with an athletic built that indicated regular physical activity. That day was Mahashivaratri and Krishnam had turned thirteen.

'Where were you going? Nobody is allowed to move around while Baba is conducting his puja,' said Krishnam. 'What is your name and where have you come from?' he asked.

She looked at him, startled and replied, 'Rhea' as she broke down and started crying. She did not seem like a stranger, not even this first time, thought Krishnam a little mystified.

He looked at her for a second and then embraced her. 'What happened? Don't cry, Rhea…'

'Who is it, Krishnam?' asked a deep-throated voice, from a distance. The sadhak who spoke had a body of a warrior, and looked like royalty, with thick long hair falling over his shoulders. His skin glowed like that of most sadhaks and his eyes were full of tenderness.

He was wearing a black robe and a long rudraksh necklace, with a huge pendant that bore the image of Goddess Kamakhya coming out from the naval of Lord Shiva.

'Baba,' they replied in unison.

'Rhea lost her way and came here by mistake.'

Satya picked up Rhea; she looked at him and stopped crying.

'She has made no mistake, Krishnam. She has come to her home,' replied Satya, with a warm smile.

He was Satya—the truth. Truth is always simple. One, however, has to be simple to understand what is simple and that's the toughest part.

The next day, the newspaper carried a small article on the local page, stating that an NRI couple had met with an accident on the highway; it was a couple of kilometres away from Shaktidham. It involved a head-on collision with a truck loaded with LPG cylinders. Both the vehicles and its passengers were burnt to ashes. The couple had come to visit Varanasi with their only daughter.

A month earlier

As Rhea drifted into the world of dreams, she would often live the future before it actually manifested into the material world. She would know of significant events that would unfold in the future. She would wait anxiously for the time when her dream unfolded itself into the present time and space. People love to know what the future holds; she did not wish to know, but ironically, she had no choice. She waited for that moment when her dream would unfold into a reality, which was inevitable. Every living moment was fearful and traumatic after that dream she had tonight.

'Mom, I saw a big fire. Both you and Dad were burnt in it,' said Rhea. She had woken up and gone into her parent's room, seeking her mother.

'Oh, my poor darling, you had a bad dream!' said her mother, pulling her onto the bed.

'Mommy, it was not just a dream,' replied Rhea in frustration and fear.

'Oh darling, sleep now, Mommy is with you.'

To know and wait for an impending disaster is more painful than facing the final moment. Unpredictability of events in life is a blessing. To not know is a gift and to know is pain; only someone who has experienced this pain can understand it.

Nevertheless, one can acquire the power through Tantra, to change the unwanted, as one then realizes that the future exists in probability. The outcome of an event can be altered, or its effect reduced or enhanced, by altering the actions, which lead to a probability. The power to alter comes with an understanding of what can be changed and what is inevitable. A person who possesses this power also understands when actions need to be altered and when they must let the events take a natural course, to achieve the desired results.

Like any other raw power, this power comes with immense responsibility. Its channelization lies in the wisdom of its user. To know how to use power is the most critical aspect of any power. Tantra is a field of raw power, and can be used to destroy or heal. No action is bereft of consequences; it is a universal law, and Tantrics are no exceptions to this law.

Rhea was admitted in grade three, in the same school as Krishnam, who was in grade eight. It was one of the best public schools in the city.

2

THE WEATHER WAS getting warmer in April, by which time Rhea was slowly settling into her new environment. Satya and Krishnam had been taking care of her since her arrival, a month ago.

Rhea's dream came back one night, and she kept murmuring something in her sleep. Satya heard her, and came at once. He placed his hand on her head, which seemed to calm her down.

Since her childhood, Rhea had known that her dreams manifested into reality. In the realm of science and logic, such things remain unexplained. In her dream, she would see a cottage painted in saffron, two idols of Goddess Kali placed on a platform; Goddess Kali had her right foot on Lord Shiva. She saw that the idol on the right had a serene expression and the one on the left had an aggressive expression; both had their tongues out. There was a huge brass lamp that was always lit.

Rhea had seen various other things in this recurring dream. She saw a pair of khadau (wooden sandals) on the side, below the platform on which the statues stood. A black wooden snake was kept beside it. At times, she saw a havan vedi with firewood burning in it. At other times, in front of the idols of Goddess Kali, she would see the silhouette of a petite woman with long curly hair falling to her waist. She could almost smell the distinctive fragrance of that space—which was a mix of fresh flowers and sandalwood; the smell was so vivid in her dream, it felt as if it was real. Rhea could identify that fragrance, if she was ever to encounter it.

The next day, Krishnam and Rhea were sitting on either side of Satya at the breakfast table, having a glass of milk with honey.

'This is awesome,' said Rhea.

'Haven't you had milk and honey before?' asked Krishnam, surprised.

'No, Mommy used to give me chocolate milkshake,' she said

ever so softly and started crying.

Satya picked her up and put her on his lap. 'Devima has blessed Rhea with a new family. Come on Krishnam, you take her to the gaushala (cowshed), go with Chander. Show her the cows and how they are milked.'

'Baba, can I show her that massive beehive in the woods?' asked Krishnam. Satya nodded in affirmation, emphasizing that he goes only with Chander.

'Rhea, come I will help you with your shoes,' said Krishnam, holding her hand and leading her towards the room that the three shared. Satya smiled looking at them. Krishnam took her to the washroom first and washed her face. 'There is no point crying in this situation, you have to accept it,' he said, as he helped her with the shoes.

Chander was Satya's most trusted man. He was six and a half feet tall, very fair with blond hair up to his shoulders and deep blue eyes. He was extremely fit, with a well-developed body, and not an inch of fat. His forehead bore a scar indicative of an earlier deep wound.

In other words, Chander was his shadow, and he had Satya's instructions not to hesitate using his weapon whenever necessary. He was well versed with weapons and their usage; he always carried a loaded gun on him. Particular about his weapons, he oiled and cleaned them often, as he wanted to be sure that they fire when required, without hindrance. He also carried a broad knife, concealed under his clothes. Chander spoke Hindi with a foreign accent.

Looking at Chander and Krishnam, Rhea was amused, and asked, 'Have trousers and shirt gone out of fashion here?'

Krishnam replied, 'The ashram's dress code is dhoti and kurta. It is the most comfortable outfit and doesn't restrict body movements.'

Krishnam then held Rhea's hand as they were walking towards

the cowshed. Suddenly, something caught Rhea's attention—it was a small cottage painted in saffron. She stopped in her path and asked, 'What is that?'

'It is Baba's sadhanasthal, where he conducts his pujas.'

'What's a sadhanasthal, Krishnam?'

'The place where sadhaks conduct pujas and rituals to pursue their spiritual path is called a sadhanasthal.'

'Can I go there and see it?' questioned Rhea.

'No, I can't allow you to go there without Baba's permission.'

'Have you been to the sadhanasthal ever?' asked Rhea.

'Yes, I am Baba's shishya, so I have the permission. Today too I will go there to clean it, as I have to make preparations for the puja,' he replied.

'Can I also help you clean the place?' asked Rhea enthusiastically.

'Sadhanasthal is a place where only sadhaks are allowed to go,' replied Krishnam.

'But I have visited the sadhanasthal many times,' she said softly.

'In your dreams!' replied Krishnam, amused. Rhea kept silent as they ran to catch up with Chander.

Shaktidham was spread out over an area of 40 acres. Krishnam held Rhea's hand tight as they entered the heavily wooded area to see the huge beehive. They were following a trail and the two walked behind Chander. Rhea stopped for a moment; she stood silently looking at a huge tree. Krishnam stood with her and felt the cool breeze blowing through the woods.

'Isn't it quiet?' she said in a whisper.

'Does it scare you?' asked Krishnam.

Rhea looked at him in astonishment and replied, 'No, it's silent, but it is throbbing with life.'

He looked at her, astounded, but said nothing.

Krishnam pointed towards a beehive, standing in front of a

tree. 'In a couple of weeks, there will be enough honey in this hive, and then it will be extracted.'

Chander stood behind them, smiling. On their return, they went to the cowshed, where Krishnam explained the milking process to Rhea. It was the first time she saw cows being milked.

'So, do you like your new home, Rhea?' asked Satya, on their return.

'Yes, Baba, but I loved the forest the most.'

'Why?' he asked.

She replied, 'It is full of life and untouched by humans.' Satya looked at her and smiled.

A few days passed by in their regular chores. One day, Chander was teaching Krishnam karate.

Satya and Rhea were watching, when she asked, 'Baba, what does karate mean?'

'Karate as a word means 'empty-handed' in Japanese. It is a martial art in which you fight an opponent empty-handed,' he replied, while looking at Krishnam's movements.

They sat watching Chander and Krishnam practise. Before and after the bout, the two opponents bowed to each other.

Satya explained, 'Rhea, karate is an art that emphasizes on attitude over technique. This procedure of bowing is called Rei. Bowing to your opponent is an expression of courtesy; it is an acknowledgement of the fact that decorum must be maintained.'

Rhea was now settling in, adapting to the pace of life at Shaktidham. One night, she had her recurring dream again.

She saw Satya in the saffron cottage in front of Goddess Kali.

She was rattled by her dream and woke up in a trance. 'Baba, take me to that cottage in saffron with the two idols of Ma. Take me to Ma!' She stood on her bed stiff and described the sadhanasthal, as she had seen it in her dream numerous times.

'Baba, she hasn't been to the sadhanasthal, it is always closed!' exclaimed Krishnam, astounded.

Satya silently picked her up, held Krishnam's hand and took them straight to the sadhanasthal. It was the most sacred place on earth for Satya and Krishnam. Krishnam hurriedly opened the doors. There were two statues of Goddess Kali depicting both aspects of the Goddess—the benevolent, and the slayer.

It was exactly what she had seen in her dream. She recognized everything, even the fragrance. All the objects were in their exact position, from the khadau to the snake, the vedi, and even the oil lamp.

'Krishnam, she had been to the sadhanasthal in her dream,' said Satya. 'Finally she has come...'

'Who, Baba?' asked Krishnam, flabbergasted.

'She is the new face of Tantra. She will reach the heights of sadhana that no one has ever reached in our lineage; the Goddess herself blesses her. She is gifted, but will have to understand how to use her powers wisely. Our culture and times have changed and she will have a tough battle.'

Rhea slowly walked towards the statues, still in a trance. She reached and hugged the statue on the left which depicted the slayer form of Goddess Kali.

'Baba, isn't she just supposed to touch Devima's feet?' Krishnam was totally perplexed. Satya signalled him to stay quiet. Rhea then bent down to touch the feet of Goddess Kali.

'Baba,' whispered Krishnam, 'I can't comprehend what is happening here.'

'The sacred Tantra Shastra, which originates from Lord Shiva, is being maligned as never before. She will be the protector of the lineage and the vidya, so she has to be protected and initiated. The fire in her eyes has to be transformed into compassion. She has a streak of destruction in her just like her Mother Goddess; this streak if channelized can destroy egos, and help transform and recreate. It is a streak which without direction and balance would be a wild fire.

'This amavasya I will initiate her, starting her with the first steps of sadhana,' said Satya, with a sparkle in his eyes.

'Baba, I do not understand anything,' said Krishnam.

'You will when the time comes,' said Satya.

3

THE SUMMER HAD set in completely; as usual, May was dry and hot. The afternoons are extreme, as hot winds start blowing across the northern plains of India. Schools across much of Northern India close for summer vacation and reopen in July.

On the morning before amavasya, Satya called Krishnam and Rhea to the sadhanasthal and made them sit facing Goddess Kali. 'Rhea, you have a lot of unanswered questions; I can show you the path that will answer all those questions. The path is of sadhana, but it requires complete faith, dedication and perseverance. There are no shortcuts and it will not be easy. Physical and mental fitness is mandatory, without which you will not be able to perform or progress in your sadhana. I can only show you the path as a Guru, but you will have to traverse it alone. I can initiate you on the path of sadhana if you wish to, on amavasya night i.e. tomorrow. '

Rhea, who was listening to him intently, got up, and touching Satya's feet, said, 'Baba, I will not let you down.'

Satya put his hand on her head to bless her and said smilingly, 'A guru's pride is his shishya.'

The next day, Rhea was excited, and it showed. She was up and about since morning, in anticipation of what was going to come. Her day didn't seem to pass, everything seemed slower than its normal pace. She had her lunch as usual, but Satya had told her and Krishnam to eat light now, and maintain an empty stomach before coming to the sadhanasthal that evening.

While they were cleaning the sadhanasthal that evening,

Rhea told Krishnam, 'The fragrance here is exactly as it was in my dreams.'

After finishing, they both showered and got into their clothes for the sadhanasthal.

The evening was a little pleasant after a short dust storm. Both the shishyas (disciples) waited for Satya, their guru, to accompany him to the sadhanasthal. Satya entered first, followed by Krishnam and Rhea, as if in order of their positions. Satya bowed in front of the idols of Goddess Kali, with his right hand on his heart, and the disciples followed it too. Satya sat on his asana, he asked Krishnam to bring his and a new one for Rhea.

As Krishnam handed the asana to Rhea, Satya said, 'This is for you Rhea, you will be using this asana for your sadhana.'

Both of them settled in their places.

Satya looked at Rhea and answered some of the questions which were going through her mind. 'Let me start by explaining to you the significance of initiating you on amavasya. The Hindu calendar follows the lunar cycle; amavasya is considered a night of the new moon and it signifies the start of a new lunar cycle. It also symbolizes the start of a new phase of your life. During amavasya, the combined gravitational pull of the moon and the sun, creates subtle vibrations which are conducive to spiritual growth.'

Satya explained, 'The first lesson I am going to give you is on "Om" and how to chant it. Om is a complete mantra in itself and represents all that manifests and all that is unmanifested. Om is a combination of three sounds, "AA", "AU" and "MA", and together they make AUM or Om. The three vibrations represent creation (Brahma), preservation (Vishnu) and destruction (Shiva) symbolized by the Trinity as per Hindu dharma.

'Now observe my lips when I chant Om. The sound of Om starts with a circle and ends with the lips converging at a point. The lips are open wide in a circular pout with "A", they slowly start closing in with "U", and then converge to a point with "M".

The outward expansion of our lips symbolizes the outside world, and when the lips converge to a point, it symbolizes our journey inward.'

Satya closed his eyes, started chanting Om to demonstrate, and then asked them to join in. Both Krishnam and Rhea chanted Om twenty-one times in unison with him. The sadhanasthal resonated with the vibrations of their chanting.

Satya opened his eyes. 'Regular practice of Om ceases the discordant chatter of your mind,' he said.

'Every day before breakfast and dinner, you should practise the chanting of Om with Krishnam,' said Satya.

4

IT WAS THE second week since school had reopened, and both Rhea and Krishnam were back to their routine. On the weekend they were given a new room with two separate beds. Satya's room was across theirs, through the kitchen and dining area. By now they were quite attached to each other; each morning Krishnam would wake Rhea up by tickling her feet, and she would wake up laughing. Krishnam's face was the first one she saw every morning, and she was getting fond of him. Upon waking, she would look towards the small statue of Goddess Kali on her bedside and bow to seek her blessings.

Like diligent disciples, each morning they would chant Om at the sadhanasthal, and then proceed to school after breakfast.

Krishnam was an academically outstanding student and was exceptional at sports. He was therefore popular with the students and staff, but he was also reserved. Sports—to a large extent—not only builds your character but reveals it too.

Krishnam was playing football along with some children during the school recess and Rhea stood watching the game. As

Krishnam dribbled the ball to the goalpost, a ninth grader tackled him deliberately, tripping him. Krishnam got up, brushed himself and his clothes, but did not react. The game resumed with a penalty, which Krishnam converted into a goal.

The game carried on and Krishnam's team was again in possession of the ball; they were closing in towards the opponent's goalpost. This time, another player from his team was closing in to try and score the second goal. The same ninth grader, Rahul, attacked the boy by pushing him; he fell face down on the ground. The game came to a halt and everyone around was at a standstill. Some of the boys rushed to help him to his feet, after a moment's shock. The boy was in a lot of pain. He cried loudly as he got up and it became clear that his lips were bleeding profusely.

Couple of students rushed him to the infirmary. Nobody dared to say anything to Rahul, who had hurt this boy and engaged with Krishnam earlier. Rahul had a reputation of a bully; he was the principal's son and was also well built, therefore everyone kept distance from him at school.

Rhea stood there watching in shock and anger. She saw Krishnam walking towards the bully. Krishnam caught Rahul's hand; he tried to jerk himself free from his grip and tried to strike Krishnam with the other. Krishnam caught his other hand too in flight towards him. By now Rhea was rushing to Krishnam's aid. The rest of the students were shell-shocked and just gaped at them. Krishnam now held both his hands; Rahul tried his best to free his hands and kept cursing at him.

Finally, Rahul gave up struggling and that's when Krishnam released his hands. Krishnam turned to leave, and right then Rahul pounced back at him; Rhea intervened by putting herself in the way. Rahul pushed Rhea with his full force in anger. Krishnam managed to catch her before she hit the ground though. Before Rhea or anyone else could realize, Rahul lay on the floor, unconscious. Krishnam had struck Rahul under his chin with lightning speed.

Rhea continued to blend in with her new environment at Shaktidham; her new life was now emphasized by self-discipline. She was regular with her morning and evening meditation, which required consistent practice. Apart from going to school in the morning, Rhea and Krishnam would also go for a run in the evenings; this was a part of their daily routine.

Their evenings would be spent together, as they sat to complete their work from school, with instrumental music playing in the background. Krishnam also taught Rhea how to play chess. He would often read out paragraphs from the books he was reading and ask Rhea to comprehend, then ask her to explain what she had understood. Rhea would often watch Chander training Krishnam in karate or shooting. Even cleaning the sadhanasthal was something Rhea and Krishnam did together, before their evening meditation.

One morning, Krishnam tickled Rhea's feet, but she woke up without her usual laughter.

Her face was expressionless. He knew she wasn't her usual self. 'What happened, Rhea?'

She looked up at him and said, 'I saw a dream last night; a European woman was teaching you; the surrounding landscape was lush green mountainside and the air was cold and crisp...'

Krishnam asked curiously, 'How would you know that the air was cold?'

'If only you would let me complete... In the same dream, I saw you sleeping at night, and you were shivering as your quilt had fallen off you,' she replied.

'Ah, intelligent!' he said, pulling her nose.

A few seconds later, understanding the implication of her dream, she asked, 'Krish, will you leave me and go?'

Their eyes met. 'Will you come with me if I go?' he asked. She had tears in her eyes and didn't need to say anything.

'I will come back to you, Rhea, wherever I may go. I am not time,' he replied softly, sensing her sadness.

He offered her a hand and helped her out of bed. 'We have to rush, else we will be late for school,' he said, trying to sound cheerful.

On their return from school, they would invariably find Satya sitting by himself on the swing in the veranda, waiting for them. Rhea would always rush to him and hug him. Krishnam would sit beside him, while Rhea would narrate all that had happened in school.

After Rhea would finish, Satya would ask Krishnam about his day. Krishnam always had the same answer, 'Good, baba.'

5

WINTER VACATIONS CAME and went by; there was little change in the routine, except that the duration of their meditation, both morning and evening, increased by 45 minutes. By now, Rhea had completely accepted her new family. The thoughts of her biological family were fleeting and had stopped affecting her adversely. Satya had made an effort towards Rhea to show his love and affection. On Sundays, Satya would often sit with them and play board games. He would even narrate stories to them and encourage discussion. Rhea frequently asked him to repeat stories of Lord Shiva.

Satya would often have meaningful conversations with them. 'Discipline is what sets you free,' he said once, during a discussion.

It was the dreaded day in February of the year 1981. Rhea overheard a conversation about Satya planning to send them to a boarding school in the hills.

Rhea refused to go to any boarding school, saying, 'Baba, I want to study here and be with Devima and you.'

Krishnam was definitely going; he was in grade nine now,

starting his new session in July. Rhea yet again saw her dream manifest itself into reality; there was nothing she could do to change it. Krishnam was going to leave her.

The final exams got over. Rhea stayed in the same school and went on to the fourth grade. Krishnam was to leave in a couple of months and Satya was making train reservations.

'Rhea, would you like to go and drop Krishnam?' asked Satya.

'No, Baba,' Rhea replied, looking away from him.

'I will be back for winter vacations in just four months,' said Krishnam, trying to salvage the situation, as he recalled her expression on the morning when she had dreamt of him going away.

Rhea became quiet and temperamental as the day of Krishnam's departure drew closer. About a week before Krishnam's departure, she was very quiet and even refused to meditate that evening. 'I am tired, Baba, I don't want to meditate. I would like to eat right away and sleep thereafter.'

Satya looked at her with a straight face. 'Rhea, the greatest victory lies in conquering yourself, and when events cannot be controlled, controlling oneself. It is fine if you do not wish to meditate. Too much of discipline leads to bondage.'

Finally, the day came when Krishnam had to leave. Rhea missed school. Before leaving for the station, all of them went to the sadhanasthal and Satya blessed Krishnam with a tika on his forehead, from the ashes of the vedi. Krishnam touched Satya's feet to seek his blessings.

He hugged Rhea and said, 'I've told you, I will be back soon.' Tears were streaming down Rhea's cheeks. She couldn't bring herself to say anything.

Satya walked out and left them alone for a moment. Krishnam hugged her tight, not a word was spoken. He then kissed her on the forehead, turned and left.

She collapsed in front of Devima and did not leave the

sadhanasthal. Long after Krishnam had left and she did not return, Satya finally had to come to get her for dinner. He saw her on the floor; she was fast asleep. Satya let her be.

Since Krishnam left two days ago, Rhea would return from school, hug Satya, but say nothing.

On both days Satya asked her how her day was, and she just replied, 'Good, Baba.'

A day later, Rhea returned from school to find a man sitting on the veranda with Satya. He had with him two baskets with two pups each.

As Rhea entered the veranda, Satya asked, 'Rhea, would you like to keep a dog as a pet?'

Rhea's expression brightened. She was thrilled by this idea and picked out a black fluffy pup.

The man addressed Satya, 'Maharaj ji, this pup is a Rottweiler; he will need to be trained well and proper social interaction is a must for this breed. They are a breed of strong and loyal dogs. The temperament of the dog depends on how they are trained and they do not do well in isolation.'

By this time, Rhea had already taken the pup to her room.

Atila was frisky and mischievous. He would sit on the veranda near Satya's feet, waiting for Rhea to come back from school. As she entered, he would run towards her to greet her. She would pick him up, caress him, and then go to meet Satya. In the evenings, she would take him with her for a run. He would sit by her side when she studied, and wait outside the sadhanasthal while she meditated. At night, he would sleep in Rhea's bedroom on a small mattress placed for him on the side.

Back at the boarding school, Krishnam had been feeling homesick. He had been there for two months now, and many a night, he lay awake until late, haunted by Rhea's crying face. He was making new friends at school, but his attention often diverted to one thought, 'What would Rhea be doing now?' He would smile thinking of her. There were students from different cultures in the school, as it had an International Board and catered to different nationalities.

One day on returning from school, Rhea finally spoke to Satya other than the two words. 'Baba, I made a new friend and his name is Neel.'

'Good. Is he from your class?' asked Satya.

'No, he is a year senior to me,' she replied.

Satya asked, 'How did the two of you get talking?'

Rhea replied, 'He had come during the recess to ask for Krishnam. I told him that he has joined a boarding school in the hills. Neel also joins us now during recess and the four of us share our tiffin. Nethra and Barkha like him too.'

'That's good,' replied Satya, sensing her lack of enthusiasm while mentioning it.

October passed with their daily routines. Deepawali was around the corner. One evening after dinner, while Rhea was sitting with Satya, she asked out of the blue, 'Baba, when will Krishnam be back?'

'During his winter vacations,' Satya replied.

'I meant to say, when would he be back forever?'

Satya looked at her with a smile and replied, 'After you have completed your education.'

'Oh, until which class do I have to study?'

'My little girl, education is not just about the classes you study in. It has a lot to do with the person you become in life. I would like my children to respect themselves for who they are, and make me a proud father. We all have to go through lessons in life; we learn from them and have the opportunity to grow.'

'Baba, when will I start to learn how to fire a revolver?'

Satya replied, 'I have already told Chander, he will start with your lessons tomorrow.'

Rhea's was excited about her first lesson with Chander. He

explained to Rhea about the mechanical functioning of the revolver, its rules of safety and all the dos and don'ts.

'Before you use any firearm, it is important that you understand it well,' he said, as he explained the workings of the firearm. He told her to always keep the muzzle pointed down and at a safe direction.

'Never point the muzzle towards anything you do not intend to shoot and always be very careful while loading and unloading it,' he emphasized. The lesson ended with the focus on its safety and the handling of a revolver.

A week later, after Deepawali, Rhea was allowed to fire the revolver. Chander placed targets in the shooting range at about 10 metres, and explained to her how to aim and shoot. He made her aware that there would be recoil from the weapon; therefore, she must use both her hands to stabilize it. He knelt beside her, positioned her arms and she took her first shot. Even though she missed her target, it was the most exhilarating experience—'What raw power.' She could not hit the target even a single time.

'Chander bhaiya, I couldn't hit the target,' said Rhea, irritated.

'It's about practising, my child. Behind any accomplishment and skill are years of practice, dedication and discipline,' replied Chander.

The vacations were about to start and November passed quickly. Satya could sense the excitement building up in Rhea while awaiting Krishnam's arrival. The night before Krishnam arrived, Rhea could not sleep and sat with Satya in his room, talking to him.

'Baba, why does Krish have to study in the boarding school?'

Satya looked at her and smiled. 'There is a world beyond Shaktidham and we should not confine ourselves within its boundaries. There will be a time when you will have to go out into the world and seek opportunities to grow.'

'I will not leave the ashram to go anywhere,' she said firmly.

Satya looked at her and just smiled.

After sometime Satya said, 'So you address Krishnam as Krish?'

Rhea nodded her head, observing Satya as he ruffled her hair affectionately.

'Baba, what does Krishnam mean?'

'Krishnam is derived from the name "Krishna" which essentially means "dark". Lord Krishna is a deity in the Hindu religion. Traditional beliefs say that he was the incarnation of Lord Vishnu. I will give you a book to read on Lord Krishna,' Satya told her and then asked, 'Do you know what your name means?'

'No, Baba,' she replied.

'In Greek language it means "flowing". It is a beautiful name which relates to movement and movement is fundamental to the universe,' explained Satya.

She was sitting after her evening meditation at the sadhanasthal, when Krishnam tiptoed in and covered her eyes with his hands. She felt the hands and knew it was he, Krishnam.

He was back for his winter vacations. She exclaimed in joy and they embraced.

6

3 years later: 1984

SATYA AND KRISHNAM were practising their karate. There was boldness and confidence in their movements. Rhea noticed both had a strong presence of gentleness too. After they finished their practice, Rhea told Satya, 'It seemed like a rehearsed dance performance and was gentle.'

'It seems paradoxical, but it is the balance of gentleness with the confidence that creates harmony,' said Satya.

It was a full moon night. Krishnam and Rhea made all the preparations for Satya to conduct his rituals tonight. The full moon night is significant because the gravitational pull of the moon affects the large waterbodies on earth. It is this cosmic arrangement which makes the environment conducive to our receptivity. Conducting rituals during the full moon night aids spiritual growth.

He asked them to accompany him to the sadhanasthal that night.

After they had settled in their asanas, Satya told them, 'It is now time that you are acquainted with the deeper knowledge and meaning of the sound Om and the vibrations from it. It's an understanding in relation to our states.

'Sound is a very potent form of energy; it is a bridge between the known and the unknown. The frequency of audible sound is a level above the frequency of solid matter. A sound is essentially a vibration; it consists of waves oscillating at a particular frequency. Sound defines the abstract energy in our material world. It is the thread that connects thoughts and manifestation,' explained Satya.

'Meditating and chanting Om ceases the discordant chatter of the mind and slowly leads to rearranging thoughts like a beautiful symphony. As we know and understand, relaxing sound heals and a discordant sound destroys,' he added.

'The three syllables of Om (AUM) symbolize the three levels of one's mind: A—conscious, U—subconscious, M—unconscious. "A" represents normal waking consciousness, in which the subject (observer) and the object (observed) exist as separate entities. This is the level of science and logical reasoning. The vibration of "A" is the heaviest and corresponds with matter, as matter exists on a tangible level; it is steady and slow to change. Tangible, or gross matter is the heaviest, and is everything that we can see and experience. It entails from the finest nebula to the heaviest precipitation, of which our earth is one.

'The sound "U" represents the level of dream consciousness. Dream and imagination are within us. The object (observed) and the subject (observer) become intertwined in awareness, both of which reside within us. Matter becomes subtle, flowing and fast-changing. This is the realm of our inner world.

'"M" is the third element, humming with lips gently closed. This sound resonates forward in the mouth and buzzes all through the head. This sound represents the realm of deep, dreamless sleep. There is neither an observing subject nor an observed object, as all are one. Only pure consciousness exists, unseen, pristine and dormant. This is the cosmic night, the interval between cycles of creation and the womb of the divine Mother. As I have always mentioned "A" symbolizes Brahma, the creator, "U"—Vishnu, the sustainer, and "M"—Shiva, the destroyer.

'After chanting Om, the silence that follows represents the state that transcends the previous three stages, i.e. superconsciousness,' said Satya.

Rhea and Krishnam sat absorbing all that they had just heard. To make sense and be able to absorb this in its true essence would require a clean slate or an empty bowl. They could now relate to it, after four years of practising the mantra Om.

'But Baba, why do we pray to Lord Shiva, the destroyer?' asked Rhea.

Krishnam interjected 'Every act of creation is first an act of destruction.'

Satya smiled and asked, 'Rhea, can you explain what Krishnam said?'

'He said for anything new to come the old has to go. For example, he had to leave us to go to a new school. He had to destroy his existing life to be able to embrace his new life,' replied Rhea, as Satya and Krishnam looked at each other.

'But Rhea...' Krishnam said and Satya signalled him to be quiet.

'Yes Rhea, you have explained it well,' said Satya. 'We will now chant Om and meditate together.'

The sadhanasthal reverberated with intense chants. Both Krishnam and Rhea were exhausted after the long meditative session with Satya. They slept until midday, but woke up excited as they were going up to Gangotri in the Himalayas. Satya was taking them on this picturesque trip.

Gangotri is where the river Ganga originates, as the holy river starts at Gaumukh from the Gangotri glacier. According to Hindu mythology Goddess Ganga, the daughter of Himalaya, took the form of a river after King Bhagirath's severe penance to absolve the sins of his ancestors. Lord Shiva reduced Ganga's force of fall from heaven by receiving her in his matted hair.

The drive from Varanasi was 1083 kilometres approximately. In the first leg, they drove until Rishikesh, which is at the foothills of the Himalayas. Rhea was going to the mountains for the first time and was excited. By the time they arrived at Rishikesh, everyone was tired from the travel and road conditions, even the jeep was heated up. The next morning, refreshed from their sleep and after breakfast, they headed out to get to their final destination. As they moved closer to their destination, they were awed by the beauty of nature—as the beauty surrounding them was pure and unscathed. The mountains stood tall and majestic; the air got fresher, as the Himalayas were free from human overpopulation and pollution.

Gangotri is a small Hindu pilgrimage town on the banks of the river Bhagirathi, and 3400 metres above sea level. They were staying at a government guest house near the river in Harsil, about 25 kilometres from Gangotri town.

Satya and Chander had a room each; Krishnam and Rhea shared one. They settled in their rooms, unpacked and then met for an early dinner. As the journey had taken a toll on everyone, they retired early to their rooms.

The night was cold. Rhea got out of bed and shook Krishnam.

'What?' he asked, half asleep.

'Krish, I am feeling cold and I cannot sleep.'

'Get into your bed under your quilt.'

He got up, went to her bed, and felt her hands and feet, which were ice cold. As Rhea lay under her quilt, he rubbed her feet one-by-one until they were warm and then did the same with her hands. She was asleep by then. He placed her hands inside the quilt and sat at her bedside watching her sleep, for a long time.

Krishnam was the first to wake up and he woke Rhea up from her deep slumber. That morning, everyone woke up at their own pace, and had their breakfast after their meditation. When they left to visit Gangotri, it was almost noon.

The original Gangotri temple was built in the nineteenth century. That was the first place they visited to seek blessings from Goddess Ganga, admire the temple and its architecture. Next, they walked through the town of Gangotri till the banks of the river Bhagirathi. The gushing river with its continuous thunder like sound was overwhelming and almost frightening. The water was extremely cold as it came from the Gangotri glacier, about 19 kilometres away from the Gaumukh.

That night as they slept, Krishnam didn't realize when Rhea came into his bed and got under his quilt with him. As he woke up he found his arms around Rhea, while she was cuddled next to him with her legs over him. He gently moved her legs and slipped out of bed, without disturbing her. Rhea was still sleeping.

They walked to the riverside after breakfast, strolling and taking in the natural beauty that surrounded them. They didn't speak for a while.

'Krish, why are you so quiet today?' asked Rhea.

'Rhea, you should not have come and slept in my bed at night,' he said, but didn't look at her.

'But why, Krish? I was very cold, and you were sound asleep so

I didn't want to wake you. Why can't I sleep in your bed with you when it is so cold at night?'

'Rhea, I am older than you and I know what I am saying. I am not a child anymore and you are growing up too.'

'I know, Krish. You are in grade eleven now, but what does that have to do with my sleeping in your bed when I am cold?'

'Stop this argument, Baba will get upset if he gets to know,' he snapped in irritation.

Rhea was shocked and started crying. This was the first and last time that Krishnam ever got irritated with her.

He wiped her tears with his hands and said, 'Rhea, be strong, why these tears like a little baby? It's a sign of weakness. There will be plenty of things that we will face as we grow in life.'

'Why did you talk to me like that?' asked Rhea.

Krishnam was quiet.

'You screamed at me, Krishnam.'

'Oh ho, is this screaming?' he said, softly pulling her cheeks.

Nobody had ever snapped at her at the ashram and least of all Krishnam.

'Okay, Rhea, I am sorry. Now smile.'

He looked into her eyes and said, 'I am your Krishnam. I will always say and do what is good for us, please just trust me completely.'

He paused for her reaction and asked, 'Will you?' Then he extended his hand to shake hers as a sign of a promise.

She responded with a hug and said, 'I trust you, and always will, but never get angry with me.'

He put his hand around her slowly and held her. The soft fragrance of her body enveloped his senses.

That evening, Chander explained to Rhea some vital weak points of the human body in self-defence. While Rhea and Chander were busy, Satya and Krishnam had a long chat. Later, they all sat by the banks of river Bhagirathi and watched the sunset in silence. At night the room was warm, Krishnam had already switched on the heater. When Rhea went to bed, he gently rubbed her hands and feet, and she drifted into sleep.

The four of them had an early start the next day, as the plan was to trek to Gaumukh from the town of Gangotri till where they would drive. They had a light breakfast and packed whatever was necessary for the trek. They had brought with them the required gear, including shoes, for this trek which involved rocky terrain and there were patches of snow on the way leading up to the glacier.

Krishnam and Chander led the group up to Gaumukh; the 19 kilometre route has an altitude of about 610 metres above Gangotri town. During the trek, they stopped briefly for a couple of breaks. As they arrived, there was a distinct change in temperature because the glacier was nearer. The icy breeze cut through their clothing, even though they were fully clothed. It was a sight like no other; there was only snow all around them. They had reached the spot from where the mighty Ganga originates.

The next two days, Satya and Chander mainly stayed at the guest house; they were relaxing and taking it easy before the journey back, catching up briefly on the topics never discussed during their busy schedule. Rhea and Krishnam took long walks into the mountainside, following trails through this breathtaking and beautiful nature reserve. Their conversations were never ending, as this was a rare opportunity where they had each other's undivided attention and enjoyed every moment.

They picked up their belongings, and loaded them into the jeep. Satya sat in the front with Chander, who was driving; Rhea and Krishnam sat in the back. Not too much was said as the holiday came to a close. Now it was back to the heat and pollution on the plains, but the silver lining was that they were going home to Shaktidham.

They broke journey at Haridwar to sleep the night off and continued the next day to Varanasi. They arrived at Shaktidham late that evening; everyone was tired by this journey. Krishnam and Rhea brought home many beautiful memories, gained experience, enjoyed nature's flavour in the mountains and bonded further with each other.

7

KRISHNAM HAD TO rejoin school in a few days; he had been studying hard during the rest of his holidays as grade twelve is a defining year. He was focused on his goal to study law at a top university in the US. Rhea had already joined grade eight, and was back to school as her holidays ended.

This time when Krishnam was leaving for school, he requested Rhea to start writing letters to him regularly. 'I won't reply to your letters, but you please keep writing. I will reply to all of them when I come back in the holidays.'

'Okay, Krish.'

'And from now on, I want to see a smile on your face when I leave. You have to be strong.'

'Okay, Krish.'

When Krishnam was leaving this time he saw Rhea smiling, but there was sadness in her eyes.

The week after Krishnam left was eventful for Rhea as she entered puberty. She wrote to Krishnam about it.

My Krish,

How are you? Dr Rageshwari had come today, as I woke up in a pool of blood and my clothes were drenched in it. I called Baba and showed him my clothes. He told me not to worry and said that nothing will happen to me.

The doctor told me that girls go through a biological process of growing up and this is supposed to be natural, and many more things, which I will tell you when we meet. I do not know if this is a natural process for all girls, so could you please find out and let me know. There is no need for you to worry.

Lots of love,

Rhea

One night at the sadhanasthal, Rhea lost track of time, with the vibration of Om resonating through her entire body. After she was exhausted and couldn't go further, she left the sadhanasthal and later had dinner with Satya.

As usual after dinner, they sat in the veranda and talked for a while. She said, 'Baba, it has taken me four years just to get the primordial sound of Om right, the first sound of Mantra Shastra.'

'Four years is a short period in sadhana,' replied Satya.

'Baba, high frequency sound waves can break up solid matter. Kidney stones are broken by these high frequency amplified sound waves; I had read this in an encyclopaedia. Is it a coincidence that omnipotent and omnipresent contain the word Om? Atom in physics too has Om.'

'What is an atom?' asked Satya, with a smile.

'Atom is the basic structure of matter,' replied Rhea. They had a brief conversation and retired to bed.

Dear Krish,

How are you? Guess what? Since the rains stopped at the end of August, Baba is getting new construction done on the first floor. New rooms are being made for us; we will each have a separate study, and attached bathrooms with tubs in them!

Baba will continue to stay downstairs in his room. He told me that I should start reading a lot, because reading is an exercise for my mind just as the run with Atila is an exercise for my body. He told me if we do not apply our mind it gets junked! School is fine. Neel was asking about you, Nethra and

Barkha are all good too. Once the rooms are complete, Atila
too will sleep on the terrace at night.
Lots of love,
Rhea

One night, as Rhea slept she was dreaming... A person in the
sadhanasthal is sitting in front of the statues of Goddess Kali. She
heard her chants, which were creating powerful vibrations that had
the power to purify all that could endure, and burn all that could
not. Suddenly, she saw the statue of Goddess Kali in the aggressive
form come alive, but then her expression changed and she became
soft, like a mother who was overflowing with love for her child.
Goddess Kali embraced her, the person who was now standing in
front of the statue. Rhea actually felt the warmth outside of her
dream; it flowed into her soul. She opened her eyes and came back
to the present.

Her room was dark; it was absolutely silent. The dream felt so
real, as if it was her who had been embraced by Goddess Kali. The
warmth couldn't be expressed in words; it had to be felt. She went
immediately and knocked on Satya's door.

'Rhea, what happened?' asked Satya.

She narrated the entire dream to him. 'Baba, I actually felt the
warmth.'

Satya put her back to bed and told her that he would speak to
her the following day. He knew the time had come.

That evening, after Rhea finished meditating and chanting,
Satya came to the sadhanasthal and placed his hand on her head.
'Rhea, the time has come to initiate you on the path of Tantra.'

Satya sat down and began explaining, 'Tantra is a Sanskrit
word which means "to weave". The word symbolizes that in reality,
the entire creation is interwoven and interdependent. We as
humans are as much a part of the creation as every other fragment.
Nothing exists in isolation. The cosmos is a web that is created by

the interweaving and interdependence of its creation. Be aware of all that goes on inside you and you will understand all that goes on outside you; therefore, what exists inside you will exist outside in your world too.

> My Krish,
>
> I got 100 per cent marks in maths and 98 per cent in physics in my midterm tests. Baba was very happy for me. I told Baba that I want to celebrate my birthday this year. Every year there is only prayers and havan, so this year I decided to have a party with my friends. We will decorate the hall for the party and Neel will help me with the games. Baba asked me to go shopping with Dr Rageshwari and get whatever I want, so I bought a new, pink dress which I will wear on my birthday! I will write and send all the details to you after the party. Just two days to go and I am very excited. I wish you were here too. I miss you Krish.
> Love,
> Rhea

It was the fourth of October and Rhea was all excited to go to school on the morning of her birthday. She even carried a bag of sweets, for her classmates and teachers. She distributed the sweets with the permission of the class teacher; everyone wished her 'Happy Birthday'. After school, she came back and rushed through lunch, as Neel would be coming early to finalize all the games. It was going to be so much fun!

Neel arrived five minutes later than the appointed time; Rhea was impatient and told him he was late, so he explained he was stuck in traffic. She held his hand pulling him towards the hall, where the decorations were almost completed. Neel was shocked to see the large hall where they were going to celebrate her birthday.

'Wow, this is a big hall you have! We don't need to step outside even to play football!' he exclaimed.

They arranged the games as Barkha and Nethra would arrive soon, half an hour before the other friends. They waited for them, chatting away; meanwhile the birthday cake was arranged. It was nearly time for the rest of her friends to come; Neel and Rhea went to make calls to Barkha and Nethra.

'Hello aunty, may I speak with Barkha?' There was a long pause.

'Okay,' said Rhea, replacing the receiver.

'What happened?' asked Neel.

'Barkha is not coming. Her aunt has come from out of town and she has gone with her father to meet her.'

She dialled Nethra. 'Hello, is Nethra there? I am her friend Rhea speaking.' A voice at the other end answered.

'But... but she was supposed to come for my birthday,' said Rhea.

At last she said, 'Thanks,' replacing the receiver.

Neel, observing Rhea's saddened expression, was anxious to know what happened.

It was 6.30 p.m., and time for Neel to go home. His driver was waiting outside. No one came to the party. Rhea stood up and didn't say a word. Her face was expressionless. Neel hugged her and wished her once again, before he left.

Dear Krish,
I am very unhappy about my birthday party; no one came for it except Neel. All my classmates who I had invited wanted to come, but their parents refused to send them as they felt that Shaktidham is not a safe place. Some of them were told that we kill young girls and boys, and sacrifice them to please Goddess Kali.

Krish, why do people say such nasty things about our ashram and our Devima? When has anyone been sacrificed to please Ma?

I told them that it was not true and it was their choice to come or not, but to never ever repeat what they just said about the ashram. I think it was a bad idea to have a party and I do not intend to ever have one again.

Lots of love,

Rhea

The ink had smudged at various places on the letter, indicating where her teardrops had fallen.

My dearest Rhea,

A single weakness of a person is stronger than all his strengths. These are small obstacles which you have to overcome. This incident is unworthy of your tears. I want my Rhea to be strong. What people say or think about us is unimportant; who we are is important. Focus your energies on what you want to be.

A tight hug to my princess.

Lots of love,

Krish

'Baba, what is the significance of human sacrifice?' asked Rhea, while sitting with Satya on a Sunday afternoon.

'Sacrifice—human or animal—was practised ritualistically in many ancient cultures. Sacrifices were made with the idea that it appeased the Gods. Human sacrifice became rarer, as it came to be looked down upon. It was termed barbaric as the human race evolved with time.

'However, these practices have reformed with the changes in society. Personally, I think that the Gods never expected these sacrifices for their appeasement. In our Indian context, Sati pratha is also a human sacrifice which was prevalent until the nineteenth century, after which it was banned. There have been incidences reported even up to the twentieth century. These rituals are completely misplaced in today's context,' replied Satya.

'I am amazed, Baba, that people seriously believe that God made these rituals of sacrifice?'

'All rituals are man-made and need to be reformed with time by man himself. Even today, one hears of stray incidences of sacrifice of humans and animals in the name of religion, and most of these are linked to Tantric traditions. Rhea, you should know that Tantra has always been mystified and maligned due to the lack of authentic knowledge about it.'

Dear Krish,

I had gone to Neel's house for lunch today. I met his father and he is an extremely warm person, and we had a long conversation. I met his mother Kritika too; she is a very elegant and pretty woman. She completed her degree in fashion designing from the Fashion Institute of Technology, New York. She designs apparels for, and manages, their garment factories in Varanasi and Delhi, from where it's then exported. The meeting with her was brief, as she was leaving for the factory.

She asked me what my parents did. I could see Neel and his father getting uncomfortable. I told her Baba is a Tantra sadhak and the head of Shaktidham. She asked me who a sadhak is. I told her that a sadhak is a person who practises sadhana. Then she asked what sadhana is. She had a warm smile throughout our conversation. I told her that it is a systematic procedure of praying. She said that she would love to meet Baba and that she could see a sadhak in the making.

Oh by the way, she told Neel that he had a lovely friend. She left saying she had to meet a deadline. Neel's father had commented after she left that she always has a deadline.

Krish, Neel's father has someone other than her in his life. The woman is a divorcee and an easy-going woman. Neel's father is unhappy with his wife as she is overambitious. He even asked her for a divorce, but Neel's mother has refused. They are together, yet not together. Neel feels like he is a victim of his parents.

Neel told me his father is fine until he flies into a rage! I liked his mother. Krish, you know, I wish I were normal like you. I do not wish to know anything about anyone. I wonder what people would do if they knew I could know so much about them. Be wary of me? No, they'd probably hate me. People do grave things in life and they wouldn't like anyone to know about it.

I have been blabbering only about I, me, myself. I hope you are well!

Lots of love,

Rhea

PS: I didn't miss even a single target today, and got a pat on my back from Baba.

◆

Satya was teaching Rhea the sunrise ritual.

'The earth receives light from the sun and the moon. The earth also receives constant radiations, but they are invisible,' said Satya.

'Stand facing the rising sun, Rhea, in a star posture. Spread your legs as wide as your shoulder, with your head slightly bent backwards, and your arms extended out upwards of your shoulder height, with palms towards the sky, absorbing the energy from the cosmos,' instructed Satya.

'Hold this position for as long as possible; practise it for up to a minute, and later you can increase it as per your comfort and requirement. The essence of this ritual is that you are a vessel that absorbs the cosmic energy. You have to be open, mentally and physically, without which nothing will be achieved.

'This procedure of recharging will have a strong uplifting

effect. Sunrise and sunset are the times when the strongest presence of cosmic energy can be received and absorbed. Cosmic energy is the least at midday, when the sun is directly overhead and midnight when the sun is under the feet,' explained Satya.

Dear Krish,
Well guess what happened? School was adventurous today! During recess a bunch of seniors stood in the hallway and as I was crossing them they called me a 'witch'.

As I went ahead, they said loudly behind me, 'They sacrifice young children at Shaktidham. She is a witch and her father is a Tantric, who kills for power.'

I stopped, turned around and confronted them. I told them to 'shut up' and said that they were a bunch of fools. They complained to Miss Sarkar, the spinster, who screamed at me without listening to me, and took me to the principal. She narrated her distorted story that I misbehaved with the seniors and her too.

I told the principal the truth, who let me go saying that she understood the situation, but I need to be more respectful towards my teachers! She, however, held the seniors and Miss Sarkar in her office to speak with them. Thank God she is Dr Rageshwari's friend. On my return, I told Baba everything and he said that it was good that I stood up for myself. He told me we all have to fight our own battles.

Lots of love,
Rhea

On a night, a week before Krishnam was expected back for his vacations, Rhea got up with a sudden jolt in her dream. She only remembered the blurred images of Neel's mother wearing a white sari and saying, 'I did love him' and the words of a doctor, 'he is no more'. She described her dream to Satya the next morning.

As expected, a week later Krishnam returned for his vacations to Shaktidham. Rhea's entire demeanour changed on Krishnam's arrival. Her laughter could be heard all around Shaktidham. She chatted endlessly only with Krishnam; otherwise she was more of a listener. She even told him about the most insignificant things which happened while he was away at school. Neel too would drop in once in a while. They would sit to either play a board game or go to the field to play football. Both of them let Rhea score goals and watched her be happy and childish on scoring them. Krishnam was devoting much of his time to his studies, as his final examinations were a few months away.

Rhea knew what Neel would go through, but there was not much that she could do.

'We all have to live through situations. How we interpret and respond to a situation shapes our lives. We also have a choice whether to learn or not from them. We also have a choice to become better or bitter,' Satya told Rhea and Krishnam listened in, as they sat together.

'Baba, is this it? One comes from nowhere and then departs as if he never existed? After death, a living being's identity ceases to exist and is deduced to merely a body in an instant? Is this the grandeur of life? Is this what we all keep running for?' asked Rhea, feeling dejected.

A couple of days later a huge idol of Natraj was placed in Rhea's room while she and Krishnam had gone for a run.

'Hey Krish, come and see what Baba gave me for my room. It's a huge Nataraj, cast in brass,' Rhea said, pulling Krishnam's hand and taking him to her room.

'Do you know what it symbolizes, Rhea?' asked Krishnam.

'What?' she asked.

'The dancing Lord Shiva (Nataraj) is a metaphor of the dynamic movements of the cosmos. It symbolizes the endless rhythms of creation and destruction. Through the dance he creates the new and destroys the old, from the destruction unfolds creation. The fundamental nature of creation is flow, movement and change. The smallest thing in nature, however insignificant it may seem, has its importance and role, and is a part of the balancing process,' said Krishnam.

8

NEEL'S FATHER PASSED away within a month. The doctor diagnosed the cause to be a cardiac arrest.

Neel was shocked by the news and boarded the train back to Varanasi. He never got a chance to make up with his father or undo what had transpired. He never had the chance to see his father alive again. The last day with his father had ended on a bitter note; he was extremely angry with his father, when he had boarded the train to visit his aunt in Mumbai during his holidays.

A week earlier, it had started with his father getting angry over something trivial, which was not uncommon. When Neel's father got into a fit of rage, he lost all control over his sensibilities and reason. Neel had to face the brunt of his father's frustration, as he was an easy victim. He would hit and shout at Neel, which was a sure sign of a weak man. His father was suffering for reasons best known to him, but Neel was not interested in knowing the reasons.

The fact was that both his parents had contributed to his miserable life. His mother was aloof; she was busy with her ambitions and in fulfilling her life. She neither had the time nor the inclination towards Neel or their home. He witnessed ugly fights between his parents as they called each other names, which was unbearable.

One evening, his father was physically beating his mother; the brawl ended that night after his mother had pulled her pistol on him, and told him that the only reason she was not pulling the trigger this time is because she did not want to go to jail. Neel could never shut out the memory of that night.

Neel had stood trembling in the corner, watching it all in shock. His mother left and locked herself in her bedroom; he had heard her sob the entire night. His father went hysterical and started hitting his head on the wall, shouting and asking for a divorce as he loved someone else. She made it clear that she did not love him; however, she would not divorce him either. And if he ever dared to raise his hand at her again, he would be a dead man. Since then the two were merely strangers living in a house together.

After that night, Neel's mother had immersed herself in work. Some days his father did not return home at night. There were nights when Neel could not sleep hearing his mother's sobs. The three stayed in different rooms, seemingly indifferent to each other.

Anger has several faces; it kills different people differently. Neel did not understand that his father was angry with himself. It had very little or nothing to do with Neel. Maybe Neel's life would have been different if his parents were in a peaceful marriage, maybe if horses could fly.

As the train moved, tears started rolling down Neel's cheeks. All the good times he had shared with his father came rushing back to him. They had played cricket and football together when Neel was younger. All had nearly been lost in the sea of anger. Neel felt a sense of helplessness. His father had to be cremated before Neel could arrive. The body couldn't be preserved until his arrival, due to the hot and humid weather. Neel could not get a flight or a train ticket to be able to return on time.

In no time a person becomes a body which has to be destroyed immediately, Neel thought helplessly on his way back.

Life may never give us a second chance, but then again there are no answers on the back of the 'book of life'. One can never travel back in time, except in thoughts. Thoughts, which can cause regret, guilt and pain. The past can cling in a way and at times, all we do is close ourselves to our present and future.

Krishnam left Shaktidham in February for his school. He had scored very well in his GRE and LSAT exams and now had to concentrate on his final results. He was determined to put in his best so he could study law at an Ivy League college. Rhea tried to maintain her composure, but as always stood crying when he was leaving. Krishnam kissed her on her forehead and left the sadhanasthal without turning back. Rhea just stood there like a statue, without moving for a long time.

◆

'As Veda is said to be recited from Brahma's mouth, Agama Shastra or Tantra is said to have come from Lord Shiva. Tantra is said to be revealed by Lord Shiva as the specific shastra of Kalyug (the fourth yug). It is designed to meet the needs of the human race of this age. Tantra is also known as Sadhana Shastra and Mantra Shastra,' said Satya, after completing their meditation in the morning.

'There are many paths and many scriptures, but all lead to the same destination. Whichever path a river might take, its final destination is the ocean, where it merges to become one.

'Tantra embraces all humans. There is no religion other than humanity. Tantra deals with the power of will, the power of action, the power of knowledge, and to apply that knowledge with wisdom is Tantra. There are rituals to attain liberation, sought by the sadhak. Such rituals generically are termed as sadhana, their essence has to be practised, understood and mastered. Every ritual has a meaning and a spirit; a ritual without meaning or spirit, is dead. To evoke a spirit and have a meaningful ritual, it cannot be diluted. There are no shortcuts and even the smallest gesture has to be followed with precision in the whole sequence. Every step of sadhana requires the complete presence of your entire being. You have to understand the monistic truth by living in the dualistic world. Live every moment, but to live YOU (self) will have to die. This is the quintessence of sadhana.'

'Baba, are rituals modified and changed with the times?' asked Rhea.

'Yes, Rhea, it is mandatory and the modifications can be brought about by someone who has mastered the spirit of sadhana and understands all its rituals well enough to mould them.'

A month after Krishnam had gone back to school, one evening, when Rhea went to practise her shooting with Chander, he said, 'Rhea, I will show you what is the power of concentration.'

He made Rhea tie a blindfold on his eyes. He then asked Rhea to stand 15 feet away from him and throw empty bottles up in the air. Chander shot each of the four bottles with his eyes blindfolded.

'Chander bhaiya! How can you do this? This is incredible!' exclaimed Rhea in disbelief.

'All I have to do is focus and follow the sound,' replied Chander.

'Oh my God!' she exclaimed. 'You must have practised hard.' Her eyes were wide in astonishment.

Chander took off his blindfold. 'Come, Rhea, let's sit somewhere.'

They sat under a neem tree. 'Rhea, there is a part of my life that was very dark. I was not the Chander bhaiya as you see me today.'

Rhea sensed an uneasiness in him, as he continued. 'I was a trained killer, an assassin. I was a part of an organization in which men and women were trained to be assassins; I was the best they had. This organization operated out of Eastern Europe and had operations all over the world. The organization took up high-end jobs for assassinating heads of states, political figures, high net worth individuals, etc. There was no political alignment of the organization; its only motto was to be the most renowned in the business. Their only alignment was with money. There was no easy entry in the organization and for sure no one had exited alive ever.

'I had many names and still was nameless. I am a citizen of no country, but I have the citizenship of many. I then fell in love with Megan; she was new in our organization. We were in love for about two years, before we wanted to quit; we had dreamt of having our own family someday. The organization came to know of our plans to leave and they got after us; they would have executed both of us, if we didn't run away. We came to India in search of a new life and a new identity. We thought we had escaped the shadows of our past.

'We were followed; they traced us to India and sent assassins to eliminate us. That night, we were taken unaware, sitting at the banks of Ganga. It was past midnight and we were clueless about the lurking danger. A bullet went through Megan's head while we were talking. She dropped dead that instant. I used her body as a shield to save my life and then swam in the Ganges downstream, until I could no longer swim. At the end, I was exhausted by this ordeal. I swam towards the bank, and at a short distance saw someone in white. I lost my consciousness. That day, Baba saved me. I had not even realized that I had been shot in my shoulder. Dr Rageshwari gave me medical help and he nursed me back to health. Baba gave me a name, a home and a purpose.'

Rhea was listening silently.

'After recovering I was very angry, my entire world had transformed in a split second. I wanted to go back and kill them all. Baba saved me again; he told me, if revenge would get Megan back, I should go ahead. He asked me to wait for a while until my anger subsided and I could reflect clearly. As time passed, I saw my past life as a spectator; it reflected on my truth, which stopped me from going back. I would have killed them all or been killed. As far as the organization is concerned, I am dead.'

Chander took a deep sigh.

'What had I done? Killed so many targets and I didn't even know any one of them. I recollect some of the faces as time has passed, but never needed to know their names. I just followed orders to kill; I never questioned them. The only priority had been to assess and identify my target, never to miss. I never thought of my targets as being human, or people like me who had a life and were connected with other lives. In a split second, I was responsible for taking their life and altering the life of their loved ones. Power is heady, any kind of power. In my case, it was the power of being better than most in my chosen work of destruction. I felt that I had control on lives like no one else.

'I had never failed at my job. I excelled in killing, but failed miserably when it came to saving just one target, even though she meant the most to me in this world.'

Chander had tears in his eyes. There was silence; the chirping of the birds could be heard in the background.

Finally Rhea asked, 'Chander bhaiya, by what name did Megan address you?'

'Mike.'

◆

'In life, certain memories remain alive until our heart beats its last. Behind every face there is a story which shapes them into what they are. Most people are the creation of their circumstances,' said Rhea to Satya and Krishnam, who had just come back after appearing for his final exams from school, as they sat having morning coffee.

'Whatever be our circumstance, our attitude is always in our control,' said Krishnam. 'We shape ourselves to what we are; we are responsible for our actions and have to live with the consequences,' he added.

'Every human being has the potential to rise above any circumstance and shape himself the way he wants, as it is never too late to begin,' said Satya.

'Rhea, always try to analyse a situation by detaching yourself from it, even if you are in the midst of it. It helps you to be honest with the situation and gives clarity,' Satya said, looking at her.

◆

It was in August, Krishnam was leaving for the US to study law. He got into the university of his choice. Satya and Rhea put a tika on his forehead.

As he was leaving, Rhea caught his hand and said, 'You are going far away, Krish.'

He smiled and pulled her nose. 'Rhea, far away from whom?'

She looked at Satya. 'Baba, why is he going to the US for law?'

Satya remained silent. Certain questions float in the air, waiting for an answer. Some answers can only be revealed when you are ready for it.

'Rhea, no tantrums. Please smile for me, I am going to study,' said Krishnam, with a smile.

Rhea blushed and hugged him tight. Satya left the sadhanasthal and let them be. Tears didn't stop from her eyes and she kept holding on to Krishnam. He held her too and caressed her hair.

Finally, he said, 'Rhea, I will not go. I will tell Baba, I cannot leave you in this state.'

Rhea stepped back and wiped her tears. 'What has to be done must be done. I will be fine.'

He kissed her forehead, looked her in the eye, then turned and left. She had never seen him off, as she always stayed back at the sadhanasthal.

She ran to him and held his hand. 'I am coming to see you off.'

She looked up at him expecting an astonished look, but was shocked to see tears in his eyes. 'Stay here, Rhea,' he said and walked off without looking back. Rhea froze like a statue.

Rhea still kept writing letters to Krishnam, but her frequency decreased, as Krishnam would now call regularly to speak with Satya and Rhea.

Dear Krish,

It was good to speak with you on Sunday. Baba explained to me about the shooting club, but I still can't imagine it. Please send me photographs of the club and your karate classes. Do write to me in detail about it, when you send them. I also want to tell you that I rarely miss my targets now, finally after so many years!

Yesterday, I saw Raaga give birth to a baby calf. It was quite an experience, to see and comprehend the process of a new life being brought into this world. The calf has such lovely eyes and she is so skinny and tiny.

I was talking to Barkha and Nethra about you and was telling them what you are doing in the US. They are very curious about you and want to meet you. They were asking me what you are to me.

Neel said Hi! He is also doing much better now.

Lots of love,

Rhea

'The beauty of life lies in experiencing it with full awareness. Use all your senses to comprehend every experience and object. The experience of anything in life with all our facets of awareness will have much greater beauty and significance. Heightened awareness heightens our joy of living,' Satya told Rhea, while they sat in the veranda after her school.

Chander brought the day's mails, which the postman had just delivered. Rhea was thrilled to receive Krishnam's first letter from the US. She went to her room and opened it anxiously.

My dearest Rhea,

What did you say to your friends when they asked you what I am to you?

Yours,

Krish

She smiled and put the letter in her cupboard, where all the letters he had ever written and other memorabilia of Krish were preserved.

It was a Puranmashi night and Rhea was with Satya at the sadhanasthal.

'With your focused thoughts, mantras and yantras, i.e. thought, sounds and shapes in Tantra are combined to achieve the desired result.

'The thoughts have to be strong and focused, the sound has to be perfect to create the intended vibration, the yantra has to be designed specifically to act as a catalyst,' Satya was telling Rhea.

'To materialize our thoughts, we harness the power of sound, but it has to be perfected to create the intended vibration.

'Sound is the mantra and the word "mantra" is derived from Sanskrit. It is a combination of two words, first one being "manas" or mind and it provides the syllable "man" of man-tra; the second is "trai" meaning to protect or to free from something. So the literal meaning of man-tra means to free from mind. This journey to freedom expands and deepens our understanding of the self and with it comes the knowledge of cosmos. The power of mantra is tangible and wieldable; its effect can be experienced by a sadhak who chants it. Mantras are powerful and produce a strong vibrating energy, and when accompanied with strong intention, they add to the realization of its result. Continued practice leads the sadhak to pitch up to the energy state represented by the mantra.

'In Tantra, we use "Beej Mantra" which may also be called "Seed Mantra". These mantras do not have a direct meaning, but each sound has immense power. For example, we use "Shrim" as a Beej Mantra for Goddess Laxmi, the Goddess of Wealth.'

'Baba, could we say that "Shrim" is Beej Mantra, for the principle of abundance and when chanted by the sadhak will attract the abundance sought by him?' asked Rhea.

'True, these are mantras that are specific and powerful. Yantra in Sanskrit means an instrument. Yantra is derived from the root word "Yam" in Sanskrit, which means to hold the essence of a concept. The syllable "tra" comes from an Indo-European suffix meaning instrument. Therefore, it is described as an instrument to hold the essence of a concept. It is therefore the visual representation of vibrations,' concluded Satya.

As time passed, Satya introduced Rhea to further advanced rituals; these required more time and energy. She had to be physically fit to be able to conduct these rigorous rituals. There were days when she was at a heightened energy level and even sleep eluded her. There were days when she would exhaust herself, after many a night practising her rituals and then sleep those mornings, until the next day. Satya accepted it, if she could not make it to school on some days, as he was grooming her to be the next heir—heir of the sacred path of Tantra—and she was coping well with her academics too. For him, everything was secondary to the sacred path of Tantra.

Rhea's time in the world outside was limited, with her devoting most of her time to conducting advanced rituals at Shaktidham. Her friends Neel, Nethra, and Barkha constituted her outside world. Neel would still visit Rhea at Shaktidham occasionally and spend a couple of hours on a Sunday. Since his father's death, his mother's brother, who was younger than her, had joined the company and managed the finances of the business. He was appointed a director in the company and had swindled off a huge sum, bringing the entire business and Neel's mother into a precarious situation. She was tough and was struggling even harder than before to bring the company back on its feet. She wasn't going to let go of it so easily.

'Only success and money matter to her,' said Neel.

'Maybe not. At times, reality may be far from what it seems,' replied Rhea.

Barkha's parents had nothing in common, other than the three children they had together—two daughters and a younger son who was pampered and spoilt. They would have been a different family, if their father had seen beyond his son. But we all know that one of the definitions of love is that it is blind. Barkha always yearned for that love and credit from her father, which she thought she deserved. She was good at academics and helped her mother in the household chores. She had a dream of becoming a fashion designer; she was very talented and had gifted a set of delicate embroidered handkerchiefs, each to Nethra and Rhea, which she stitched herself.

'These are amazing, Barkha! We know for sure you will make it to the fashion school,' they told her.

Barkha's parents had no clue about fashion designing. Her father was a wholesaler of food grains and lentils. Early marriage of girls was the norm. College was unimportant, as it was expected that a woman should excel in her household work. Sons were considered a blessing and daughters a liability. Barkha's mother quietly encouraged both her daughters to study and be financially independent.

Nethra's childhood was spent in a palatial house, with a lot of domestic help available. Her parents were perpetually busy as both were doctors, and they firmly believed in logic and reasoning. For Nethra, truth was more than reason and life was more than what was tangible. Shaktidham and Rhea's father being a Tantric perturbed Nethra's parents, even though they thought of Rhea as an intelligent girl and a good influence on their daughter. However, they avoided bringing up this topic in front of their daughter.

'In a certain space, reason and logic have their importance, but then some aspects have to be felt. The sun is a star made up of hot gases, eight light minutes away from the earth. However, the beauty of the rising sun has the promise of a new beginning, which can only be felt and experienced. Human life results from a sperm impregnating an ovum, which is logic, but beyond that it could be the result of shared oneness between a male and a female. Truth is multidimensional and to comprehend its entirety one should have the ability to go beyond what seems obvious,' Rhea said, making perfect sense when she had a discussion with Nethra.

Gradually with time, things were developing and taking a different shape at Shaktidham. The requirement of Shaktidham for its grains, vegetables and fodder was now being met by the cultivation of the forty acres of land, which had been developed over the last few years. All that was excess was sold in the market. Mostly the crop was good; a fair amount of money was made in the good years. The produce was more than the consumption by the inmates of Shaktidham. The inmates cultivated its fields and looked after the gaushala. Satya was getting a temple constructed, near the entrance to Shaktidham, which was just off the main road; it had been decided that the statues placed would be of various forms of Shakti.

Shaktidham employed landless poor people as workers, who were way below the poverty line and were either paid very poorly or had no work at all. These were people who couldn't support their families and were given a place to live, food to eat and wages with which they could support their families. There were thirty rooms in all, with four common washrooms and four toilets for the workers, away from the main residential area, nearer the fields. Everyone knew that Rhea could come at any time and inspect the toilets and washrooms; therefore, they were kept clean at all times. Satya had taught and inculcated the need for cleanliness, also why fields aren't meant for littering with faeces. Each room had a wooden charpoy woven with rope made from coconut fibres, and also had an open closet inbuilt, which had concrete shelves to keep clothes and other belongings.

Chander had a separate suite to himself, with an attached

bathroom in the main residential area. He had a sitting room and a study, while his bedroom had a double bed with an iron safe in the wall. There was also a small pantry with a refrigerator.

Chander and a few of the staff members had an office space, which stood at the entrance of the private office of Satya. To go into the residential side where Satya, Rhea and Krishnam had their living quarters, one had to walk through the office. The door of the reception office led into a corridor, at the end of which was the veranda with the iron swing. Alongside the corridor were Satya's room, dining area and kitchen. The room adjacent to the kitchen was converted into family lounge; this had previously been Krishnam and Rhea's bedroom. The family lounge had a music system, television and shelves full of books. It was also stacked with board games and a chessboard for Rhea and Krishnam. A flight of stairs from the veranda led to the landing on the first floor; Krishnam's room was across the landing and to the right was Rhea's room along the terrace.

Atila had to be shifted upstairs on the terrace whenever someone came to meet Satya or Rhea, as even with all the training he was not good with strangers. None of the workers of Shaktidham ever came into the private office of Satya, as they feared Atila. If it weren't for Rhea, he would have attacked one of the workers who once came to deliver milk instead of the milkman, who was unwell. Rhea had shouted 'stop' in the nick of time and Atila obeyed the command. However, he'd stood like a barrier between the worker and Rhea, growling and in position to attack the man until he left. The only people who could come near Rhea and Satya in Atila's presence were Chander and Krishnam. Rhea took Atila for her runs; Chander would also accompany them, but maintain a safe distance behind them.

9

ONE HUMID SUMMER morning, Rhea had a dream in the wee hours. Satya was in his car that was speeding on a highway and suddenly there was a loud noise of a collision. The loud bang of the collision woke up Rhea.

Satya was to leave today for Delhi, in his newly bought jeep to receive Krishnam, for his summer holidays. She ran downstairs, straight to his bedroom and woke him up. He heard her and then simply asked her to pray with all her faith for his safety to Devima. He had already taught her the procedure on how to avert it. 'I will have to go to receive Krishnam, as there are no reservations available because of the train collision in Bihar, and the trains remain cancelled on this route,' he said.

Later that morning, Satya sat in the car and Rhea at the sadhanasthal. Rhea calmed herself down and sat on her asana, in front of Devima. She gathered herself to concentrate and began with reciting the mantra Om. In between came thoughts, like 'What if anything happens to Baba?'

After her thoughts were more focused, she started reciting the Shakti Mantra, which is a Beej Mantra; when coupled with intention, it creates strong and powerful vibrations, and can change what seems inevitable.

'Everything in this creation is a probability apart from two facts—birth and death. An aware individual can enhance one probability to negate the other. We as individuals deep down are co-creators of our lives. We always have a choice that we make for ourselves; our actions are a complete reflection of our choices,' she remembered Satya's words.

Rhea increased her intensity to elevate the vibrations, as she chanted the Shakti Mantra and focused her thoughts to visualize that Satya had reached his destination safely.

The doubt had disappeared completely and was replaced with faith in Devima and that she will take care of everything. With that came a strong affirmation that Satya with everyone else had reached their destination safely.

'The time has come, Rhea, when the intended result is for you to choose and create. Pray with your faith whichever way you want and you shall be able to achieve the results you intend,' Satya had told her before leaving.

She knew if Satya had said she could, she would cross all barriers to do what seemed impossible. Later that evening, she finally got a call from Satya; she had been anxiously waiting near the phone in anticipation. He briefly conveyed to her about a light collision with another car, which happened on the way to Delhi; however, no one had suffered any injury.

The next day Rhea went to bed early. She was sleeping, when she heard someone knocking on her door. Half-awake, she wondered who could it be, as she opened the door. Before she could see who it was Krishnam picked her up in his arms. Rhea could not believe herself, she closed her eyes shut and was giggling with happiness to see him. Krishnam placed her back in bed.

She sprang out, rubbed her eyes and pushed him. 'You liar, you said that you were coming tomorrow!'

He laughed and picked her up again. 'That's an aggressive welcome, princess. I wanted to surprise you and see your reaction.'

He carried her to his room in his arms and sat her down on his bed, telling her that he had bought some things for her. Rhea went through all the dresses and perfumes and loved each one of them.

'I hope they fit, Krish!' she said, holding a long black dress.

'They will,' he replied.

There was playfulness in the air with some silly arguments and Satya's intervention was prompt. That night came to be dawn before they finally went to bed; Krishnam was fighting his jet lag still. Though no one wanted to sleep, all of them were very tired and were fighting it.

The afternoon was spent chatting and talking about the different experiences that Krishnam had at his university. The different interactions and how people and students in general are different in the US, as compared to India. As the evening set in, Krishnam told Rhea that he had brought some beer for himself and he wanted to have it in the fields, after everyone had retired to their rooms. Rhea was all excited about having beer for the first time. They sneaked out after midnight, when in all probability everyone was asleep.

There was sufficient light coming from the half-moon; it was a clear night as Krishnam and Rhea walked through the fields.

'Ah, it's good,' Krishnam said, after a sip of his beer.

'Can I have a sip too?'

'It isn't meant for kids,' he replied teasingly.

'Krish, you are only four years older than me. Can I please... please...please...please?'

'All right, take a sip, but remember I didn't give it to you.'

'Yuck, it tastes horrible,' she said, spitting most of it out.

'I told you, Rhea.'

'You did not say it tastes horrible. Why are you having it?'

'Because I love it,' he replied, stressing on the word love.

'You love all the horrible things, Krish.'

'That means you are horrible?' he said teasingly.

Both were suddenly quiet. There was a realization of what he just said. He caught her behind her neck and pulled her closer; she closed her eyes and he pecked her on both her eyelids. They walked further away from the residential area.

After a brief silence, 'Oh, by the way, what did you tell your friends, who am I to you?' asked Krishnam. She said nothing, as she was swimming in exhilaration.

He reached out for her again and they embraced each other.

She could hear his heart pounding; he softly kissed her forehead and then walked ahead as he leisurely finished his beer.

'Come, let's head back now and go to sleep, it's late.'

They walked back in absolute silence. Krishnam held Rhea's hand until they were out of the fields.

Rhea entered her room and said loudly, 'You mean the world to me.' She shut the door behind her. The entire night, she kept tossing and turning in her bed.

Nearly a week passed by in catching up with the past year. Krishnam was physically fitter and was regular with his karate practice. He had been giving a few tips to Chander too while they practised together; it was all the learning from the Karate Club he had joined in the US. Krishnam boasted about his proficiency in karate to Satya too and Satya challenged him for a match to assess it.

Rhea was looking forward to the karate match today with Satya and Krishnam as opponents. They came in full attire dressed in black for the match, which started with the bows. Chander was the referee. Both were mindful, both exercised swiftness when required and it all seemed effortless. Both were aware of their strengths and weaknesses. Both fought to win. In their fluid movements of extending and contracting their bodies, it seemed to Rhea as if it were a dance performance, where both were in harmonious engagement. Rhea witnessed the coming alive of the principle of Aiki, the beauty of which was breathtaking. Aiki is a principle of martial arts, whereby one attunes physically and mentally with the opponent to avoid a direct clash of force.

They first joined together in the flow of movements and then in the intention. Both intended to overcome the will of the other and then redirect their motion and intent. Both were cautious not to harm the opponent. The fight culminated with a Rei, a bow. Both were equal.

'It did not seem like a combat, Krish. It was like a spectacular dance,' said Rhea, completely taken aback. The magnificence that she had experienced was difficult to express in words.

After they finished with their karate, everyone dispersed to do their own things. In the evening, Krishnam and Rhea went for a run with Atila, but Chander did not accompany them.

Krishnam and Rhea did their meditation before dinner that evening. While on the way back from the sadhanasthal, Krishnam told Rhea what was the reaction initially of other students, when he chanted the mantra Om in the campus hostel. How the students had mostly been inquisitive and receptive. After they finished dinner, the three were sitting as usual in the veranda and chatting.

'Baba, the karate match today between the two of you was an exhibition of skill and graceful movements,' said Rhea.

'The aim of karate is self development through self discipline,' said Krishnam. 'What you witnessed was not an actual combat.'

'We have to exercise conscious control over our movements. One of the principles of any martial art is to find stillness in movement, and movement in stillness. Any martial art has a spiritual significance and works towards developing both, the body and spirit. There is never a lookout for the first strike. This is akin to the principle of Tantra,' said Satya.

'Is there a strike in Tantra?' Rhea asked, totally flabbergasted. 'Baba, how can we use Tantra to strike?'

'We don't use it, but every power has the strong potential to be greatly misused. It happens in Tantra too and you will understand this with time.'

Rhea got up to receive the phone, it had been ringing for a while. She spoke briefly, hung up and told them, 'Tomorrow Nethra and Barkha are coming over for a picnic with Neel. It will be their first visit.' Rhea was filled with elation.

In a while, Satya retired to his room and the two of them went for a walk.

'They are eager to meet you, Krishnam,' said Rhea, stressing on eager.

'But why?' asked Krishnam, with naughtiness in his eyes.

'They want to meet my Krishnam,' she said, as she ran into the field being prepared for paddy.

Krishnam ran behind her and caught her by her waist, and came to a halt. He looked down at her, bent over and kissed her at the nape of her neck. He turned her around to face him and caressed her face with the back of his hand.

'Can you tell me what you see in my eyes?' he asked, whispering in her ears. She looked in his eyes as if in a far-off land. 'You will always be mine,' he whispered again.

Krishnam thought of what he was doing; he turned to walk away.

'Krish,' she called out.

He stopped only for a second and then continued to walk away. Rhea stood still, not understanding what had just transpired and what was it that ticked Krishnam off.

As scheduled, Rhea's friends came the next morning. The episode of her birthday was still very vivid in her mind. She wasn't sure if they would actually make it, as Neel was picking them up on the pretext of going for another friend's birthday. She offered them thandai, which had been made in Shaktidham. It was Neel's favourite and each time he came he would ask if there was some. They savoured every drop of it.

They went out to the grassy area just outside the veranda, as by now the sun had been covered in clouds. Nethra noticed that there was no noise, she could hear the birds chirping loud and clear; the air was fresh here unlike the city.

'Look, the clouds are moving, it seems they are in a race,' said Nethra.

'Yes, similar to human beings,' replied Rhea.

They gazed towards the clouds and tried to decipher their shapes, relating them to various things.

'Look at the vast expanse; I remember looking at the clouds as a child and trying to find faces in them. I feel I am reconnecting with my childhood,' said Nethra.

'Do you realize that we should remain connected to certain things in our lives and treasure them, but we tend to lose out on them?' asked Neel.

'Memories of my childhood are coming back to me; I loved the rains, getting drenched in it; the paper boats we made and floated; dancing in the rain and splashing water collecting in puddles. When did I forget how much fun it was and the joy it gave me?' said Nethra, reminiscing.

'Whatever gives us joy should be a part of our existence,' said Rhea.

'Do we choose pain?' Neel asked Rhea.

She replied, 'Yes, it is a choice that we make.'

She took them out to the fields to show them around; they sat under a tree, looking at the serene surroundings with lush green fields. They saw a tall figure approaching at a distance, as Rhea pointed out with a naughty smile and raised brows, 'Krishnam's coming'.

'Oh my God!' said Nethra aloud.

'He took my breath away,' said Barkha, looking at him as he came closer.

He was walking towards them leisurely and there was something inexplicably striking about him. It was impossible to remain untouched by it. Neel smiled, observing the reaction of the two girls towards Krishnam, as they greeted each other with a warm hug and he introduced Krishnam to the girls.

The food was served for them under the thatched shelter in the fields.

'The food tastes so different!' remarked Nethra, while they sat having lunch, which was served on banana leaves.

'The food is made using ingredients from our own fields and is cooked in earthen pots on cooking cakes made out of cow dung, though it is slower to cook,' said Rhea.

'No wonder it tastes so different,' replied Barkha.

'You do not use gas?' asked Nethra, totally shocked by the conversation.

'We do have a gas in the kitchen, but it is mainly used to make tea or coffee, or is used if Krish or I wish to eat something other than what's cooked in the common kitchen for everyone.'

The girls were staring at Krishnam intermittently, when they thought that he was not looking. Rhea was aware of the unnerving effect he had cast on her friends, but paid no heed.

'The curd too is naturally sweet and is delicious,' said Barkha.

On their way back, Rhea took them to where some workers were making cakes from the cow dung and she added, 'A part of the cow dung will be used to make these cakes for cooking fuel. These will be dried in the sun before they can be used and the remaining cow dung will be used as manure for the fields,' Rhea explained to them.

Krishnam was looking at her smiling.

Nethra commented, 'You live in a beautiful place.'

'Baba says stay as close as you can to nature and all that is natural. The well-being of our human race is dependent upon the well-being of our Mother Earth. Nurturing and preserving our environment is the only way of preserving the human race. Our ancestors recognized the importance of our interdependence with nature. There are many hymns that seek the blessings from the five elements that constitute nature.'

'That is fascinating, Rhea,' said Neel, 'what are the five elements?'

'Earth (prithvi), water (jal), fire (agni), air (vayu), and space (akash). The most interesting thing is that the human body is constituted of these same elements and in similar percentage respectively. These five elements are the universal components of all matter. These elements are actually metaphors for what they represent at a subtle level and cannot be understood literally.'

'Rhea, can you explain it more simply?' asked Nethra.

'I think it is crystal clear,' said Neel.

Krishnam was observing Rhea with complete attention.

'Nethra, I will try and articulate it for you,' said Rhea contemplatively.

'I am going to take a walk with Neel, you and Nethra can continue your discussion at length,' said Barkha.

'I would like to be a part of this conversation,' said Neel.

Barkha pulled his hand. He resisted, but then gave in and both walked into the fields.

'The five elements are the foundation of the universe and constitute all material reality, be it the universe or the human body. The element "earth" is the material body of any situation. It represents the quality of stability. In a human body, bones, flesh, and the sense of smell represent earth. It is the foundation of life. For matter to exist, it has to be interconnected in respect to each other and various forces interplay to hold it together,' said Rhea, looking at Nethra.

Nethra stood nodding in agreement.

'The element "water" by its very nature results in forming connections. It brings about flow and change in any given situation, and from its movement results the coming together and drawing apart. In a human body, blood and all other fluids are a manifestation of the element water. It also represents the sense of taste.

'The element "fire" represents energy, which may be latent or manifested. Every situation has its potential, as there is a process of transformation from latent to potential. The old state is consumed to create the new. In a human body, it is represented by digestion. It consumes to create what is nourishing for the body. Fire also represents the ability to see.'

'No wonder there is the phrase, "fire in the eyes and fire in the belly",' replied Nethra.

'Element "air" is movement. Life is continuously moving, and with every situation, forever changing. The element air in the human body is represented by respiration, and voluntary and involuntary movements of our body.

'"Space" is the element that enables all others to exist. It is the backdrop of all creation and just is. In a human body, it exists as cavities and orifices. It is responsible for the sense of hearing. The human body is the micro of the macrocosm,' continued Rhea.

Krishnam was listening with complete concentration, as Rhea went on explaining further.

'For an integrated optimum functioning of all elements, they have to be in harmonious balance with each other internally as well as externally. We human beings are a part of a larger system and this system needs to be integrated too. When we exploit nature, we in turn are in a self-destructive mode or disintegration.'

'I understand what you are saying. It's different to see life from your perspective and you have explained it very well,' said Nethra, looking at Krishnam and expecting him to say something. He remained silent.

Rhea's friends met Satya and they touched his feet. This was the first time that both the girls had met a Tantric and visited his abode. Their visit to Shaktidham had been an extremely refreshing and pleasant experience. They had not encountered anything that screamed or hinted caution. Everything seemed to say 'may peace descend on you'. They came back feeling good and happy.

'You will make a very good teacher,' said Krishnam to Rhea, after all of them had left.

'Teacher!' she exclaimed, bemused.

'Yes, my princess,' he said, ruffling her hair.

That night, Rhea could not sleep, so she decided to try out the outfits and footwear Krishnam had gifted her. She got into the black dress first, which fitted her beautifully. She slid on the black stilettos, secured its straps and sprayed the perfume. She was admiring herself in the mirror, when she heard someone knocking on her door. She smiled at her reflection and walked to open the door.

Krishnam was stunned looking at her and without taking his eyes off, he said, 'Wow, it did fit you well! Will you try on the other dresses as well?'

He just sat and kept looking quietly, as she came out wearing different outfits from her dressing room.

She had finished trying them all and came out in her pyjamas, when he asked, 'Are the stilettos comfortable?'

'Yes, they are beautiful and very comfortable,' she replied.

'Oh my God, it's 2.30, let's get some sleep now. Good night.'

He gave her a peck on the forehead and walked out of her room.

10

A WEEK LATER, Nethra and Barkha came to Shaktidham again, giving an excuse to their parents.

'Something in you comes alive, Rhea, when Krishnam is around,' Nethra said, while they were taking a walk in the fields.

Rhea just smiled.

'I have seen love in Krishnam's eyes for you and it's different; he looks at you with startling tenderness, which is impossible to miss out on.'

Barkha added, 'Your Krishnam is so good-looking. He seems straight out of a dream. He has a very intense earthy presence and there is a palpable energy around him. There seems something incredibly mysterious about him and he looks like a younger version of your Baba.'

Rhea just kept smiling.

'Girls, how do you find Neel?' asked Barkha, looking at Rhea with a twinkle in her eyes.

'We have known him since childhood; he is a wonderful person, but what about him?' asked Rhea.

'Okay, well, I think I should tell both of you about it; I am in love with him,' said Barkha hastily, in a single breath.

Both Rhea and Nethra were quietly looking at one another, to judge if this is another frivolous delusion of hers.

'It's a beautiful feeling and I feel so light; it seems I am always floating,' she said dreamily, with a grin.

'Love is a serious word!' said Rhea, with uncertainty.

'Now, what is that supposed to mean, Rhea?' questioned Barkha, with a bewildered look. 'Gosh, why are you are so complicated,' she further added, the frustration in her voice all too apparent.

'What does love mean to you, Barkha?' asked Rhea, looking straight into her eyes.

'What the heck, Rhea, I know what love is and I know that I love Neel. I am not getting into any philosophical discussion about it.' Barkha said, irritated. 'And what does it mean to you, Rhea, can you please enlighten us? I am rather curious to know now!' she asked, with a smirk.

'Your question to my question does not answer my question,' replied Rhea.

'You don't seem to be happy about my feelings for Neel!' said Barkha, infuriated.

Rhea nodded her head slightly and said nothing. Nethra didn't know how to react, she quietly stood listening and watching the two. An uncomfortable silence prevailed, which marked the beginning of a change in their relationship.

Later at the dining table, Nethra was trying to keep the conversation going between the three, as there was an unpleasantness that could be felt. Things were wrapped up in haste and the friends dispersed on what seemed like an ominous note.

A few days later at night, Krishnam and Rhea were having a discussion, while sitting with Satya, and Krishnam asked, 'Rhea, have you thought of what you want to do in life?'

'Obviously pursue my sadhana,' she added, 'and be the best.'

'You want to be the best?' asked Krishnam, amused.

He waited for a moment, then added, 'There is only one way to be the best—it is to put in your best effort to pursue excellence in what you do. Sadhana is a path, where you only compete with yourself and strive to make a better you. There are no opponents to overcome, but yourself. The destination of Tantra is self-understanding and no one can claim to have arrived.'

Satya told them, 'A Tantra sadhak must strive with one's whole being towards self-understanding. One must be aware of every emotion one is capable of and every appetite must be understood. In Tantra, there is no fight or struggle to beat our bodily desires. Every aspect must be understood, before we can comprehend the whole.'

'There is a time for silence and there is a time for motion. The motion is as important as the silence and so is every step transiting from one to the other. There comes a point when the entire effort becomes effortless and that is the starting point for a sadhak. That is a point from when the sadhak seeks nothing; there is no seeker and there is nothing to be sought.'

◆

Rhea was perplexed about what will happen with Neel, as she knew Barkha was extremely possessive of her relationship. She carried and harboured her insecurities from the atmosphere at home, where just by being a girl she was devoid of any appreciation or attention. It was also time for Krishnam to return to the US for the next semester in a few of days.

Rhea was lying in bed with mixed thoughts and emotions going through her mind. She finally got up and knocked at

Krishnam's door; it was past midnight.

'Come in.'

'What is it, Rhea?'

'I can't sleep.'

'I am trying to study. Why don't you lie down here and sleep,' said Krishnam.

'What are you studying?'

'Indian laws, as they are different from what we are studying at the university. I was trying to make sense of the laws here.'

'Why does time pass in the blink of an eye when you are here?' asked Rhea softly.

He closed his book.

'I wonder, Krish, why did Baba decide to send you to an American law school, when the laws are totally different here?'

'Yale is considered one of the best. Not everyone can get this opportunity,' said Krishnam, avoiding her question.

'Baba always has a reason, a strong reason,' said Rhea, contemplating and lost in thoughts.

'You are right, princess,' he said, looking at her sad face.

Would you like to play truth or dare?' asked Krishnam, trying to cheer her up.

She looked at him and smiled, 'Sounds interesting.'

'Head's your call, tail's mine,' she said.

Krishnam flipped a coin in the air.

'Tail's,' said Krishnam.

'Truth or dare, Rhea?' he asked, looking into her eyes.

She looked back in his eyes and said, 'Dare.'

He put his hands on her eyelids and closed them; he asked her to keep them closed. His fingertips then moved from her face to her neck, only stopping at the collar of her nightdress. He then picked her up in his arms. She did not know where he was going to take her and why.

She could hear his heartbeat, hear him breathing; smell his

scent, feel his touch. He lay her down on the cool floor. His lips touched hers; he kissed her softly and she responded. He let his tongue explore her mouth hungrily, then moved on to her neck. He held her hand and kissed each fingertip, one-by-one.

He kissed her eyelids and said softly, 'Open your eyes.'

Her first kiss was in a place, which was most sacred for both of them; it was the sadhanasthal.

◆

On the day of Krishnam's departure from Shaktidham, Satya, Krishnam and Rhea stood in front of Goddess Kali. Satya put a red tika on Krishnam's forehead. Tika is symbolic of blessings of the deity worshipped. He touched Satya's feet and hugged Rhea and kissed her on her forehead.

'Why don't you take Rhea along with you next time for a month? Both of you can see and explore the US together,' said Satya.

Rhea looked at Satya in disbelief and said, 'No Baba, I don't want to leave you and go.'

'It is good to travel, Rhea,' said Krishnam calmly.

'I don't want to go,' she replied adamantly.

Satya put his hand on her head and smiled, 'You should, Rhea, as you stay confined in a completely protected environment. The world is a field; it offers experiences which will aid your growth.'

'With Krishnam, I will still be in a protected environment,' she replied. 'I will go when I am older.'

Both Satya and Krishnam were silent.

The day after Krishnam left, Neel called Rhea. He sounded distressed and he informed her that he was reaching Shaktidham. On his arrival, he was escorted to the veranda, where Rhea was waiting for him.

Neel hugged Rhea as they met. She could sense that he was stressed out. His body language reflected his agony. She asked him to take a seat and if he would like some coffee.

'Yes please.'

Rhea asked him about school, she also told him that Nethra and Barkha had come to Shaktidham a couple of days earlier, to which he nodded in acknowledgement. Neel inquired if Krishnam was still there or had left already.

The coffee was brought to them.

'What has happened, Neel?' asked Rhea, as they sipped their coffee.

Neel was silent for a few moments. 'Rhea, I told my mother that she was responsible for my father's death,' he said, suddenly breaking his silence.

'Daddy would have still been alive had she divorced him. She killed him!' he said, looking at the floor in disgust.

Rhea looked at him perplexed.

'How can you be so certain about it?' she asked, once Neel had gained composure.

'Had she divorced him, you could be sitting here and blaming her for splitting the family. Could it be that she loved you and was afraid that your father may take you away? Maybe she was hopeful that their marriage could work out. Or maybe it was your father, who was threatened by her persona. Maybe, he was the one who wanted someone to follow him, rather than stride with him.

'Neel, not everything in life is black and white, some areas are often grey. Well, I may not be wrong in saying that, to a large extent, we are all responsible for our own lives. We always have an option to choose; one can choose love over resentment. What has transpired in your life has made you bitter; you blame your mother for it, whereas, it is your own inability to cope up with the situation.'

Neel listened to her without responding and both remained silent. He put his hands on his forehead and slumped in the chair looking down.

'I believe that the day you take responsibility for your own life, you will have no one to blame.'

Both sat in silence. Rhea wanted to change the topic after a considerable amount of time had passed. 'By the way, Barkha said that she is in love with you,' said Rhea, with a smile.

Neel looked up and smiled back, 'God knows what love is all about. What do you think love is, Rhea?'

She answered, 'For me, love means Baba and Krishnam.'

'Do you get a sense of completion with Krishnam?' asked Neel.

Rhea looked at him and replied, 'No one completes us, only we can complete ourselves. If we seek completion from someone, we end up in disastrous relationships.'

11

Four years later

Whenever Rhea went out with Atila into the fields for a run, there wasn't reason enough for Chander to tail her by 50 metres, though Chander saw it as a good opportunity to exercise, other than his workout.

Satya agreed with him and had said, 'There could possibly be some wild animals around.'

However, to date Rhea had never spotted one.

The fields had beautiful golden stalks of robust wheat. As she was running, she thought she heard a voice. Atila stopped in his tracks and growled. She sped behind Atila, who was leading her to this voice.

It sounded like the voice of a small girl who was repeating, 'Yes, harder, harder, I love it and I want more.' The girl was reciting it like a poem, without any emotions.

The sight Rhea saw made her freeze. 'Chander bhaiya, stop. Do not come any further.' she said loudly, raising her hand to signal him.

Chander stopped, but took out his revolver as a reflex action. A girl was lying in the middle of a pile of crushed wheat stalks and a scrawny-looking middle-aged man got off the girl on hearing Rhea's voice. The man was struggling to straighten his clothes. The girl seemed barely nine or ten years old. Her clothes were covered in mud and she had a blank expression.

Atila was getting uncomfortable. He had never seen so much commotion around. Rhea felt the chain loosening from her hand and Atila's growl getting louder. She tugged at his chain as she moved closer to the man; holding the girl by her arm, she looked into his eyes and lost the grip on the chain. Atila was off. She moved away and closed the girl's eyes and turned her around. The man screamed; then a short cry and then silence followed. The law of the jungle allows the stronger predator to survive. Nature has its way to create a balance in what meets the eyes as chaos.

The girl was malnourished and her face had a deadpan look, but she looked better after a shower and a meal, when Chander brought her to meet Rhea. Rhea gestured Chander to leave.

Rhea hugged the girl and said, 'You are safe here.'

The girl stood, exhibiting no emotions. 'What is your name?' asked Rhea, softly taking her hand in her palms. The girl looked at her and Rhea saw a flicker of life in her inert eyes. The girl did not reply, but made no attempt to free her hand.

'Will you stay here? You will be safe,' said Rhea, looking gently into the girl's eyes.

The girl nodded in affirmation and replied, 'Didi, my name is Meena and I have no one to go back to.'

After a brief pause she said, 'He used to force me...nearly every day and made me do dirty things.'

She pulled up her frock, pointing and revealing her burn

marks. 'See, he burnt me with his bidi one day.'

Then she added, 'Today our relatives had come for a wedding in the village, so he brought me here.'

A pause and then she spoke again, 'My mother died a few months back, while giving birth to my sister, who died too. He would beat up my mother often and would shout at her to "have a son this time around". One of the days my mother wasn't well and she slept downstairs in the only room we had, as she had a big belly. I slept with him on the same charpoy on the roof…he then put his finger in me, rubbed me, and he asked me "how does it feel?" I said okay, as I was scared of him.'

She continued, 'The next day he made my mother sleep on the roof and took me inside. He made me take off all my clothes and was staring at me for a while. He then made me lie down with my legs apart; he told me that he would give me a good time…'

Silence prevailed for a bit.

'Didi, that day he did it for the first time. I was in pain, I told him that I was hurting and begged him to stop. I was in tears, but he didn't stop and bit me hard here,' she said, pointing to her undeveloped left breast.

'He told me, when he is doing that to me, he wants me to repeat, "Do it harder, I love it and want more". After a few days, while he was having sex with me, he asked me "Enjoying, bitch?" and I said "No". He stopped and sat up abruptly; he lit a bidi, took a few puffs, and put that burning stub in my inner thigh at different places over and over again. He then forced me to repeat many a times "Do it harder, I love it and want it more". I kept repeating and crying all the while he hurt me.'

By now her eyes were moist and her throat choked up.

With a heavy throat, she continued, 'Since that day, whenever he hurt me, I continuously repeated, "Do it harder, I love it and want it more". I never failed to repeat it. Didi, your dog killed my father and I am relieved.

'Didi, I am a Shudra,' said Meena, her head bowed and eyes looking down. 'Can I still stay here?' She looked up at Rhea, with tears running down her cheeks.

Rhea, looking at her, said, 'In Shaktidham, all human beings are equal.'

Apparently, the next day a body of a man was found about 50 kms away from Shaktidham, on the highway ahead of Mughalsarai. He was beyond recognition; a convoy of lorries had crushed him. There were unexplained animal bites too on the body. The unclaimed body was cremated by the administration.

The day after, Satya came out of his three-day maun-vrat (vow of silence). Maun-vrat was a time when he neither spoke nor met anyone. Only Rhea had the liberty to access him in this period. However, it had to be a catastrophe and only if she failed to handle it. This time before Satya went into maun-vrat, he had instructed Chander that from now on, in his absence Rhea's instructions would be followed, and whatever she says must be obeyed as his word.

Rhea was curious about the caste division, which Meena had stated. She wanted an insight from Satya, who explained it to her, 'Caste was a division of the Hindu society based on the occupation of the family and by virtue of being born in that family the next generation carried it forward. Hindu's were divided into four distinct classes. The Brahmins were ranked the highest in society, who were educated and performed sacred rituals. Next came the Kshatriyas or the warrior class, who protected their people. The Vaishyas or the business community came next, followed lastly by the Shudras or the labour class. The Shudras were deprived of all the privileges, which were enjoyed by the other three castes in their order of ranking. They were treated as lowly and were discriminated at every level of their existence. A large population of India is still in the grip of this age-old system, even when occupation is no more based on caste and the economics too have changed. The caste system still creates a strong divide in the society. Many gruesome crimes owe their birth to this still prevalent caste system.'

That same night after dinner, Rhea sat with Satya and he explained to her, one of the principals of Tantra. 'A Tantric lives in a dimension of vibrations, where nothing is right or wrong. The deeper you go, you realize it simply is. A Tantric must live in harmony with nature; nobody is greater than nature, as its laws can neither be modified nor broken, just complied with and revered,' he said.

In the days that followed, Meena was admitted in a school that was close by. She was staying at Shaktidham and helped Rhea in her personal work; she was paid a salary, which was deposited at the bank. Other than that, Shaktidham took care of Meena's needs.

The days passed by, after Rhea's grade twelve board examinations, for which she had appeared about a month ago. Rhea and her friends were now awaiting the results of the exams they had written. Rhea had decided to pursue physics, as it was a subject that fascinated her.

Nethra and Barkha wrote various entrance papers for their chosen fields. Nethra had joined coaching classes. Barkha was facing some issues at home but was going about her preparation as best as she could. After the results of twelfth grade were announced, Rhea applied to the university for a bachelor's in science.

My dear Krish,

I wish you could have been here for my holidays, but I know it was important for you to not take this break due to your commitments at work. I have taken admission at the university and I will be starting classes from tomorrow. Once I graduate, I think I will pursue post-graduation in physics.

Nethra got selected in a medical college and has already joined. Barkha too is leaving; she applied and got admission at a school for fashion designing. It was a herculean task for her mother to convince her father to let her go to Delhi and study fashion designing.

I met Neel yesterday; he was here for his semester break and will be completing his course in business management next year. Stock market speculation seems to be Neel's new interest. He asked me to convey his 'Hi' to you and he also said it's been a long time since he saw you.

I hope the telephone department fixes the lines, which they have been promising for the last three weeks since the work on the highway is in progress and they destroyed the lines during excavation. It seems such a long time, since I heard your voice...

Oh I have to tell you about this new girl Meena too who has joined the ashram, and is a very charming little girl. I will tell you the rest when we speak. Hopefully soon...

Lots of love,

Rhea

It was Rhea's second day in college, seniors were ragging the new students; one of them asked her where she had come from.

She replied, 'Shaktidham.'

Hell broke loose amongst the students. 'It is that Tantric's place,' said someone.

'That is scary,' said another.

'They have powers to possess people and are destructive. I have heard Tantrics are dangerous people,' said someone.

'What do you do in a place like that?' asked another guy.

The group turned curious; a bombardment of questions followed. Rhea was looking at them silently; all of them saw her observing them; there was silence and a kind of fear.

'I am a student of Tantra and my Baba is a Tantric,' she replied calmly.

'You mean you live in Shaktidham and he is your father?'

asked a short guy, who stood behind a few students.

She replied, 'Yes.'

Everyone dispersed in silence, as if in mourning.

That was the first and last day any senior came to rag her. There wasn't any interaction thereafter with anyone in the college. Everyone maintained a distance, except Devraj and Ishaan, who could not see each other eye-to-eye.

Rhea became the hottest topic for discussion in the college.

Gossip went from pillar to post and did many rounds of Rhea's antecedents and lineage as a Tantric.

Some were scared and said, 'Keep off her, we are ordinary people living our lives, why unnecessarily complicate things for ourselves.'

'I had a different image of Tantrics. She is beautiful and striking.'

'Isn't it intriguing that an occult practitioner is a science student?'

'Look at her eyes, I am sure she can hypnotize.'

There were all kinds of deliberations going on about her in the college.

On Sunday afternoon, Rhea told Satya in detail about all that had happened in the days since the ragging incident and the gossip going on in college. She was amused by the opinions of people and their lack of knowledge.

She even told him about the college canteen, where a group was discussing about the Tantric girl from Shaktidham joining their college.

'I know Tantrics are into black magic,' said one.

'Do you know what black magic is?' asked Ishaan.

'Yes, it means that they have magical powers which they use to destroy.'

'If that is true, couldn't they use this power to construct as well?' asked Ishaan, as he walked off in disgust at their narrow thought processes and superstitious minds.

Satya told Rhea after listening to what she had experienced, 'Remember that any display of power frightens people, whatever good you may do. Frightened people will attack you in any way possible for them. The practice of Tantra will enhance and develop certain faculties, which when used will be looked upon as miracles by people. A person who displays power by performing miracles, attracts attention to fan his ego, which leads to destruction. Ego is the biggest enemy of oneself; it is what separates one from experiencing oneness with the entire existence.

'An exhibition of power can easily put you on a pedestal, but then it is like a prison; it's a lonely place. The road of Tantra is such that it will take you where you want to go. You are to make a choice at every step, as there will be many probable paths. Therefore, you are a decision maker, who then lives with the consequence of your own chosen path.

'A Tantric has a kind of power, which is difficult to comprehend, but remember, my child, you should have the wisdom to do or not, and where to do what. You will realize in time that you can enhance, reduce the effect of, or change things. But not everything can be changed; only a wise person knows what can and cannot be changed, which he must accept. With every decision, you will either choose to take a step towards understanding oneness, or towards creating a wall of ego that will destroy your reason for sadhana. We live in a realm, where each action has its consequence and every seemingly insignificant act also bears its implication.'

12

FROM THE TIME Rhea joined college, whenever Devraj saw her he would pass a remark audible enough for Rhea to hear. He was a certified goon and an aspiring student leader with the support of some local political party. For some, even a bit of power gets difficult to handle. Rhea would evade him, by simply ignoring him and his remarks. Her being indifferent irked him further, as he wanted to extract her reaction.

Ishaan too was a student leader of the college. No sooner did he file his nomination than he requested Rhea for her vote. 'One vote may not matter, but I look forward to your winning the election,' she had replied.

One day, Devraj took a step further and stopped her on her way to the lecture room. Ishaan intervened and Devraj left after a mild altercation.

Rhea looked at Ishaan and told him, 'Please do not fight on my behalf, I can take care of myself.'

Ishaan looked at her flabbergasted, and said, 'I would have done that for anyone in your situation.'

She said, 'Don't do that for me; I can fight my own battles.'

He shrugged his shoulders and walked away.

A few days later, a professor intervened as Devraj tried to stop Rhea on her way, and he had to leave again. One day, however, he got the opportunity which he had been anxiously waiting for. Rhea was alone and the corridor of the first floor too was empty. She came out after her lecture was over. Devraj was standing with a couple of friends near the stairwell leading to the ground floor. As he saw Rhea walking down that corridor, he started walking towards her. His friends exited, taking the stairs.

'Rhea, why don't you talk to me? You know I am interested in you and your being indifferent towards me is driving me mad,' Devraj said to her.

She did not respond and stepped to the side to walk ahead. He intercepted her again, and caught her left wrist. Rhea did not struggle.

Calmly, she looked at him and said in a tone icy enough to freeze fire, 'Devraj, leave my hand.'

He held her wrist even tighter and said, 'What if I pull you into the class and have some fun with you, you think you can do anything?'

Rhea made no effort to free her hand. The grip was hurting her wrist. He pushed her to the wall and looked her in the eyes. He then suddenly let go of her wrist, turned and walked away...

Everyone wondered how he managed to slip and break the elbow of his right hand, while going down the stairs and got a deep cut in his head that required about ten stitches. He was kept under observation for the next forty-eight hours since it was a head injury. He was advised complete bed rest for a few days.

Ishaan's most serious opponent was Devraj; but Devraj withdrew from the election five days prior to it. The nature of action is that it concludes in a consequence.

Rhea didn't come to vote on the day of polling and Ishaan won the election to become the president of the students' union. This was, however, going to be the last election that the college witnessed, as the new vice chancellor, who came to the university in the next term, saw it as an unnecessary evil. A students' body would be formed, with the students who excelled in their respective fields to represent the relevant issues.

As time passed, the talk of Rhea in the college also dwindled considerably.

Ishaan was sitting with his group of friends in the college café and discussing his party for winning the election. He told them he would go to Shaktidham to enquire why Rhea hasn't been coming to college for the past three days and also invite her for the party.

'Ishaan, why are you going to Shaktidham? Have you taken leave of your senses?' asked Ajay.

'Have any of you been to Shaktidham?' he asked Ajay, who he thought fitted so well in the role of an advisor, when it came to others.

No one had a reply.

'Have you ever met a Tantric?' he asked, with irritation. 'Only Rhea!'

'There is something very mysterious about her, she is dangerous,' said Rajneesh.

'Oh will you shut up! Just let her be,' screamed Ishaan, in irritation.

'I will only have the party if Rhea comes and I am going to invite her,' said Ishaan.

'Someone seems to be counting the days of her absence!' mocked Ajay.

Ishaan didn't respond to the statement.

He said, 'Rhea does seem different from us, but I want to see where she comes from.'

'She is strange and some things are better left alone Ishaan, don't mess with them,' said Rajneesh, and added, 'I have never seen her hanging around with anyone in college. Whenever I have seen her she is alone, which is not normal.'

Ishaan just left without saying anything further.

◆

'A sadhak is protected, but we too are gifted with life, which is fragile. This is a universal truth without any exceptions,' Satya told Rhea, after she had told him what happened to Devraj. 'Tantrics flow with the rhythm of the universe, treating it as a manifestation of the Mother Goddess. They open themselves to receive universal energy and become a reservoir of those energies. When a Tantric blesses or curses, it materializes as accumulated energy, which when thrown at someone has a massive impact.

'Firstly, he has to be positive in thought; secondly, his speech should reflect that positivity; thirdly, his action should be constructive. As long as he follows these rules, the universe will take care of such a Tantric. A Tantric who has failed to eliminate negativity within, goes wrong, because he lacks the wisdom to use his accumulated energy positively. Such a sadhak has defeated the purpose of practising Tantra,' Satya explained.

Ishaan reached the gates of Shaktidham; its enormous entrance gates were overbearing, and there was a bit of hustle bustle in the new marketplace, which seemed to be quite unoccupied yet. The high walls of Shaktidham seemed to fortify it.

As he entered the gates, the panorama transformed completely, with acres of green land. It was quiet, barring the occasional sound of the temple bells. It was impossible to comprehend from the outside that it would be a place like this. He thought how wrong it was for everyone to pass a judgment and therefore one should never conclude without knowing all the facts. A temple bell disrupted the flow of his thoughts as he walked. He saw a huge temple to the left and entered. It had various smaller enclosures, which had statues of different deities. The walls of the main temple had geometrical illustrations painted on it. Each statue was beautifully carved out of marble, and adorned in fine jewels and clothing. At the centre was a small enclosure, where a beautiful statue of Goddess Kamakhya was placed. A statue of Kaal Bhairava caught his attention.

He walked out of the temple, walked further and observed a yagyashala (a place to conduct yagya), which was triangular in shape; further ahead were lush green fields full of paddy. He found a signboard with the direction of the office on it.

It was quite a walk before he came upon the office building. A middle-aged man dressed in a saffron kurta was at the reception; from his looks he seemed like a foreigner, smiling and with a pleasant demeanour. Ishaan expressed his wish to meet Rhea. He went out of the back door to seek permission. He came out a while later and escorted Ishaan through the same door that led into a passage. They entered the veranda and he was asked to sit in the row of chairs, arranged perpendicularly on either side in front of the swing.

From the vantage point, he saw that the veranda opened onto a garden area, surrounded by trees. Ishaan saw a beautiful huge neem tree at some distance, under which was a Chabutra. Under the tree was a trishul, covered with a bright red cloth. Placed below the trishul was a stone depicting Lord Shiva. The place made Ishaan feel very calm and tranquil. His thoughts weren't scattered, he was simply in awe of the place. He had come to meet and seek Rhea's father's blessings, as he had won the college election.

Rhea came out to meet him; they had a brief conversation.

'Thank God, Rhea, I listened to myself and came to Shaktidham. It is indeed an experience coming here. It is so peaceful, calm and quiet here. I really wonder why people fear Shaktidham.'

'People fear the unknown,' replied Rhea, with a smile.

He later asked Rhea if he could meet her father.

'He is a recluse and doesn't meet too many people,' replied Rhea.

'Please, Rhea, it will be an honour.'

Satya came to the veranda to meet Rhea's fellow student from college. He walked in wearing a dark red robe, smiling, and Ishaan looked at him in awe. Ishaan touched his feet as he sat on his swing; he felt an overwhelming feeling of goodness flow through him. Rhea observed Ishaan was addressing Satya as Baba ji, throughout his conversation and seemed very comfortable in his presence. Satya conversed with him in fluent English, which made him gape in wonder.

After the brief conversation, Satya left and Ishaan asked if Rhea would show him around Shaktidham. Rhea nodded and took him around, with Chander following them.

'Why do people have such weird notions about Tantrics?' asked Ishaan.

'There is a difference between a quack and a qualified doctor.

A quack too is considered a doctor by a lot of village folk,' Rhea told Ishaan, while they walked through Shaktidham.

'All those who claim to be Tantrics may not be one. Tantra is a vidya which, in today's day and age, is practised and mastered by only a few. It has been exploited and misrepresented by self-proclaimed Tantrics.

'In layman's language, it is important to complete the prescribed course and clear an examination to be granted any degree. Similarly, any person can become or claim to be a Tantric only after completing his sadhana under a guru, which at the end is still an endless road. Someone claiming to be a Tantric without completing his sadhana is like a quack proclaiming to be a doctor. Such a person is sure to make blunders, but the medical fraternity cannot be maligned for that. Even for increased proficiency one requires to keep acquiring greater skills and it never really ends. A neurosurgeon is trained for specialized skill and if an ordinary doctor attempts to perform a neurological surgery, neurosurgeons cannot be maligned.

'Tantra is a field of practice and is handed down from a guru to a disciple and it originates from Lord Shiva, who passed it to Goddess Parvati as his shishya. Therefore, ignorance and judgement cannot go hand in hand,' said Rhea.

'Rhea, I have heard that Tantra is a path that advocates sexual freedom and the practices are largely sexual in nature. I have heard that Tantra sadhaks, in order to acquire powers, even go to the extent of using corpses to perform their rituals.'

'No, there is no truth in it and this has nothing to do with the true nature of sadhana. If anyone indulges in pervert activities under the garb of Tantra sadhana, Tantrics can't be maligned for it. Nothing or very little is known about this field, as its masters in today's time can be counted on one's fingertips. In my knowledge, except for Baba, the balance few Tantrics live far away from civilization.

'As I mentioned earlier, Tantra is imparted through a guru-shishya parampara, which in today's social structure has lost its essence and is difficult to understand. Guru actually means the one who brings light into our lives, by removing darkness, which is a symbol for ignorance. In the older times, when the guru-shishya relationship was prevalent and it was followed in its true spirit, the position of a guru was considered above God. It was the guru who showed one the path to God; he always sought the best for his disciple and it was a guru's discretion to accept an individual as a disciple. Similarly, in Tantra, it is the guru who chooses the shishya. If at any given point the guru feels that a shishya is not meeting the required parameters, he withdraws. It is a field where risks are best not taken.

'Coming to the other part of your question of sexual practices in Tantra, it is a path which does not ask to abstain; instead it is a path that requires a Tantric to recognize every aspect of his existence, as one is a part of the whole and must live it with awareness. The complexity of this statement can only be understood when it is lived. You can see for yourself that this philosophy has a great potential to be misunderstood.

'In Tantric tradition, "Shiva" and "Shakti" or "Purusha" and "Prakriti" represent the two fundamental forces that sustain the universe; all that exists is interplay of these forces. Shiva being the masculine aspect also represents focused energy and Shakti being the feminine represents the creative force. A human body, irrespective of the gender, is also an interplay of these energies. Each one of us has a unique ratio of the two energies, which when balanced completes us. The essence of male and female union in Tantra is in fact the union of the two energies within a human form, which is misinterpreted. Each aspect represents certain qualities: the masculine aspect represents our rationality, reason and linear thinking; the feminine aspect refers to emotional qualities like nurturing, caring, compassion and love.

'Goddess Kamakhya is the deity of Tantra. She represents the sacred act of creation and we as sadhaks pray to her divine form. The act of procreation is a representation of that principle; the male gives and the female receives, then nurtures and gives birth. Sex between a male and female also brings about creation, leading to progression of the species, and represents the interplay of the two forces. This whole concept can be perceived in numerous ways. Hence, you can imagine it being perceived simply at a sexual level,' explained Rhea.

After assimilating what he had just heard, Ishaan said, 'I found the statue of Kaal Bhairava in the temple very mesmerizing. I have not seen it anywhere.'

'Kaal Bhairava is a form of an expression of Lord Shiva, fierce and fiery. Kaal Bhairava is a form, which is beyond the understanding of time known to humanity. He is a destroyer as well as the protector, and remains unchallenged. This form is also called Kshetrapala or the guardian of a temple, where symbolically the keys of the temple are given after the temple closes, and taken to open the temple the next morning.'

'Rhea, who is Baba ji's disciple?'

'I am,' she replied.

They were silent for a few minutes. 'Rhea, I had come to invite you for a victory party that I was planning on throwing, but now I don't think I will invite you.'

She thanked him and congratulated him once again.

He said, 'The party is not worthy of your presence and neither are the people who are coming there.'

Ishaan had come to visit Shaktidham, to see it, feel it and then form an opinion for himself. Shaktidham was a sacred place. Satya was a person who could evoke only reverence and had a strong aura of wisdom around him. He had been on the right track about Rhea. The energy that surrounded her was conspicuously very powerful; Ishaan had felt it since his first interaction and could feel it even more at Shaktidham. Rhea was completely self-assured and beyond any doubt, comfortable in her person.

The summer holidays of 1991 went by. Neel, Barkha and Nethra met Rhea very briefly; the three went back to the cities they were now residing in and the girls rejoined their respective colleges, which restarted in July.

Neel's urge to speculate in shares kept him busy. He was speculating forward in the stock market, betting and making money as the market was rising. With money came arrogance and the lack of respect for hard work. Nothing comes easy in life, surely not money, and it is a well-known fact that everything has a price. In his case, the price was loss of sleep and appetite. He was caught unsuspecting in a whirlpool which sucked him and others into its dark depths. You may only come out of its depths alive after you have lost it all.

His day started and ended with the anxiety of the price of shares. The fate of the Indian cricket team only mattered to him if he had placed a bet on that day and if it was for or against them.

'Rhea, I made lots of money today,' he said, talking about the cricket bet he won that day.

She replied, 'Spread it on your bed and sleep with it, maybe it will give you a good night's sleep.'

'Rhea, why the hell are you being so sarcastic?'

'It's good that you understand the sarcasm, and Neel, you need to get a grip on your life,' she said and then disconnected.

Neel sat wondering why Rhea was losing it; he had no time to waste on contemplation though, as he had lots to look forward to. His day was spent at the stock market. After a gruelling day, he would let his hair down partying, drinking with friends and sleeping with nameless and faceless women.

◆

Dear Krish,

Hi, sorry about the abrupt reply when you enquired how Neel was doing. Honestly, I don't know what is happening to Neel. His sense of direction has warped completely since Barkha walked out on him. After completing his business management, he became a part of a race, where everyone seems to be clueless about where they are going and why. He is running, but he does not know where. He is running away from his mother and also from the fact that Barkha simply walked away. He just seems to be running, falling, getting up and then running again. Barkha even told him that they do not have a future together. He is heavily into speculation in the stock market and there is a crazed restlessness about him. He is basically in denial of Barkha leaving him; his relationship with his mother makes him feel that he isn't loved either and he still holds her responsible for his father's death.

I spoke with Baba about Neel. He told me he will need time to realize things and experience them on his own, before he comes to face the facts of life. He will need to fight his own battles and grow as a person through them.

That is why I didn't tell you about Neel this morning when you called, and was abrupt. So I am writing to explain what is happening with him. In any case, I am very perturbed with his situation and don't want to see him in this state.

Lots of love,

Rhea

Rhea had understood after speaking to Neel and Barkha over the last few months that Barkha had moved to New Delhi. She was amidst people who lived a faster pace of life and was trying hard to catch up. To her, it seemed as if it were only these people who understood her creative ability and she deserved a place amongst them. Her life was filled with glamour and was moving at a fast pace. In her new-found life, she was losing Neel, as there was a lot more in the offering and she couldn't picture him in the new scenario.

Rhea was concerned about Neel; there was only so much she could do, to hear him and give him an opinion on what he must do as an individual. Rhea related what was happening to a book she was reading on quantum physics, which stated that 'particles appear to be waves, it means that they behave in a certain pattern. The smaller the area of confinement of a subatomic particle, the faster will its speed be. A confined particle reacts by increasing its motion. This is the fundamental restlessness of matter.'

◆

It was Sawan ka Somvar, Monday of the month of Sawan, as per the Hindu calendar. People were thronging to the temple of Shaktidham, as prayers to the almighty Lord Shiva is a ritual followed by many on every Monday of Sawan, which means the monsoon season—a season of celebration, festivity, love and poetry. Nature comes alive with colours and greenery, rejuvenated after the scorching and blazing summer months.

Satya was sitting on the swing in the veranda, and Rhea on the chair beside him.

Chander came in and said, looking flustered, 'Maharaj ji, there is some trouble outside.'

'What happened?' asked Rhea.

'A man tried to molest a young girl; he had taken her to the fields, where we caught him, but he is refusing to divulge his identity. He won't utter a word. He is a middle-aged and fairly well dressed man. The girl is sitting in the office and we are trying to locate her parents, as she got lost in the crowd,' he replied.

'Get the man in here,' demanded Rhea. Satya remained silent.

Chander quickly went and came back with him; Rhea noticed he was wearing an expensive watch and a branded shirt.

'What is your name?' she enquired.

No reply.

She repeated the question firmly, without any response from the man.

'Chander bhaiya, remove his wallet.'

The man resisted, Chander slapped him, which sent him reeling to the floor. There was an ID card that revealed the fact that he was a branch manager of a nationalized Indian bank.

'Strip off his clothes, including his undergarments and then throw him out from the rear gate,' Rhea instructed Chander.

Chander nodded confirming he understood. The man was stunned and silent; he fell at Satya's feet and started sobbing.

'Maharaj, please forgive me.'

'I am sorry,' he said, turning towards Rhea.

'The deity of Shaktidham is Shakti and you have dishonoured her, your actions have consequences,' said Rhea.

Satya and Rhea got up and walked away.

13

RHEA HAD GONE through her second year in the college; the first quarter of 1992 was nearly over, when she dreamt about another jolt which Neel would have to go through in life. One night, Rhea drifted into the future. The bourse was empty and she could hear wailing sounds all around. She saw Neel sitting and crying hysterically.

'I think it is time to sell. Do not indulge in further speculation,' she said to Neel, that morning over the phone.

Neel had thought otherwise—after all, what did Rhea know about the stock market? God, why doesn't she keep to herself and her Tantra! He was certain of his knowledge about the market and the trend was bullish.

He had gone along his usual ways, not paying any heed to what Rhea had warned him about. The market had given gains until the trend had been up. He had made the right decisions and maximized his profits by knowing when to buy and when to exit. There wasn't anyone better than him is what he thought.

Unexpectedly, the market turned around and started to slide. Every day he hoped the market would bounce back, as it was only a market correction. However, the market kept creating new lows every day. He was now in a trap, never to get out of it; he lost money each time he had to exit contracts, as the share values were crashing. He lost every cent he had ever made and there was still more to be paid. The balance of the debt was paid from his mother's hard-earned money.

Many declared themselves bankrupt and many people disappeared without a trace.

Everything that goes up has to come down. There are no shortcuts in life. The only good thing about a shortcut is that it is a shortcut. After losing all the money, he realized that money couldn't buy sleep, appetite or peace. A purpose and a goal are the propelling forces in life. A life without purpose is like a rudderless boat lost in the vast expanse of an ocean.

Neel returned to Varanasi, depressed and dejected, and often went to Shaktidham to spend time with Rhea, as he also didn't have many friends left.

'Love may have hurt, but be open to it and it will flow into your life again. Someone may have broken your dreams, but healing is mandatory, and restoration possible,' said Rhea.

'Move on to save your own self. The truth is that forgiveness is a very selfish act, as one forgives and moves on to be able to live in the present moment. The baggage from our past is the heaviest to carry and we all knowingly or unknowingly hurt people,' she said.

'The difference lies in "knowingly or unknowingly",' said Neel, filled with bitterness.

'Neel, the opposite of love is not hate, it is indifference,' said Rhea.

Dear Krish,

Missing you a lot. After what has happened with Neel, I realize that probably there is no way we can ever save anyone; experience is the only way people are willing to learn. Krish, even after warning Neel it did not help the situation in any way—this fact stares me in my face. Was Baba right in saying that you probably cannot save anyone, even if you know what is coming?

But then it is a challenge—especially if the person is a loved one—to know and behave ignorant, and to watch them suffer helplessly. It is very hard to let the person keep walking a path, knowing that there is a pitfall lurking ahead. Some lessons are best learnt with experience. Very few learn from others' experiences, the rest of us have to be those others.

Yours,

Rhea

Rhea had yet to accept the fact that one could only help those who wanted to be helped. According to Satya, one has learnt only if the learning had been applied in life and the mistake never repeated, but if repeated it no longer remains a mistake, it becomes a choice.

A month later, Neel's mother came to meet Rhea.

'Didi, a woman by the name of Kritika has come to meet you,' announced Meena, while Rhea was taking a nap in her room.

Kritika had a toned body and was wearing trousers which flattered her figure. She looked different from a stereotypical image of a mother. She was a part of that rare category, where women apart from being wives and mothers had an identity of their own; it was still not accepted in the city of Varanasi.

Varanasi, considered the heart of the mystical world, was also a house of widows, living as corpses, and continuously being exploited by men adorning saffron. Varanasi was a place that mirrored the ugliness that we so effectively construct in the name of culture, religion and society. Each of us has the ability to create beauty, but then majority of us choose to create ugliness, as it is much easier.

Kritika was an exception, as she was a successful and rich widow. That day, Rhea realized that behind the façade of confidence and arrogance was a woman who was vulnerable. She realized that it was not time that heals wounds but love. Behind the strength demonstrated is always a part that remains vulnerable. It is a basic human need to love and be loved. Kritika wanted love and care too.

Neel came to Shaktidham a day later and was taking a walk with Rhea.

'Life cannot be a directionless run, there has to be a meaning to it, which only we can lend to our lives and you will have to find that meaning,' said Rhea.

'Rhea, have you decided what to do with your life?' he asked.

'My calling is what I am doing. I am a student of Tantra and I manage the affairs of Shaktidham. I know I am in this world to do what I am already doing.'

'Is that why you did not leave Varanasi for your studies?' he asked.

'Yes,' she replied.

'What is failure for you, Rhea?' Neel asked.

'It is foremost for one to decipher what one loves to do; if you love your work, it transcends the definition of work, and you can never fail. To me, failure does not mean things which have not turned out the way I hoped or wanted; failure to me means if I do not recognize my mistakes. Making mistakes and learning from them are a part of one's experiences, which is mandatory to succeed. I don't think that any man is a failure unless he fails to succeed in something he loves to do.'

Neel finally decided to join his mother in their family business. Rhea had told Neel over the past few weeks that his mother unquestionably needed him, as often the truth is different from what it seems. Each and every one of us without exception has a need which is universal—the need to be loved and cherished. She, however, had not mentioned to Neel that his mother had come to meet her.

'Remember, Neel, money is important, but it is equally important to strike a healthy relationship with it. Its value and its purpose are to be understood,' Rhea told Neel.

'Now, my affair with money will start again and I hope this time it endures,' said Neel.

'Yes, I want to see the start of this successful relationship,' said Rhea, with a smile.

It was the month of October and Navaratri was around the corner. Navaratri happens twice a year—at the commencement of spring and autumn. These are considered very significant junctions of climatic and solar influences. Navaratri is taken to be a sacred opportunity to worship the Mother Goddess. The word Navaratri literally means nine nights in Sanskrit and symbolizes the victory of good over evil. During these nine auspicious days, nine forms of the feminine energy Shakti are worshipped. During the second Navaratri, which usually falls in the month of October after Vijaydashmi, on Ekadashi, a yagya was organized at Shaktidham.

According to Hindu mythology, a demon named Mahishasura earned a boon from Lord Shiva after a tough penance. The boon gave him power whereby 'no man or deity would be able to kill him'. The powers of the boon lead him into indiscriminate killings. He defeated Lord Indra and captured Devlok, the abode of devtas.

Goddess Durga possessed the unique individual powers of ten deities, which is symbolized by her ten arms. When Mahishasura heard of Durga's beauty, he wished to marry her and sent her a marriage proposal. The Goddess replied that she would marry him on the one condition, that he is able defeat her in battle.

Mahishasura was completely intoxicated by the powers of the boon; he readily consented to the battle not knowing that Durga, being a woman, could kill him. The battle went on for nine days and nights, and resulted in the beheading of Mahishasura on the tenth day. The nine nights came to be known as Navaratri. The tenth day was called Vijayadashami, symbolizing the triumph of good over the evil.

Shaktidham was glowing; it had been decorated with beautiful coloured lights. It seemed that a bride wearing vibrant red had replaced a serene quiet woman in white. People came there from all walks of life.

Eleven pundits in red kurtas sat and chanted Vedic hymns in sync, while the yagya was performed. The aroma of the havan samagri spread throughout Shaktidham. Just listening to the chants could relax the most troubled souls. After the yagya, the devotees sang bhajans, they even danced on devotional songs. Satya delivered a discourse, just that one day of the year.

A woman, while the bhajans were being sung, had suddenly stood up and started behaving oddly, as Rhea could see it. She was going hysterical, shaking her head and rolling her eyes. The woman became the centre of attention. Her long hair was open, her head shook violently and her mouth seemed to froth; there were some muted whispers.

'*Iss pe Devi aa gayi* (the spirit of Goddess has gotten into her),' somebody shouted from the crowd.

By now, the woman had removed her sari pallu and before she could go further, Satya got up and slapped her hard across her face. Everything happened in the blink of an eye and the impact was strong enough to send her toppling over.

Satya believed in communicating with the person in the language understood by them. It avoided wastage of time and energy. The woman came to her senses immediately; she touched

Satya's feet and begged for forgiveness, then was escorted away by her relatives. Rhea had witnessed this episode for the first time, but had heard stories about such things happening.

'Rhea, there is no such thing as a Goddess entering anyone. The incident you witnessed was the manifestation of an unattended psychological issue and it is a way to seek attention,' Satya explained to Rhea.

Satya added, 'The woman had been repressed beyond doubt. At times, people get carried away by an inherent devotional spirit; they sing and dance, and may even start crying due to temporary loss of self. But this all perfectly natural.'

The next day onwards the Vidai started. Satya spent time with every family that came to attend the yagya from out of town. It was tiring, but it was a custom which he followed without fail. The devotees took this as an opportunity to discuss their problems. They also interacted with Satya and spent some precious moments with their guru. He would sit on his swing, patiently listening to everyone.

One day, a young boy touched Satya's feet and sat down.

'Maharaj ji, I am Devraj and I have come to apologize for my behaviour with Rhea. I owe an apology to you and Rhea.' Satya placed his hand on his head, stood up and walked away.

Rhea came into the veranda and Devraj stood up. 'I am sorry, Rhea,' he said, looking into Rhea's eyes with his hands folded.

Rhea's smiling face and the tenderness in her eyes said it all. She extended her hand and said, 'Friends.'

Devraj held her hand. 'That day I wanted to see fear in your eyes, but I saw pity. You made me seem so small in my own eyes,' he said, 'but Rhea, I love you and it has taken me a lot to muster up the courage to come and face you and your father.'

'Other than pity, anger was the other emotion that day,' said Rhea.

'Is it so easy to forgive me? I see no bitterness in your eyes.'

Rhea smiled and replied, 'Forgiveness has nothing to do with you. I love myself, therefore, I hold nothing that may be detrimental to me. If I hold resentment and anger for you, it would affect me first.'

'My search in life will be to find a Rhea for myself, which I know I will never get. But still I will not give up,' he said, laughing.

They sat together for a while and Devraj mentioned about his political aspirations after college was over.

'One of the hardest things in life is to say I am sorry while meaning it too. Devraj is a man of courage,' said Satya to Rhea, after everyone had left.

'Baba, everyone comes to you with problems. Has anyone come to you as a seeker?' she asked.

'No one has ever come to me asking me to initiate the person on the path of sadhana. Rhea, this path is for the chosen one. Only you are my disciple in the true sense. A recipient has to be worthy of it; it is not a path for the masses and the responsibility to carry on the lineage now lies on you. It is of utmost importance for a guru to pass on such knowledge only in worthy hands. If he does not find such a disciple, he would rather not impart such knowledge.'

'But Baba, how does a guru recognize the chosen one?' questioned Rhea.

'That is the final test of a guru and if he fails this, he fails himself. I still have to take this test and I know, my child, that you will not let me down. Vidya going in unworthy hands can be disastrous, as no one escapes from the consequences of her actions. Never ever misuse or exhibit your powers. Remember that they are incidental to our path. Our path will compound your gifts, which you have received from the Goddess. It can become a boon or a bane depending on the choices you make, so always be aware,' he added.

Rhea was quiet for a while. Then she asked, 'Baba, what if I ever make a mistake unknowingly?'

'There are no mistakes, only actions and consequences. In your words, if you make a mistake, you will have to bear its consequences. The ultimate power rests with the person who is absolutely aware,' he said, looking straight into Rhea's eyes.

14

IN HER DREAM, the calendar, which hung in a room, showed the date of Sunday, 29 November. There was someone in bed, but she could not figure out who; she only saw a shadow tossing in bed, taking her name. She could not place the room in her dream and was getting curious to see the face. She got up with a start from her dream. She had seen this dream for the last two consecutive days. Hundreds of questions crossed her mind: where this place was; who was this person was; and what was about to happen on that date. She could not sleep that night and a few nights after.

On a bright sunny day, a call came at an unexpected hour. The phone rang until Rhea answered it.

'Hello,' said an excited voice, from the other end.

'Hi, Barkha,' said Rhea recognising her voice, still half asleep.

'Hi, Rhea,' replied Barkha cheerfully.

The moment Barkha said, 'Hi Rhea', the face of the shadow from her dream cleared. It was Barkha. She realized that today was Saturday, 28 November. 'Oh no,' thought Rhea.

'Rhea, you seem to be preoccupied, are you there?' asked Barkha.

'No, no, nothing Barkha, what are you doing tonight?' asked Rhea.

'Going to a rocking party, it's going to be awesome,' she replied, with excitement in her voice. Rhea was quiet.

'I am wearing a black short skirt with a really sexy top, which I designed and got tailored,' she said, even more enthusiastically.

'Rhea, why are you so quiet?' asked Barkha.

'No, Barkha, I was just wondering if you could stay at home and watch television instead?'

Barkha was quiet for a second and then replied curtly, 'Rhea, my life is different from your life in Shaktidham. I thought you would be happy, but it seems my closest friends are getting jealous of me.'

'What are you saying?' asked Rhea, completely in shock.

'I think I know what is best for me. This is so typically a small-town mentality, interfering in other people's life. Anyway, I don't think you can relate to it.' She banged the phone and it got disconnected.

Rhea sat shaking in her bed, holding her head with tears in her eyes.

'My child, it is not important that people understand you, but it is very important that you understand yourself,' said Satya.

'Yes, Baba, you were right; you cannot save anyone. They will do what they want, so be it.'

'No, it is not black and white; there will be a lot more opportunities in life to learn that not all people are the same and neither are all situations. It is your wisdom to recognize the faith of the person you are dealing with, which is the utmost essential ingredient. I know it's tough, but you must accept the fact that you will be misunderstood, if there is lack of faith. Only experiences can teach you and it is not always pleasant. People see things as they themselves are, they do not see things as they truly stand. If they lack faith in you and things happened the way you said they would, then people would be fearful of you,' said Satya.

Rhea was still upset with all that had happened. She told Krishnam when he called over the next weekend about the whole incident with Barkha and how she wanted to caution her.

Krishnam heard her out and at the end explained to her, 'It

is well known that children who have grown up in authoritarian households often rebel and lead totally different lives from their upbringing. To keep their newfound freedom is their only priority and anything in contradiction is viewed as a threat. In this case, probably Barkha felt you were trying to control her life. She perceived it as you being jealous of her lifestyle and success. She possibly also felt that you were upset with her for breaking up with Neel and resented her for having a good time.'

Barkha left for the party with her friend; she was all dressed up for the evening. They arrived at the apartment, which was shared by four boys, two of whom were from her college and had thrown this common party. The music was loud and the bar was full; there were all kinds of alcohol and the bartender was mixing cocktails. The party was an expression and show of wealth, which was a trend of sorts in Delhi among the college students. There weren't many familiar faces in the crowd; in any case it was difficult to see. The party was spread throughout the apartment; the bedrooms were full of people too as it was impossible to be in the drawing area where people were dancing to the trance and psychedelic music, played by a college friend. The party was going wild into the night already by 11.30 p.m.; some of the guys and girls were getting drunk and throwing up too.

Barkha went up to the rooftop terrace with some friends to get some fresh air, where there were already some people smoking. One of the boys lit a joint of marijuana and it was passed around the group. Barkha wasn't going to miss out on all the fun; she sat with them on the floor for hours. From the rooftop rose smoke clouds of marijuana and grass, with boys and girls getting high under its influence, mixed with alcohol.

The party went on until the wee hours of the morning; though it was still dark it was time to leave. Barkha's vision was hazy and so was her mental state. She couldn't distinguish between people and was falling all over them; she had lost control of herself.

Barkha just remembered vaguely telling someone to stop stripping her; the two unknown boys, who had offered to drop her back to her apartment, raped her in her apartment before they left. She was not oblivious to the fact that she was being raped, but could put up no resistance in that inebriated state.

Her head was spinning and the calendar showed Sunday, 29 November; she tossed around in the bed, repeatedly calling out Rhea's name.

On 1 January 1993, at 10.30 in the morning, there was a call for Rhea.

'Hey, Rhea, happy new year!'

'A very happy new year to you too, Nethra. Where are you calling from?'

'I came to Varanasi day before yesterday; I only have a week off. Barkha is in town too.'

Rhea did not respond.

Nethra added, 'She has been here for a week, you guys must have spoken, right?'

There was silence. Rhea still did not respond.

'Is something wrong between the two of you?' Nethra questioned Rhea, sounding concerned.

Rhea still did not respond. What had transpired with Barkha could not be explained.

'I am having a small dinner for just the four of us tomorrow evening. Will you be able to come, Rhea?' asked Nethra.

Neel came to pick Rhea up for the dinner; they drove in silence to Nethra's house.

As they were about to get to the entrance, Neel said, 'I am meeting her for the first time since we broke up.'

The discomfort was palpable, as they all put in an effort in what used to be effortless earlier. Everything had changed now and the ice could not be broken. The dinner was laid early, as Rhea had to leave and in any case the evening was a drag. After a rushed dinner, Rhea stood up to leave. Neel too wasn't keen on staying and preferred to leave immediately to drop Rhea back at Shaktidham.

Nethra looked flustered when she came to see off Rhea and Neel at the door. 'But what has happened, will someone tell me?' she asked.

Rhea looked blankly in space for a moment and then replied, 'Nethra, it's pointless, some changes are irreversible. Accept the change; it will be easier, since we cannot fight it. It will never be the same between Barkha and me.'

Barkha later said to Nethra, 'Isn't it very apparent that Neel and Rhea are in a relationship? I don't want to meet them again, it makes me uncomfortable.'

'You are crazy, they are just friends, and Rhea likes Krishnam,' said Nethra, in defence.

'Well, has Rhea ever acknowledged that she loves Krishnam?' questioned Barkha.

'You are getting it all wrong,' said Nethra, in resignation. 'I feel it's best to resolve the issue, as we all have been friends since childhood,' she continued.

'Did you ask Rhea what happened?' asked Barkha anxiously.

'Yes, I did ask her, but she did not reply.'

Barkha looked up at Nethra, feeling relieved and said, 'Nethra, you are too simple to understand what has transpired. Rhea was the one who was instrumental in my break-up with Neel and she knows she is guilty. Anyway, I always found her a little weird.'

Nethra looked at her in disbelief.

The next afternoon Satya woke up late, because of the ritual he performed every Saturday night. Rhea told him how awkward her last evening was with her friends.

'Rhea, within us exists our own world; it is through this world that we access the world outside us. One's world outside is directly dependent on their world inside, which is constantly changing due to their ever-gaining experiences. Relationships too change constantly and can never remain the same. The nature of creation is ever changing. Therefore, change is a natural constant,' said Satya.

'Yes, Baba, I understand we as individuals, our bodies, the people we know, our relationships, all come under this natural law,' added Rhea.

She had realized there were things that she could not explain, not even to people she had grown up with. She had learnt to only be a mute spectator to events in people's lives, unless it was someone who had complete faith in her. Satya and Krishnam were the only two who understood the world in which Rhea lived. Nobody else would ever understand where she came from, and she was learning to accept this fact.

One has to accept the unchangeable and move on. Life exists in movement. Past is to be learnt from, present to be lived for, and future to be dreamt and hoped for.

◆

The vibrations emanating from Rhea's sadhana could be felt in the world of a handful of Tantra sadhaks. She was emerging with a strength that was getting impossible to ignore. They were Tantrics, who were masters in the field and practised Tantra as a path leading to salvation.

However, the great Tantric Bhairava was getting particularly uncomfortable with this new woman entrant. But he knew challenging Satya meant losing, as he was the master of masters.

'A strong person exhibits tolerance and endurance. A strong person even with the power to destroy his opponent will choose to forgive. However, a weak person demonstrates his weakness by using a canon where a stick could have worked. We lose balance the moment we let our ego prevail,' Satya explained to Rhea one day.

15

IT HAD BEEN a couple of years since Rhea started being present during the discussions Satya had with people about their problems. They were people who had faith in Satya, and if he did assure them of a remedy, they knew they would be relieved of their problem. Rhea had understood that however rich or successful any person is, after all he is a human, with the same emotions. Each one of them wanted to keep their pain at bay and be happy. She often thought that it was an impossible target. Pain was an undeniable truth of life, which had to be accepted with equanimity. Happiness as a constant state was impossible for any human being, even for the greatest sadhak. One could only ask for strength to overcome their phase of pain and seek happiness in little things that life offers.

The people coming to meet Satya and seek his blessings belonged to all walks of life. Some of the people who came to meet him were politicians, corporate heads, celebrities and socially influential personalities. Rhea met with all those people too who were achievers in their respective fields, and it had become a part of Rhea's life. These famous faces came to Varanasi under cover, driven to Shaktidham as a lone passenger in a car with tinted glasses, entering from the rear gate to stay out of public view.

A Hollywood actor had called some time ago requesting an appointment with Satya, to seek his blessings. He wanted to schedule his trip to India according to this appointment. His itinerary had to be kept away from the media and he was advised to ensure extreme confidentiality about his visit to Shaktidham. He was the romantic icon of Hollywood, crazed by women of all ages. The night before, Rhea could not sleep out of excitement.

'I can see how excited you are to meet him, remember those

are just characters he plays. You know he is staying with us for two days,' said Satya, laughing.

Hi Krish,

I have been on pins since I knew he was coming. I couldn't recognize him, as he came with a baseball cap and large sunglasses; if I had not known it was he, I would have walked past. He is such an intelligent guy; I had a great time speaking with him. Remarkably, he comes across as someone who has been able to strike the right chord between power and money.

He said something very interesting, that the desire for money or power may essentially stem from the desire to continuously grow and expand. We all seek freedom, power and money. But when even power and money are not enough, it leads to further discontent, because what we were searching for in the garb of money and power was the limitless and infinite expansion, which eludes us even then. It is important to strike the right chord between money and power and then use it as a stepping stone for our growth. Normally, we get entangled with this concoction and live our lives dissatisfied in spite of all material pleasures. Promiscuity is the desire for the right partner, which again is the desire to complete and expand our self. Baba had just said one thing in the end, desire can never be destroyed and we can purify it. Desire is innate to human nature.

It is extremely cold and foggy here again, you know how January is, and I hate the cold. Yesterday, we gave blankets to the needy and homeless.

Baba was insisting that I apply for my passport and visit the US before you return for good. I told him that I don't wish to go right now; I will go when I am older. He got upset and said that my problem is that I cling to him and you! I asked him how I could cling to Krish, as you sent him away a long

time ago and you obviously haven't visited in so many years.
He started laughing and said, but I still do cling, whatever that
means!
Lots of love,
Rhea

Satya, Krishnam and her sadhana gave Rhea a sense of stability,
and the assurance that in this dynamically moving existence
some things may still remain the same; an illusion again. Nothing
remains the same…

The earlier one learns to flow with the change, the earlier he
learns to live with the eternal truth. A simple truth may be so
difficult to absorb and could take an entire lifetime to understand.

Neel's focus had shifted towards his work; he was completely
transforming into a new man. It had only been about two years
since he joined his mother. He had begun travelling internationally
for the company and there was great learning from his travels. His
confidence and self-worth grew as time passed, and his persona
had become extremely attractive. In any case, he had an inherent
flair, which is normally difficult to acquire.

His business acumen grew sharply; he had clarity of his goals
and worked tirelessly towards them. He modified his lifestyle too;
after work every day he would play squash to release his stress,
thereby cutting out the need to go out with friends in the evening,
which would eventually end up in drinking.

Neel made a large contribution towards the limb camp—
an annual feature organized at Shaktidham—and preferred to
remain anonymous. The underprivileged were donated limbs or
wheelchairs free of cost. Neel was the only person who wished
to remain anonymous as a contributor. The person who mattered
to him knew it. Rhea and Neel's friendship over the years was
developing into a deep bond of trust.

'Strive to find yourself and ego will cease to exist. Ego is the false sense of identification with the external world; it springs from ignorance. Being recognized for helping is a need of ego. Always be attentive of your ego,' Satya had said to Rhea.

'Rhea, I have a surprise for you, come to the rear gate in half an hour, I will meet you there,' said Neel on the phone.

Rhea was anxious; she went out and stood looking at this mean-looking convertible. Neel was standing by the car holding the door open for her. She congratulated him as she sat inside. 'Rhea, I wanted you to be the first person to see it and drive in my car,' said Neel, smiling. He buckled up and zipped onto the highway.

◆

A man stood in front of Satya and Rhea with his hands folded; he had been released a day before, after serving a sentence for twenty years as a convict. He was a gang member of dacoits in Chambal and their leader had surrendered voluntarily along with them. The dacoits had committed numerous murders, kidnappings and robberies.

The man was tall, agile and looked about fifty years old. Rhea observed him and saw that he had a childlike innocence on his face. 'Baba, I have no family anymore and nowhere to go. My mother is also no more. Please let me work for you here in Shaktidham,' he pleaded.

'What is your name?' asked Rhea.

'I have left my past behind, so whatever name you give me, Didi ji, that will be my name. We would only loot the rich and never touched the women. We had some principles and stuck to our rules. We took good care of whoever we kidnapped and asked for reasonable ransoms. It was different in our times,' he said, looking into space.

'We had been promised lot of things and land too at the time we surrendered, but none of the promises were kept by the government.'

'Did you kill someone too?' asked Rhea, looking at him.

'Yes, I did,' he replied.

'My father died when I was an infant. My mother used to work as a labourer in the fields, getting a meagre amount. For us as a family, getting two square meals was also a big challenge. Then one night, the zamindar came to our house. I killed that zamindar.'

Rhea saw him clench his fist, but he said nothing after that. There was complete silence for some time.

He then said, 'Didi, I belong to the lower class.'

Rhea was quiet for some time, thinking.

'Chander bhaiya, please give him a room. He will assist in cooking food and work in the fields too if required,' she instructed.

'Ramu kaka, do you like this name?' asked Rhea, looking at the man.

He smiled. 'Yes, Didi.'

He spoke again with some hesitation, 'Didi, the people here may not appreciate me being a part of their cooking.'

'Ramu kaka, we too have some rules.' She got up and held his hand in hers. 'Kaka, treat this as your home and it will become your home. Is there any saint who does not have a past and is there any sinner who does not have a future?' she said with a smile.

◆

Satya preferred his solitude. He would meet people in seclusion and only individually; else as per Satya it wouldn't take time to become a broker, instead of a sadhak. People closely associated to powerful people, often lose their mind along with the person himself. To maintain sanity while being in power can be an extremely tough balance to strike. Chander would get frantic calls from these powerful people to meet or speak to Satya, as per their whims and desire. Satya was not easily accessible; no one spoke or met Satya at will. He would only meet those who he wanted to meet.

The secretary told Chander that his boss wanted to meet Maharaj ji urgently and that his boss was a cabinet minister, who had to return to Delhi in the evening.

'It is impossible to meet Maharaj ji immediately,' said Chander. The secretary of the senior politician misbehaved with Chander over the phone, on being told that Satya was resting and he could give him the message only when Satya woke up.

The secretary said, 'Tell Maharaj ji, if he wants to run this ashram, he better be available to people like us. The ashrams run because of our donations. Do not think and behave like God.'

Chander narrated the entire conversation to Rhea.

Rhea silently listened to him bereft of any expression on her face. 'Please get him on the phone for me,' she told Chander.

'Secretary sahib, I am Rhea calling from Shaktidham.'

'Ah, yes Madam.'

'Kindly tell the minister sahib that he cannot enter the ashram,' said Rhea.

There was a stunned silence at the other end.

'Why, Madam?' asked the secretary, infuriated.

'Sir, that you'll have to tell him,' she said and disconnected the phone.

'There is no need to tell Baba or me if this person or the minister calls. Do not get into any dialogue, just disconnect,' said Rhea to Chander.

◆

A few weeks later, Rhea was driving to Delhi with Neel much against her wishes. It was Neel's mother Kritika's first fashion show. Neel had organized this fashion show to launch Kritika's label.

Neel sought permission from Satya and he had consented immediately, much to Rhea's displeasure. Kritika too had called Rhea and expressed that her presence would mean a lot to her. However, it was Krishnam's call insisting that she needs to move out of her cocoon, which prompted her to go.

This would be her first trip to Delhi after she came to Shaktidham, fourteen years ago. Satya had a villa in Delhi too, which Rhea had never visited; a caretaker managed the place, and Satya and Krishnam visited it. At various occasions, Satya had asked Rhea to accompany him, but she had always refused. However, Satya insisted that she stay with Neel at his place.

She stayed with Neel and Kritika at their house in South Delhi. Rhea was going to wear the dress which Kritika had made for her.

'A simple, clean cut would be best suited for you,' Kritika had said to Rhea, before creating this outfit for her.

The next day, Neel came to pick Rhea up from where the event was happening. He gaped and said softly, 'You look very pretty,' as Rhea came out of her room.

The outfit she wore wrapped her form in a lingering embrace, accentuating her femininity. Her thick, long, curly hair fell below her shoulders.

'This outfit is an ode to a woman,' replied Rhea. The colour was beige and the gown flowed below her ankle.

The Indian fashion industry was still in its nascent stage and people were gradually understanding fashion. The women were emerging out of their cars in saris. At the hotel where the event was, the media was present in huge numbers, and so were the editors of fashion magazines, photographers, and even eminent news channels.

Neel together with his brand manager and PR agency had sent invites to the who's who of Delhi. Invites were sent to the people who regularly feature on page three and celebrities too. The focus of the event was on revealing their new collection to the fashion writers and critics of the fashion industry.

The models walking the ramp were from one of the top agencies in India. The choreographer for the show was a celebrity of sorts; they had put in a lot of teamwork for the event to be a success. The event coordinator, who was responsible for the show, had left no stone unturned to make it a successful launch.

All this effort had been coordinated and executed by Neel as he had told his mother, 'You are good, but people must know about you.'

Rhea was a witness to this enthralling fashion show, sitting in the front row of this five star hotel with Neel. The ramp came ablaze with vivacious models adorned with mesmerising creations of Kritika. It was the first peep into her creativity and her flair for designing clothing. The designer seemed like a master of human form. The collection was a sharp contrast from the ethnic splendours. The clothes were chic and urban, with a sleekly tailored look. The styling was simple but elegant like its designer Kritika. She hoped to create a new look for the Indian woman. The collection had business wear and evening formal wear.

At the end of the show, Kritika came on the ramp with the models to thank everyone who came to view her line. There was a thunderous applause, which was a sign that she had arrived. It was clear that there was no stopping now. Neel and Rhea had moist eyes, which neither saw but each knew.

After the fashion show, there was a party with all the glitterati. The party was extravagant, with cocktails and a sit-down dinner organized for the invitees, models and the media.

Neel gave Rhea a glass of champagne. 'Rhea, it's champagne, you will enjoy it. Sip slowly.'

She had her champagne and sat thinking about Krishnam. She was getting butterflies in her stomach; he would be back soon, forever.

'I am here because of my son, Neel, who dared to dream big for me,' Kritika was telling the editor of a leading woman's fashion magazine. 'My first outlet in the capital will be inaugurated in a week's time.'

The editor replied, 'Yup, I heard some buzzing that a big Bollywood personality is coming to open the store?'

'Soon you will find out, it isn't too far,' said Kritika, smiling.

'Someone is missing Krishnam…' Neel said, with his eyebrow raised.

'He will be back soon, for good,' said Rhea.

'Rhea, you look stunning,' said Kritika, approaching her.

Rhea got up and they hugged each other warmly. 'Congratulations! The show was awesome and I loved the collection, it was fabulous. Everyone loved it.'

'Thank you,' she replied.

'Which outfit did you like the best?' asked Kritika.

Rhea smiled, 'All of them were fabulous, but the red one was strikingly different.'

'Rhea, I have to thank you for everything. Neel is here with me because of you,' said Kritika and hugged her again.

'I have done nothing, you have got all that you deserved,' she said.

Neel and Rhea stayed back for a week and he showed her around Delhi; they went out to eat at different restaurants and Neel took Rhea to a few nightclubs too. She had fun going to the clubs, where they had a few drinks and danced.

A couple of weeks after she was back, at the break of dawn, Rhea was taking steps backwards to exit the sadhanasthal; one is never supposed to turn their back towards one's deity, it is considered disrespectful. As she took the steps, she knocked into something, losing her balance, and let out a scream. She nearly fell, but someone caught her before she hit the floor and pulled her up. Rhea immediately recognized that touch being an integral part of her. It was these arms, which were meant to be around her and she was meant to be in them.

'Caught you in time, princess.'

Rhea gained control and said in astonishment, 'Krish, you

were supposed to come a week later.'

He helped her regain her posture.

'Wanted to surprise you.'

She took a deep sigh and said, 'You always do that.'

He had thick silky hair falling on his forehead and there was a naughty twinkle in his eyes. It was odd as he was wearing a white dhoti-kurta.

'You changed your clothes?' Rhea asked.

'Yes, I wanted to come to the sadhanasthal first thing and knew you were also here, so I did what I had to.'

Satya saw them both coming through the entrance towards the veranda. Satya was very happy to see Krishnam back. He had met Krishnam earlier, as he had been waiting for him to arrive from the railway station; it had been their secret. Satya had told him that Rhea was at the sadhanasthal.

The silence in the ashram was replaced by laughter and pranks Krishnam's return had brought alive a side of Rhea which even she had been oblivious to since he left. Behind her quiet and serious demeanour, unfolded a very playful spirit that was alien to all, and with him she was like a spoilt child. Krishnam indulged her in ways that would fulfil the needs of the child and the woman in her.

Krishnam's return brought an additional rhythm into Rhea's life; both were completely absorbed in this new-found phase. They spent time watching movies together, took long walks together. Sometimes, even Neel would join them whenever he could in the evenings in Shaktidham. On many weekends, Neel would call them over and the three would usually spend Saturday night drinking and having a good time. At times, Rhea would drink herself silly and Krishnam would have to lug her back to Shaktidham.

Krishnam would narrate episodes about his experiences in the college. His averments of the female attention towards him couldn't be ignored, whenever he spoke about himself. Even at his workplace, one of the most prestigious law firms in New York, his immediate boss, a woman, had a soft corner for him. She was a a few years his senior and a partner in the firm, and was hot and single.

On several occasions over the last couple of years, he had expressed to her his need to quit and return to India. Each time, she would propose a hike in his salary and perks to the partners. The firm kept accepting her proposals and passing on the increments, until he had to tell her finally that it was not about money, but that he had to go back to India, never to return. They made him a final proposal in which they even offered to make him a partner at the firm, but he refused and returned, leaving it all.

Both Krishnam and Neel would get on one side and pull Rhea's leg, teasing her. One night, Rhea poured a jug of water over Krishnam's head, as he went on and on about the attention he got from women. Neel was in splits about her being jealous about the fact that Krishnam got attention; he held his stomach laughing. Rhea got irritated even further and smeared a box of confectionery in Neel's face.

Later that night, she was drunk again; she binged heavily after she felt embarrassed of exhibiting her jealousy.

'Rhea, are you jealous?' asked Krishnam, on their way back from Neel's house.

'Obviously, you have any doubts?' slurred Rhea and passed out in the car.

Krishnam shook her a few times, intending to make her walk on her feet until her room at least. She was not in a state to walk and he had to carry her to her room.

She woke up the next morning with a splitting headache and had been lying with a hangover.

'You should drink only as much as you can handle,' Krishnam told her, after he gave her the third cup of coffee.

She looked at Krishnam. 'Then what are you here for?' she

asked and winked at him.

'There is an etiquette to drinking Rhea and you...' She shut him up, kissing him; it ended in a long passionate kiss.

16

THE PREPARATIONS FOR Holi were underway; the air was filled with the smell of gujiya, namkeen, and thandai being prepared for the next day. As Krishnam and Rhea appeared from their rooms for lunch, Satya saw them walking in with their heads hung.

As they finished lunch with no word spoken, it was time for Satya to say what he had held back, 'Excess of anything is bad, overindulgence in life is avoidable.'

Holi is a festival that signifies triumph of good over evil. The mythological story is about the King Hiranyakashyap, who wanted his entire kingdom to worship him. To his utter disillusionment, his own son Prahlad defied him and was an ardent worshipper of Lord Vishnu. The story goes that Prahlad was saved every time by his unwavering faith in Lord Vishnu, as Hiranyakashyap tried to eliminate his defiant son, but failed miserably. Finally, after being unsuccessful, he decided to burn Prahlad alive in fire with the help of his sister, Holika; she had been blessed by a boon that she could not burn in fire. However, when she sat with Prahlad on her lap, she was burnt alive, as she was ignorant of the fact that the boon would only work if she were alone in the fire. Prahlad came out unhurt due to the grace of Lord Vishnu.

The celebration of Holi starts on the night of the full moon and on the next day it is celebrated with colours. This day also marks the onset of spring season. Spring is a season which signifies love, romance, and beauty.

It is also called Kama Mahotsava, after the lord of desire, Lord Kamadeva. Lord Krishna, who was a charmer, started this trend of

Holi being played with colours by applying colour on the face of his beloved Radha.

Rhea got up with loud knocking on her door; it was Krishnam.

'Happy Holi!' he stooped down and in single motion picked her up in his arms and walked towards his bathroom.

Rhea struggled a little but it was pointless.'What are you doing? Put me down,' she screamed at Krishnam. The bathtub was full of water and rose petals. He gently immersed her in the tub of warm water and said, 'Happy Holi once again.'

Rhea splashed water from the bathtub at Krishnam and then picked up the hand shower and drenched him. Krishnam took off his shirt and stood in front of Rhea who was still showering him.

She saw him bare-chested for the first time in years. 'Krish, I think I will change,' she said, almost in a whisper, coming out of the bathtub, her skimpy long night t-shirt hugging her body showing each curve and undulation. He pulled her towards himself.

'Krish, let me go, I am cold,' she said feebly.

He said nothing, but his hands moved to take off Rhea's long wet t-shirt; she wore nothing underneath. His gaze did not leave her even for a second, while he wiped her. He finally looked down at her in fascination.

They were longing to enter the world of passion and sensation. He poured an entire bottle of oil on her from head to toe. He walked her into his room and spread a towel on the carpet and lay her down on it. Starting with her toes, he massaged her entire body right unto her head and front to back.

He drenched her in oil again and his fingers left no part of Rhea untouched. As his fingertips slowly ran on Rhea's bare spine, she let out a soft moan.

He could feel Rhea let down her guard gradually and their senses heightened. His fingers moved slowly over her body as if creating rhythmic music. His tongue took Rhea to new heights, which Rhea had never known before. He was enjoying the woman he loved so deeply. Rhea learnt a new facet about herself with Krishnam that day. He did not make love to her, but Rhea experienced the pinnacle of pleasure from what Krishnam made her experience.

'You are very sensual, Rhea,' Krishnam said softly, 'very beautiful and I love the way you responded.'

Rhea blushed and her heart was beating fast hearing and feeling the intensity of Krishnam's desire for her. She also had a nagging feeling that Satya would be waiting for them to wish him Holi and it was already late.

'Don't you think we should go down, as Baba will be waiting for us?' asked Rhea, trying to escape her realization of shyness that was clouding her now. Krishnam understood her dilemma. He wrapped her in the towel and escorted her to her room, Rhea went in and locked herself in and called out from behind the door, 'I'll be ready in 15 minutes, and will wait for you to go downstairs.'

Rhea waited for a few minutes for Krishnam in her room and they went downstairs, she avoided eye contact with him. Satya was in the veranda already, his feet covered in colour. They wished Satya for Holi and took his blessings touching his feet.

Touching someone's feet is a sign of reverence and respect. However, there is a proper way to do so and a reason for it too; it enables a person seeking blessings to tune into the energy flow of that person by touching their feet in an accurate way. The seeker by this method is able to receive a fraction of his energy as a blessing.

The energy level of a sadhak is extremely high and even a small fraction to the recipient adds substantially to his energy. Satya had taught Krishnam and Rhea the right way to touch his feet.

Rhea was avoiding addressing Krishnam directly and she avoided looking at him, Satya had noticed. 'Tantra is a field that says neither abstain nor be obsessed. This can be handled by a few, even if you have mastered it,' said Satya.

At night, when Rhea retired to her room, she saw a wrapped package on her bed. She unwrapped and saw that it was a book of Vatsayayana's Kama sutra. She opened the cover and it was written, 'To Rhea, with love, Krish'. The book was an English version of the Kamasutra with pictorial illustrations, which is one of the ancient Hindu scriptures and the most notable texts on human sexual behaviour.

Kama sutra is recognized as one of the surviving and original text of Kamashastra. It consists of three texts dealing with the aims of life, which are dharma (righteousness), artha (wealth) and kama (desire).

Krishnam led Rhea into the world of pure Eros and she stepped in with trust, shedding all inhibitions. They started exploring the world of sensation, imagination with passion, fulfilling the needs of their souls through their senses. In their flow together, they were lost to the world, where neither was there as they were one. With each other, they devoured so many unknowns about their desires, potential, and their relationship. Krishnam was demanding, yet comforting, as he knew just what to do and when. Their intensity of lovemaking was a trance like state; it connected them somewhere much beyond the body, what is humanly inexplicable. It opened a new chapter in their life, which was enticing, compelling, and ecstatic.

Neel was coming to Shaktidham for dinner; he had been travelling since Holi and had returned only that morning.

'Mom sent this package for you,' said Neel, as he handed it to Rhea. She gasped in delight as she opened it up.

'Oh my God! It's the red gown,' she exclaimed in astonishment. It was the one she had seen during the fashion show. Rhea was ecstatic and did a jig holding the red gown against her.

'How will it look on me?' asked Rhea, looking at Neel and Krishnam.

'Why don't to wear it and show us,' said Krishnam.

Rhea took more than forty-five minutes to change into the evening gown; she made up her hair, wore matching stilettos, and put on makeup.

There was a sudden break in the conversation and everything became mute, as she entered the room.

'So, how does it look?' she asked.

'Hello! Guys say something!' Krishnam just walked up to her and pecked her on her forehead.

'You are irresistible,' he whispered in her ear. Neel too couldn't take his eyes off Rhea.

'What? Neel, say something,' said Rhea.

'Yeah, I know Mom makes great clothes, anyone can look stunning,' he replied.

Rhea threw a pillow at him, which started a pillow fight. Rhea beat both Krishnam and Neel, throwing pillows at them, but they responded gently. Rhea burst out laughing; she was trying to catch her breath amidst her bouts of laughter. Krishnam took some photographs of Rhea and Neel caught in a pillow fight. When the fight ended, Krishnam called out for Meena to come and take some more photographs of the three of them together. This one particular photograph in which Krishnam stood in the centre with an arm each around Rhea and Neel turned out to be a favourite of the three and adorned their respective bedrooms.

17

WHEN RHEA HAD entered the sadhanasthal on the Puranmasi night, she had no idea that tonight would alter everything in Shaktidham.

Rhea came out of the sadhanasthal and the vibrations struck her like a dagger with a massive impact. She could feel the energy draining from her like a tap running full. She just managed to walk to the residential area and fell near the swing in the veranda. She mustered all her energy and called out for Satya. She could feel the warmth of the blood trickling down her nose. Atila suddenly started barking uncontrollably from the terrace, Satya and Krishnam came out of their rooms, Satya rushed to pick her up. He saw blood trickling from her nose and mouth. He shouted loudly for Krishnam; he rushed down hearing Satya's frantic call in despair, he had never heard Satya call like this ever before. Looking at Rhea, Satya instantly knew what had happened. Rhea saw anger in Satya's eyes, a destructive anger, for the first time since childhood.

'Baba, I have been struck,' barely spoke Rhea. Krishnam was shocked seeing Rhea bleeding in Satya's arms.

'Take her to Rageshwari's clinic immediately' instructed Satya, as he dialled Dr Rageshwari on the phone, 'do all that you can to save both my children. Rhea will take no one else's blood except Krishnam's, their blood groups match.'

'Krishnam, your blood group is the same as hers, give her only your blood until she does not stop bleeding, I will sit for Kriya,' instructed Satya. Kriya is an intense prayer and an extremely potent form of the Tantra ritual.

Rhea held Satya's hand, as he gave her in Krishnam's arms. 'Baba, it's my call, leave it at that,' she said and fell unconscious.

'Krishnam, Rhea will not lose if you don't, and I want both of you back, now go.'

Later, all the inmates got together to pray for Rhea didi. Something serious had just happened and she was being rushed to the hospital. Meena was sitting and crying uncontrollably. The two pundits of the main temple started reciting Mahamrityunjaya jaap. Mahamrityunjaya jaap is a Sanskrit mantra, which is believed to save life. It is supposed to be the ultimate life-saving drug in the Vedic scriptures.

Mahamrityunjaya mantra is all that could be heard.

Om trambakam yajahmahe sugandhim pushtivardhanam,
Urvarukmiv bandhnath mrityomurkshiya maammratath.

This mantra is a prayer to Lord Shiva addressed as Trambakham here, which also means someone who possesses three eyes; the third eye signifies the light of wisdom, which destroys the darkness of ignorance.

Satya's words to Rhea had always been, that according to his limited knowledge, this mantra was a prayer asking Lord Shiva to bless the person with moksha i.e. liberation from the cycle of life and death into the world of light. Life and death in this gross world is of the body.

Rhea was pale and devoid of her glow by the time she reached the hospital. Her white attire was doused in her blood. All arrangements had been made at the clinic. Rhea was immediately put on an intravenous drip and administered a drug to stop her bleeding. It was an antidote which in such a case is life-saving. The bleeding didn't seem to stop and Krishnam's blood was replacing hers.

Satya was in the sadhanasthal performing the Kriya, the effects were being negated, but it would take time. Rhea and Krishnam had to sustain it until that point arrived.

'Krishnam, we cannot take your blood any further, it will be dangerous for you,' said Dr Rageshwari. His look conveyed to Dr Rageshwari the required and she continued with the transfusion.

'She is sinking Krishnam, her blood pressure is dipping even further, her pulse too is getting feeble, and nothing is working.' Dr Rageshwari was in a state of extreme stress.

'Better call up Baba now, I think huh …we are losing her.'

'Baba is at the sadhanasthal,' replied Krishnam in an even voice.

Rhea was slipping between consciousness and unconsciousness. He heard her mumble, 'Krish, Baba will save me, don't you worry now.'

Instantly, he knew that Rhea would make it.

At no point would he stop, even if it meant giving each and every drop of blood to save Rhea. He knew that Satya would go to any extent to save them. He just closed his eyes. As they lay beside each other in two different beds, he extended his hand and held hers. Love can only be expressed through actions. Words fail to encompass its enormity. One definition of love is when one can effortlessly place the other before one's self.

Krishnam in his thoughts was sitting in front of Goddess Kali asking her to save Rhea. He had no doubt that Rhea would survive this, but he also knew that this was only the beginning, a start of a big change. He recognized the holocaust, which was about to sweep Rhea's life and would engulf him too. There was nothing in Rhea's life, which would leave Krishnam or Satya unaffected.

Satya got up from the sadhanasthal on completion of Kriya after offering Purna Ahuti. The Mahamrityunjaya chants had also been effective and saved Rhea didi. The antidote had finally worked and Rhea started stabilizing. Dr Rageshwari had stopped pondering over certain mysteries long ago. She loved Satya and understood the spaces which were not to be intruded. She heaved a sigh of relief. She knew Satya had only one weakness, his children.

Strong negative vibrations sent by a Tantra sadhak from a place called Kamroop had breached Rhea's protection. It was a village deep in the jungles of Guwahati.

Guwahati is a Shakti peeth, where the organ of worship is the yoni (vulva) of Shakti, signifying the sacred point from where creation flows. One of the most prevalent mythologies concerning the origin of worship at Kamakhya is associated with Sati, wife of Lord Shiva. She burned herself in a sacrificial fire at her father Daksha Prajapati's palace, as he was disrespectful to her husband, Lord Shiva.

According to the story, Shiva became furious and took the burnt body of Sati over his shoulder and began to dance the Dance of Death (tandava) to destroy this universe. The other Gods, afraid of their total destruction, went to Vishnu asking him to pacify Shiva.

Vishnu silently followed Shiva while dancing, but did not come close to Shiva, as he was raging in anger. He sent his Sudarshana chakra (a sharp edged, disc shaped weapon) to cut up the corpse of Sati. Pieces of her body fell as they were cut up and Shiva was left without the body of Sati. On realizing that Sati's body was no more on his shoulder, Shiva calmed down and sat down to perform Mahatapasya.

Supposedly there were fifty-one pieces of Sati, which had scattered across the Indian subcontinent. Her yoni (vulva) is said to have fallen on the spot, where the Kamakhya Temple stands today, and hence the spot has a prominent status among the Mother Goddess' temples. The yoni symbolizes the creative power of the universe and is an abstract representation of Shakti.

Bhairava sought his revenge with Satya using Rhea, as it would be impossible for Rhea to handle these vibrations and their impact. She was the shishya of Satya, his sworn enemy, progressing to become a Tantric, which was incomprehensible and unacceptable to him. If she were out of his way, Satya would lose his pride, his successor; it would completely break him internally. It would then be easy to dethrone him and Bhairava would be unchallenged in his domain. Bhairava thought he had his revenge finally.

◆

Satya's father had been the guru to both Satya and Bhairava, who had committed the most inexcusable blunder that a Tantra sadhak could. Bhairava had raped a minor girl from a nearby village; she was collecting firewood in the woods adjoining her village. It was an act of blasphemy, as a woman is considered a form of Shakti and a young girl is a representation of Devi Kamakhya, the virgin Goddess of Tantra. His guru had declared him unworthy of the vidya of Tantra and he had been asked to leave, never to return. He left feeling humiliated and with pent-up anger towards his guru and his guru's son, Satya.

Bhairava had been a young orphan named Mohan at birth. He ran away from the orphanage in Varanasi; it was due to the terrible treatment they were all meted with. At the dawn of the second day, he was hungry and resorted to begging. He was begging for food, and came upon a saint in a white dhoti coming out after a dip in the holy river Ganges. The saint brought him back to his place, a little outside the city. He fed him and took care of his needs and sent him to a local school, but Mohan refused to go after a few days. On the persistence of the saint to go to school, Mohan ran away, only to return hungry and weak, a week later.

Mohan requested the saint to teach him Tantra vidya and make him his shishya, as school was not what he was keen on. The saint finally accepted him as his shishya, a year later. Satya, the saint's son, was studying in a private boarding school and would come during vacations when he would dedicate his time in pursuing his sadhana. Satya and Mohan were almost the same age. Satya joined Delhi university after completing school.

Mohan changed his name to become Bhairava, as he wanted to shut himself out of his past. However, buried inside him were the nights in the orphanage, the caretaker, the physical abuse he had to take as a child. If only changing his name could relieve Bhairava of his excess baggage that he carried! Bhairava was angry at the world and all he sought was revenge. The saint hoped that Bhairava would gradually forgive, as time passed, and let go of his anger and resentment.

Bhairava resented Satya and his anger and resentment was reflected in his behaviour towards him. Satya's composure always averted an ugly situation. He resented Satya's looks, his education, and his peaceful demeanour, even Satya's luck.

Bhairava had not completed his path as a disciple, before he committed the unpardonable. He moved on to Kamroop, with revenge in his mind.

The family of the girl had asked the saint to be fair, as no respectable boy would marry the girl. Being the head and the guru, he was responsible for his shisya's act. The saint married the minor girl to Satya, who was fresh out of college and offered no resistance. The young girl turned out to love her husband Satya dearly and he fulfilled all his duties as a husband. She was simple and dutiful. She studied further and completed her graduation privately from the Banaras University. Satya too studied further to complete his doctorate in physics. She spoke less, like Satya.

However, she yearned to be a mother. Satya's wife gave birth to a boy after twelve years of marriage. She had disliked Satya's use of contraception as her yearning increased; her simple mind connived to deceive her husband and she lied to him about her safe days. She could not hide her pregnancy beyond the fourth month.

As Satya's wife was wheeled to the labour room, Satya asked the doctor and her assistant to do all they could to save his wife. The doctor and the intern exchanged a confused look with each other, as they saw no complication. It was a simple case of normal delivery and everything was progressing well. Satya had met Dr Rageshwari, the intern who was assisting the doctor during his wife's delivery. Dr Rageshwari was totally taken in by this handsome man, with an imposing persona, wearing a white dhoti kurta with a red tika on his forehead.

The doctors were dumbfounded as to why the mother breathed her last as the child cried for the first time at birth.

After going to Kamakhya, Bhairava had pursued his sadhana, but his desire to destroy Satya and become unchallenged in his domain was so overpowering that he completely lost the vision of his sadhana. He practised all that he had learnt from his guru and perfected it. He, of course, had stopped short of Satya, who took all from his guru, also his father. Bhairava's vidya had remained incomplete, he had missed many vital teachings, which Satya had learnt and was now passing them on to Rhea. The plan according to Bhairava was perfect, but he still missed his target.

◆

Rhea came back home, but was physically very weak. As she lay in her bed she asked for Atila. Krishnam was quiet as he sat beside her, he did not want to break the news of Atila's demise right now. He had passed away in his sleep, a few days after Rhea was admitted in the hospital.

'Krishnam, has Atila left us?' she asked pointedly.

'Yes,' he replied closing his eyes. She closed her eyes and said nothing.

Every day Krishnam looked after Rhea and fed her too; twice a day he gave her milk with turmeric, which works like an antiseptic, but she never liked its taste. In the evenings, after he had finished his day's work in the office, he would spend all his time with Rhea. He would oil her hair and massage her feet at times. Sometimes, he would just lie beside her and keep caressing her hair. Every night, she would cuddle up and sleep with him. Every day, Satya would sit for his prayers at the sadhanasthal. After fifteen days, Rhea started her walks; Krishnam took her for a short walk on the first day, the duration of which gradually increased in time.

'Neel, Rhea is not ready to meet anyone, she is still unwell,' said Krishnam, when Neel visited him during the day.

'What happened to her?' enquired Neel, concern reflecting in his voice and facial expression. No reply came from Krishnam.

'When will she be fine?' he asked.

'She will take some time to recover,' replied Krishnam. 'Her world is different and I understand because I am a part of that world. Let's leave it at that.'

Neel held Krishnam's hand. 'Do let me know if I can be of any help.'

'I will, you take care,' replied Krishnam.

Rhea hardly spoke; both Satya and Krishnam understood her silence, without it being said. She was a victim of the misuse of Tantra, which for her was a path of self-evolution and chaste. It was difficult for her to comprehend that a Tantra sadhak mercilessly tried to sniff life out of her, and had it not been for Satya and Krishnam, she would be dead. She was not strong enough to protect herself yet, in her chosen field. It was a glaring inadequacy on her part, when she dealt with paranormal forces. There is neither scope for making a mistake nor any scope for being a victim of someone else's mistake. The reality remains that you are inadequate. The defeat was a reality and the survival of the fittest is a natural law.

It took Rhea almost two months, before she could sit in the sadhanasthal. As she resumed her practices, she realized that she had a strong kavach (protective armour) of vibrations, which had been created by Satya for her. Satya would have to sit for a ritual every twenty-one days, to keep the protection strong and in dynamic state. Presently, there existed no Tantric, who had the power to penetrate this armour. In her chosen field, Rhea was still living a life of a dependent. Life for her was now sadhana and sadhana required more and more practice.

She accepted the pain of defeat and clearly understood the actions that needed to be taken. People called it the path of black magic and she would be the black magic woman, as she now understood what that magic was.

Black magic or white magic, it depends on the magician. Now it was endurance for all at Shaktidham. Every decision or step she would now take, would be decisive for the three lives intertwined together in an inexplicable way.

'Rhea, Baba has a surprise for you, come quickly,' said

Krishnam, pulling her by her hand. They rushed downstairs and in front of Satya were four pups.

'Which one does my little girl want?' asked Satya.

She was quiet and then said softly, 'Baba, I don't want to keep any.'

◆

Krishnam was lying in his bed watching the news on television, with Rhea's head on his lap and her eyes closed. He was caressing her scalp, slowly massaging her. A tear dropped on Krishnam's lap from the edge of Rhea's eye, he felt it and turned off the television. He held her at the back of her neck and helped her sit up and face him. He looked at her eyes, but she said nothing only held him and tears kept rolling down. He did not say a word and held her till she stopped. He went to the kitchen and brought up two cups of coffee.

As they sat and had their coffee together, Krishnam was concerned, 'What is it, Rhea?'

She said, 'I have failed, as I have to be able to protect myself, not be dependent on Baba.'

Krishnam says, 'What happened to you is because someone decided to break the rules of Tantra, it is not your failure.'

There was silence for a moment and then Krishnam questioned her, 'Tell me, who makes the rules?'

'Each one, their own,' she replied.

'Is it possible in any game and on the same playing field, to have different sets of rules?' he questioned.

Rhea thought for a bit, she then answered, 'No, there can only be one set of rules.'

'Then who sets these rules?' he asked.

Rhea was quiet. She had understood what Krishnam wanted to tell her.

18

THE MAJOR FORMS of the Goddess are worshipped in Tantra; Dasa Mahavidya is the worship of ten forms of Shakti, which are Kali, Tara, Maha Tripura Sundari, Bhuvaneshvari, Chinnamasta, Bhairavi, Dhumavati, Bagalamukhi, Matangi, and Kamala. Her entire focus was sadhana, she had to learn and perfect all that Satya could impart.

'Vidya is only a tool; it aids you to bring about a change within yourself. Don't hold on to this tool, only discover what lies beyond it. Perfection is a perpetually forward moving goal; therefore, one can only strive to attain it. There never comes a point, where nothing more can be acquired,' Satya said to Rhea.

Rhea's days were spent sleeping, her evenings with Krishnam and nights at the sadhanasthal. The only nights she took a break, was when Satya had to perform his rituals, twice a week. The change Rhea was going through was evident and for Krishnam to keep pace with changes was not easy. This change brought no choice, but only an unknown future for them. The only decision Krishnam could arrive at from this change, would be to tread the road of faith, that time does not diminish love and love can't be superseded by any force. The only option was to have faith, if you love someone, barring all time and space.

'Krishnam, her pace is impregnated with a seed of stillness.' Sometimes you must lose yourself to find yourself. Sages have said that when you wish to achieve something start at its opposite. To overthrow, one will have to exalt first. Rhea has understood this,' said Satya.

Krishnam was in bed with Rhea and wanted to make love to her, it had been over five months since she had been struck. He kissed her and touched her, removed her clothes to make love to her, but she was not ready and he stopped midway.

She cried for a long time with her head on his chest, 'I am sorry Krish, please forgive me.' Krishnam said nothing and kept stroking her head. It was an ordeal, which inevitably both had to go through.

Satya called both Krishnam and Rhea to the sadhanasthal the next evening. It was time for Satya to share certain facts with his children, which they were oblivious to. Satya spoke through the night, as they sat talking in the temple. Certain facts needed to be accepted and actions needed to be taken to protect the lineage and them as individuals.

At the end of it all, Krishnam asked Rhea one question, which was relevant to the three lives as they were linked, 'Rhea, what do you think you would have done, had you been in my place?'

Rhea looked up at him and replied, 'I would leave Shaktidham and go, Krish.'

Satya contributed nothing to this.

Krishnam left Shaktidham and he left Satya and Rhea. Certain choices in life are painful, but nevertheless we still have to make them. In every choice made, lies hope for happiness. They had faith that life would bring them together again, when, where, how; these questions were left unanswered.

'I shall wait for you…' were the parting words of Krishnam.

Rhea was going to undertake the longest journey, inwards, as the outside depends on the inside. Death is not always physical and Satya saw Rhea die the day Krishnam left.

Rhea didn't leave the sadhanasthal the entire day; she sat in front of Goddess Kali and cried. Satya sat on the swing; just waiting for her, understanding what she was going through. He could let her cry, but he himself could not do so.

A month went by, but Rhea would leave the sadhanasthal only to either visit the washroom or take a bath. She even ate her meals in the sadhanasthal and slept on the floor. There were times when Satya heard her scream; the pain in her screams shook his being.

Satya just let her be by herself; it was important for her to feel the pain, go into its depth, grow from it, and then go beyond it. Burying it, denying it, or forgetting the pain does not relieve it.

One night, as she slept in the sadhanasthal, she woke up feeling Krishnam's hand caressing her head, she had heard him say, 'Whatever you do affects me Rhea, you must rise to the occasion, my princess, I am waiting,' she had felt his lips kiss her forehead.

Satya was in the veranda sitting with his eyes closed, waiting for Rhea, as he did for the past month. She touched his feet and said, 'Baba, Krishnam will come back.'

Satya opened his eyes, smiled, but remained silent; he blessed her with both hands.

Neel was flabbergasted when he realized that Krishnam had left, as Rhea told him. Rhea had called him to come to Shaktidham, a few days later. Neel had come many times, but was informed by Chander that Rhea cannot meet anyone and Krishnam is out of town.

'What do you mean left and gone? Where?' asked Neel, completely rattled by what had happened

'I don't know where, but I assume he has gone back to US,' she replied looking blankly in the air.

'And when will he come back?' he asked in a confused tone, still not being able to comprehend what Rhea was saying.

'When, I don't know,' replied Rhea.

Neel held his head, 'What made him take such a radical step?'

'He will come back,' she said.

'At times, I feel I do not know you guys at all, what has happened in the last six months?' he said with a sigh.

'Is there something that I can do?' asked Neel.

'No, only I can. It is me who has to walk this long path, but I know I will arrive at my destination,' replied Rhea.

Rhea immersed herself in sadhana and everything else in life took a backseat. She was no more Satya's little girl or Krishnam's princess; neither was she Neel's friend. She was just a sadhak and all other relationships ceased to exist.

To find stillness while in motion is the paradox to accomplish, rather than just being still while in stillness.

19

Four years later, 1999

'RHEA JI, YOUR field does not believe in abstinence, you follow the path of indulgence, isn't it? How come you took up this field being a woman?' asked Vivekacharaya, the famous orator, who was visiting Shaktidham,was being cheeky.

Rhea looked at Satya to respond, but he remained silent. Rhea had to face the world directly and move out of his shadows.

'A wise man is one who knows the limits of his wisdom,' replied Rhea, with a straight look.

Swami Vivekacharaya nearly jumped of his chair, but managed to control himself, in no way was he ready to know that there was any limit to his wisdom. He had a following in hundreds of thousands and was a regular orator of scriptures on television.

In an icy-cold tone, he said, 'Well Madam.' 'Rhea ji' had turned into 'Madam'.

'We all know about the five makars, without which there can be no Tantra sadhana.'

'No, you don't know, Sir, you have just heard it and if you knew you wouldn't have questioned a woman taking up Tantra,' she replied.

'What arrogance,' thought Swami Vivekacharaya; his brash opulence was visible in his clothing and his assistants too. The thought was strong enough and Rhea caught it.

She immediately reacted in response, 'It is not "arrogance" as it is based on subject knowledge through practice.' But she knew she had made a blunder. Even if she had caught his thought, she was supposed to ignore it.

She looked at Satya, but he seemed to be unmoved by it. 'Thank you, Devima,' thought Rhea. An inadvertent statement at times would make Satya make an assertion 'You still have to learn to use your ability wisely.'

Rhea had no intention on reading his thoughts, but they were louder than words. It crossed Swami Vivekacharaya's mind that if she can do this, it is very dangerous. He turned pale, as he tried to check his thoughts. She did not respond to this one consciously. Vivekacharaya's mind was now an uncontrolled horse, as this was his first experience.

He did not know where to look or what to say.

Rhea said, 'Acharya ji, I am sorry, it just happened.'

He took time to ease out. He took large swigs at the tumbler of lassi, but Rhea could still sense his discomfort.

It was then that she said, 'I would like to explain the five makars to you Acharya ji. Masam is meat, it signifies mastery of speech. Meenum is fish, which signifies the currents of energy that flow through the body. Madiram is symbolic of knowledge as knowledge is intoxicating. Maithuna is the sexual act, which signifies meditation of the primal act of creation. Mudra denotes parched grain, symbolizing intense concentration of a sadhak. Masam signifies earth, meenum water, madiram air, maithuna the act of creation, which is result of coming together of the two aspects of energy Shiva and Shakti. The two energies may seem different, but in Shakti resides Shiva and in Shiva dances Shakti, bringing about creation and consuming creation. Mudra is the act that brings the two energies into that harmonious balance, which can create as well as destroy. Even amidst what seems chaotic, there is a symphony that balances it all,' Rhea explained the five makars to Vivekacharaya.

After she explained, he said, 'I understand your point Rhea ji. I will not ask you for forgiveness, as I do not want to embarrass you, being elder. I give you my deeply felt blessing.'

He looked at Satya and said, 'Maharaj ji, you must be proud of having a shishya like her.'

Satya said nothing, just smiled.

Rhea was trying to clarify her actions to Satya after Vivekacharaya left. 'I did not intentionally read his thought Baba, just caught it.'

'A woman Tantric! That rattled his senses! He will know now forever that his knowledge is limited to the knowledge of the scriptures. Why don't we refrain from talking on the subject that we lack authentic knowledge of? Instead of exhibiting our half-baked knowledge why don't we just simply ask, how come I did not try and talk about scriptures? When you go to an expert, first you should have no doubt that he is an expert and accept it, and then ask your questions, isn't that the sensible way?' Rhea said to Satya.

Satya burst out laughing, then said, 'Arrogance, arrogance, my dear girl is getting arrogant. Rhea, you must remember at all times that you are a sadhak. Sadhana is not just in the temple and going through your rituals, it must transform you as an individual, it should also reflect in your interaction with the world around you. Sadhana is just a tool for self-transformation.'

It had been long since she had heard Satya laugh such a hearty laugh. He rarely did since Krishnam left four years ago and no one had heard from him since. Rhea knew that he was waiting, but she still had a long way to go.

20

NEEL HAD GOT married nearly a year ago and had already filed for divorce, which was still pending in the courts. His wife asked for it and he consented to give it.

Neel urged Rhea to see him immediately one morning, a year ago.

He broke the news with a gleaming face. 'Rhea, I am getting married to Barkha. She had joined Mom as an assistant and we kind of rekindled our relationship. Things have changed and so have people.'

Rhea congratulated him, but there wasn't any enthusiasm in her voice. In any case, Rhea hardly seemed enthusiastic about anything nowadays. Her focus had just remained towards her sadhana.

Kritika had made her thoughts abundantly clear to Neel that he was making a mistake. But he was in love; he knew he was right and that Barkha was his soulmate and what anyone thought didn't matter to him.

The wedding was a big lavish affair with cocktail parties and ceremonies as would be in an Indian wedding. Neel, one of the most eligible bachelors in town was tying the knot with an upcoming designer.

They had a party in Delhi for their friends and a row of successive parties and ceremonies in Varanasi. It all seemed like a fairy tale of two childhood friends falling in love to begin with and then moving away due to circumstances beyond control. Fate brought them together again for them to realize that life was bland without each other and they decided to walk together as a family and live happily ever after.

Rhea did not attend the functions; she was preoccupied with some saints, who had come down from various parts of the country to Shaktidham. Neel insisted, requested, and pleaded, but all that yielded no results.

Right after returning from their honeymoon from Switzerland, Barkha wanted Neel to break all contacts with Rhea. That was their first fight; the beginning of their quarrels was about Neel's relationship with Rhea. Barkha put it across that she being a wife was concerned for her husband's safety and well-being. Rhea was a threat, as she was into black magic. Neel never anticipated that a problem of this nature could even come up. Rhea had a special place in his life, which could not be filled by anyone.

'Barkha, your thinking is absurd and beyond reason. Nothing will work when it comes to Rhea, least of all emotional blackmail. I think you know better than to talk like this.'

Neel, though, did not pay heed to Barkha and spent the entire evening with Rhea at Shaktidham, telling her all about the wedding and their trip to Switzerland. He mentioned nothing about his argument with Barkha.

When he returned home, Barkha cried after she realized where he had been, she accused him of having a relationship with Rhea, and out of anger flung things at him. This wasn't the Barkha Neel had married; he was in shock to react to the situation. He had tried to reason with Barkha the next morning, but all went in vain. With each passing day, things deteriorated further. Her interrogations and suspicions were making things difficult for Neel; it seemed she was perpetually suspicious.

Barkha would be certain of Neel's honesty towards her, only once in bed and they would make up for a while. Neel only wanted Barkha to understand what his feelings for Rhea were and that Rhea was not and would never be a threat to her. Rhea could never take Barkha's place in his life.

'Nobody can ever replace Krishnam in Rhea's life, even after he has left she is still sure he will be back one day,' Neel explained to Barkha, when she had picked up yet another fight.

'Why don't you tell me or explain to me why Krishnam left?' she screamed back.

'I too am unaware why and I have often wondered about it myself,' he replied.

'Oh, really! As if you don't know you were the reason,' she said, with sarcasm dripping, which shook Neel totally.

One evening, after he returned, Barkha inquired where had he been, as he was not reachable since long. 'I had gone to deliver a dress, which Mom had made for Rhea and chatted with her for a while,' replied Neel.

Barkha went into a rage, 'What is the need for your mother to send anything to Rhea. Who is Rhea to us?'

She then said spiteful things about Neel's mother.

'Even after being your mother, she is hand in gloves with Rhea to snatch you away from me.'

Barkha added, 'She obviously feels threatened by my work professionally and personally too.'

Her contorted face, ugly with anger, sent shock down Neel's spine. He looked at her in shock and sat dumbfounded with his hands on his forehead. Words failed him and her face disgusted him. He wondered what could have driven him to love and marry this woman. Barkha went even more belligerent, as she saw Neel slumped in his chair. She threw at him whatever she could lay her hands on and Neel only warded them off. Neel got up from the chair, went into his bedroom, and locked himself in. Had he not left, he would have slapped her.

Barkha kept banging at the door wildly and shouting at the top of her voice, 'Come out, the truth is you can't face reality, as it's in your face.'

This lasted for hours. That night, the past of Neel being a witness to his parents' fights surfaced. As thoughts travelled, he could somehow comprehend what his mother's situation was, more so now, experiencing this situation, he could relate to her pain.

The next day, late in the morning, Barkha had swollen eyes and Neel a throbbing headache as they sat in silence for breakfast. He left for work right after, without making any effort to strike a conversation. He had to leave for Delhi and travel onward to Paris for work that evening.

He came back home early evening; while he was packing, Barkha walked into the bedroom and said, 'So, you will be gone for a week? Is that bitch also going with you?'

Neel couldn't bear it any further; he turned around and slapped her hard right across her face. She tried to get back at him, but he grabbed her by her hands, pulling her into the other bedroom, and locked the door from the outside. He packed his bags and instructed his house help to open the door, only after he had left.

Barkha, consumed by anger, went to Shaktidham the next morning. She told Chander obstinately that she had to meet Rhea instantly.

'Sorry, she is asleep, no one can meet her at the moment, so you can come back later,' Chander told her.

'Tell her that I had come and if Neel comes here again, she will be in trouble.'

Chander asked her to leave immediately, as it would be in her best interest to avoid any unpleasant incident. 'If I ever see you in the premises again, you will be in big trouble,' Chander threatened her. Barkha left in a huff, mouthing swears under her breath.

For the first time, it hit upon her that even to access Rhea was not easy; it was different when she was a friend. Neel did not answer any calls from Barkha, while he was travelling. Rhea had got all the information from Chander about Barkha's visit. She did not react.

'Words should be soft; you never know when you have to eat them back. If you can't say anything good, refrain from saying bad too. Weak are the people who remain silent when it is time to speak and speak when it is time to be silent,' Satya had often told Rhea and Krishnam, when they were kids.

Neel encountered Barkha's hysteria on his return to Varanasi. She screamed at him how she had been insulted in Shaktidham.

'Why did you go there in the first place; and stop barking that you were insulted,' said Neel, who was mentally and physically fatigued. Without waiting for her answer, he locked himself in the bedroom.

To Neel, Barkha felt like an absolute stranger, whom he had no intentions of trying to understand.

He called Rhea apologetically. 'I am sorry Rhea for Barkha's actions and behaviour with Chander. She has completely lost it,' he said.

'I wonder, if she ever had it,' was Rhea's reply in disgust.

Finally, Barkha broke the two day silence between them and asked Neel, 'Will you leave Rhea or not, you have to choose between the two of us.'

'How can I choose, she is a friend and you are my wife? I fail to understand what your problem is with Rhea?' questioned Neel.

'Why has she never told you?' Barkha asked in turn.

'Told me, what?' asked Neel taken aback.

'Neel, you will never understand, she does black magic, and you are under her spell.'

'Oh! Please stop all this. I can't cope up with this stupidity anymore,' said Neel, in an exasperated tone.

'Just say yes or no, will you leave Rhea or not?'

'You are being irrational and I have told you that she has a different space in my life.'

She insisted again, 'Will you or won't you!'

'No, I won't. Don't ask me this ever again and this topic is forever closed,' replied Neel.

'Well, if that's your decision, then I want a divorce,' said Barkha, trying to corner him.

Neel got up and walked away; living with Barkha was impossible. Three days later, Barkha received divorce papers, with Neel's signature. She accused Neel that this action of his further proved her point that Krishnam had left Rhea, because he realized that Neel and Rhea were in a relationship. Neel thought it was worthless to get into another spat, so he walked out and stayed out, until she packed and left the house.

Barkha called Nethra and narrated all that had transpired. Nethra heard her side of the story and called up Rhea the next morning. 'How could you do this, Rhea? How could you break, your own friend's house?'

'What do you mean, Nethra?' asked Rhea.

'Come on Rhea, don't put up an act. Neel and Barkha are breaking up because of you and don't say you don't know. There is something going on between you and Neel.'

'Nethra, you have already made up your mind and I don't think I owe you an explanation.'

'What possibly can you explain Rhea, how will you escape the truth, when you know that you have wronged Barkha,' she said with repugnance in her voice.

'How come you never told us why Krishnam left? Don't you think it's all crystal clear now? I know what kind of practices you are into Rhea and I feel we are less knotted people than you for sure.'

Rhea put the phone down and sat in silence, she had heard enough.

You could spend a lifetime with people and still be total strangers. Rhea had grown up with strangers, thinking them to be friends.

The truth is that it is difficult for us to know ourselves, forget knowing anyone else. If we knew ourselves, we would have known everything required to be known.

The story travelled fast in the small city of Varanasi, more so because it was about Rhea, who had wronged a woman to possess her husband. The outside world was not of any concern to Rhea. Anyone could believe what he or she wanted, it was immaterial for her.

Kritika only had one line for Neel, 'It's never too late to correct your mistake. I am happy that Barkha is out of your life, but also sad, that you had to go through it to find out for yourself.' Neel agreed with his mother.

'How is Rhea taking it?' asked Kritika.

'I wonder Mom, I have not really spoken to her on this, and I would probably demean her even by talking about it. I don't know if anything really matters to her anymore, especially since Krishnam left. I don't even know if the outside world ever mattered to her. I have always felt that for her the world has been Shaktidham, Baba, Krishnam and maybe somewhere me.'

'She must be broken after Krishnam left.'

'A part of her died that day; it seems somewhere and at some level that time has stopped for her. I wish I could do something for her,' he said sadly.

'Neel, have you ever expressed your feelings to her?' she asked with caution.

'The definition of love for her is different,' he replied.

'Have you ever told her…?' she asked again.

'No Mom, I never saw the point in doing so. I am lucky to have her as a friend and I don't want to take any chance and destroy that.'

Kritika held her son's hand; he felt her love and concern.

'Mom, she is fighting a battle, which we possibly cannot comprehend. I am sure she will come through.'

'How do you know that?' she asked.

'At times, I feel she is like any of us, but at some level she is more than us and then at times, I feel there exists a world of hers, which is inaccessible even to me. I think, I understand certain things about her,' said Neel.

'I haven't told you this before, but her baba was my senior in college in Delhi.'

'Really Mom?' asked Neel, surprised. 'How come you never told me that before?'

'It did not really seem significant,' said Kritika.

She then went on, 'In our college Satya stood out from the rest. We all thought he was a really handsome guy. Satya probably doesn't even know me, as he remained mostly to himself and there was mystery surrounding him. Many of the girls hung around after college, to catch a glimpse of him. In the last year at college, I heard that he was from a lineage of Tantra sadhaks and lived in Varanasi. Even in college, he was a very dignified person, but he was unapproachable too. I see a strong and distinct reflection of him in Rhea. Krishnam looks exactly like him and is nearly as handsome as Satya.'

'My God Mom! That's news to me, and Rhea has hardly ever spoken about Baba with me.'

'Neel, at least speak your heart out to her.'

Neel was quiet for a long time.

'Mom, I wonder what hurts more, to say and then regret it all your life or regret all your life what you never said.'

21

RHEA GOT UP totally disoriented and ran down to Satya, he was sitting on his swing reading the newspaper and having morning tea.

Like every morning, she touched his feet. 'At night I dreamt about Ishaan. It started with me seeing someone's arms and then someone's legs float by, soon a body came into view, it was without arms and legs. As the body came closer, I recognized it was Ishaan; it was just his body floating in the clouds. Baba, I need to sort this out somehow, I will not let it happen,' Rhea was crying, as she was narrating this dream. Satya put his hand on her head.

'Have you interpreted the dream?' he asked.

'Baba, it's absolutely clear, I see a strong probability of him in an air crash!'

She preferred using the word probability, because she always believed that there were other possibilities. The truth was that her dreams were an imminent forecast. But then as per Satya the future always exists in probabilities. If one can modify an action, its probable future would change too.

'What do you think you can do about it?' asked Satya.

'I will advise Ishaan not to travel by air.'

'Until when? What will you tell him if he asks you, why so?' he questioned.

Rhea was quiet; she did not know how to answer both the questions. It was unknown to her until when and she couldn't answer if she was questioned about it.

'A perturbed mind cannot think with clarity, so first, settle your thoughts,' he told her and added, 'detach yourself from the situation, only then the task in hand will become easier.'

She sat in distress for a long time with her hand on her forehead.

'Baba, Devima will have an answer, I leave it to her.'

Satya smiled. 'Are you confident you will get your answer?'

'Yes Baba, I know I will.'

Ishaan, after his bachelor's in college, had gone on to complete his civil engineering. He had joined a corporate organisation and was posted in Delhi. Ishaan and Rhea had kept in regular touch; during each visit to Varanasi, he made it a point to visit Shaktidham. They shared a cordial and warm interaction.

Rhea was aware that he could relate to certain aspects of her world. He had respect and affection for Rhea. Ishaan never forgot about the one who did good for him; he was one of those few. Whether he was categorized as a friend or not, he knew that Rhea had the right to ask him to do whatever she felt was needed and he would.

That entire day and night, Rhea sat in the sadhanasthal. She kept a maun-vrat and nobody could disturb her.

Rhea's cell phone had been ringing in her room. She entered

her room and saw five missed calls from Ishaan between 4 and 5 a.m., on her mobile. She called back instantly.

'Good morning Rhea, I am sorry to have been trying to call you at this hour,' said Ishaan apologetically.

'I can barely hear you, there is too much noise Ishaan, where are you?'

'Rhea, can you hear me now...I am just boarding a flight to Delhi from Calcutta. I have to rush back urgently for an important board meeting. If it works out, it will be great for my career and I may get the opportunity to head the overseas operation. I just wanted to share this news with you. I know it was an inconvenient hour to call, but just could not resist the urge to speak to you before taking this flight.'

Rhea froze for a second in shock and spontaneously she screamed back, 'Ishaan, DO NOT board that aircraft.'

The connection dropped, she redialled. The network signal had disappeared on her phone, she rushed out to the terrace to try and get some signal, but it was all in vain. She ran down and woke Satya and burst out crying.

'What happened?' he asked her with caution.

He asked her to sit down and poured her a glass of water. 'Calm down, Rhea and tell me what happened.'

She kept sobbing and narrated the sequence of events. Satya sat quietly watching her and remained silent. 'Rhea if you have faith in Mother Goddess then maintain your calm,' said Satya.

It was in the morning news broadcast. A Calcutta–Delhi flight via Patna and Lucknow, a Boeing 737, had crashed just before its scheduled arrival at 7.40 a.m., in Patna. Most bodies of the passengers and crew were charred beyond recognition. The six-crew members, including the pilot, captain and co-pilot were killed too. The year was 2000. It was the flight that Ishaan did not board.

◆

Neel came to Shaktidham to see Rhea on Sunday morning, 'Don't you miss our old days? You, Krishnam, and me used to have so much fun,' said Neel, as Rhea and he were walking around Shaktidham.

'I have been wanting to speak with you about why Krishnam left.'

Rhea did not reply and kept walking quietly. Neel turned towards her and physically shook her.

'Hello, am I talking to the trees? Rhea, what is it with you? Krishnam has left long ago, stop clinging to the past and move on.'

What he witnessed, he would never forget until he died.

'He is not my past; he is my present and my future.' Rhea repeated it, screaming hysterically until she could scream no more.

The pain in those screams and in her eyes, which had tears, pierced Neel to the core. He held her and hugged her tightly until her sobs ebbed. It was the first time he ever saw her cry. There is a charm in vulnerability; Rhea lacked vulnerability, he had always thought.

That moment on, Neel's opinion changed, though he still failed to comprehend how and why Krishnam would leave both Satya and Rhea. But after he saw Rhea's state that day, he sought no answers.

Today, Neel understood that words had serious limitations. Expression of anything deep can only be felt, be it grief, bliss or love. He remembered Rhea saying that words were a poor mode of communication, to express anything that was from the soul, which the other could only feel.

He had no clue whether his praying to God would have any result or not, but if it did, he took this moment as an opportunity, to ask him to send Krishnam back into Rhea's life. Everything had stood still for Rhea for the last six years, since Krishnam left. Neel had to find him anyhow. Neel was oblivious to one reality that every step Rhea took was towards an end—Krishnam.

22

A COUPLE HAD brought their seventeen-year-old daughter to Shaktidham. For a year the girl had been having fits of violent behaviour and her face was pale. Her voice would change and she would exhibit strength, which was not possible when she was normal. Her eyes would become bloodshot and her voice would become heavier like a man's. A doctor had been treating her and she was regular with her medication, but she was still getting those fits. The girl was clearly possessed, some pundit had told the family, and they brought her to Shaktidham. Her parents requested Satya to help her, so he asked Rhea to see if she could be helped.

Rhea sat across facing her and looked into her eyes, she needed to make sure if it was genuine or just another act.

'Yes, I will try and help her,' said Rhea.

She asked the parents to get Priya in the evening for a ritual, which was required to heal her. Her parents were being inquisitive, but Rhea said nothing, just advised them to have faith and come.

Priya came that evening and was taken to the sadhanasthal, where all the arrangements for a ritual had already been made. Rhea took Satya's blessing and went to the sadhanasthal. Nobody was to disturb her during the ritual and all were made doubly aware. She could sense the restlessness rising in Priya, as she took her into the sadhanasthal. Rhea made Priya sit in a particular spot and made her relax with her eyes closed, she then took her into a state of trance but mentally alert, where Priya was ready to receive instructions and follow them. She created an imaginary protective barrier around Priya while chanting mantras and the physical representation of the barrier with bhasm (ashes). Rhea was in complete concentration, as this was the first time she was attempting this independently. She, however, knew she would be able to cure the girl. She took Ganga jal and chanted mantras sprinkling some on Priya. She instructed Priya now to remain within the circle only and not to leave it under any circumstance until instructed. Rhea said, 'Cooperate with me and you will be fine.' She then created a circle of protection around herself, chanting the mantras and sat in it.

Rhea was performing a havan, while chanting the mantras to create a vibratory conducive environment for the ritual to take effect and provoke the spirit. Priya's face started to contort grotesquely and her voice started to become husky and masculine. Rhea amplified the vibrations to evoke that energy and asked the possessor to leave her body. The spirit showed complete reluctance to let go. It demonstrated its relentlessness with anger spewing in its voice and words.

The spirit was bound in the circle of mantras and the vibrations had pinned it down. It now, would not to be able to use Priya for violence. It could not escape the bound sanctum of the protective circle.

As the havan progressed and the vibrations were gaining intensity, the spirit screamed assertively at her, 'I will not go.'

'You will have to go,' the thought vibrated through Rhea, threatening the spirit to exit in order to dispel it. Assessing the adamancy, Rhea would have liked to have Satya's help, but that was irrelevant at this moment, Satya had entrusted her with the responsibility.

She used an even more potent combination of mantras and directed it towards the target. In that split second, Priya slumped into a ball within the circle, devoid of any energy, as the vibrating energy of the mantras hit her.

It seemed that the spirit squatting in Priya had left. Rhea cautiously reached out to Priya without leaving her protective boundary, instantly Priya rebounded, still unable to breach the protective boundary. The havan vedi disgorged blistering flames in which Rhea perspired, but did not stop. She reiterated the potent chant until Priya let out a raucous scream that shook the sadhanasthal.

She analysed that the spirit was getting weaker and losing its hold. Rhea was near exhaustion too but now her faith had taken over. Finally, she heard the spirit again, 'I will leave her, please let me go.'

'Will you come back?' was the question in Rhea's mind.

'I promise never to come back ever. I promise, let me go,' the spirit was pleading.

Rhea chanted and put her hand on Priya's head, carving a window in the barrier, which created the path of exit for the spirit. Priya slumped into Rhea's arms and was out of her circle. The spirit had abided by her word and left.

Certain things one can believe only after having experienced them. Priya would never have believed, had she not been in the situation. Priya also realized that the existence of what may not have been experienced couldn't be denied on that mere basis. A while later, Priya left after she mustered enough energy to walk back. Rhea sat thinking of her experience.

'Rhea, one should never meddle with forces unknown, until you know how to control them. Energy exists in different forms, at different frequencies of vibration. A lot is unknown, but lack of that knowledge does not conclude non-existence. A whole world lies beyond what our senses can ever perceive,' were Satya's words.

At one point during the ritual, Rhea had been slightly petrified too; however, she had faith in the ritual practices, passed on to her by Satya. She clearly understood that she overcame the obstacles and could help someone, only after she surrendered herself to Goddess Kali.

What had happened in reality was that Priya invited the unknown, without having the knowledge or the power to control. She, along with one of her friends, had tried to invite a spirit using the Planchet method. It seems like a prank until one has to face the consequences. What we call supernatural is natural in another dimension. Never invite something to a dimension where it may cause trouble. We remain oblivious to its existence until it strikes us; like a virus may not be harmful until it enters a human body and causes trouble. Specialized skills, treatment, and handling are required for its eradication.

Just a few weeks later, a recently married girl came to see her. She had been coming almost each day to Shaktidham for a couple of weeks now and was requesting to meet Satya. Chander approached Rhea explaining the plight of this girl, as she seemed adamant to meet Satya. Rhea consented to meet this newly wed girl on Tuesday.

She came in a completely distraught state of mind. She was uneasy and seemed to be in haste. She butted in trying to talk about her problem several times while Rhea spoke to Chander; there was anxiety about her, which was distinctly abnormal. Rhea asked her to be patient until Chander left.

Immediately on Chander's exit she said, 'I want to eliminate my mother-in-law through Tantric Shakti.

'Tantrics do not indulge in such things, who told you so?' Rhea said amused.

'But I have heard that Tantrics have the power to eliminate people. There are mantras and rituals to destroy one's enemies.'

'I don't think you have ever met a Tantric before,' replied Rhea laughing.

She said, 'My mother-in-law is in an incestuous relationship with my husband, her own son.'

'What are the facts or evidences that support this serious allegation?'

'My husband is perpetually with his mother, even after he brings her home from work, he goes into her room with the door closed.'

'Okay, and…'

'Whenever they are speaking to one another and smiling, if I approach they become quiet, as if nothing was spoken.'

'Okay.'

'I know she is having an illegitimate relationship, I can see it every day with my eyes.'

'But that can be just a figment of your imagination, can't it?'

'No, I am telling you I know, as I am not a little baby.'

'Tell me how long have you been married?'

'One and a half months, but that's not important, I know what's going on.'

'You don't seem to have any concrete evidence on which you have based your theory.'

'I just want to know, if you can do it or not and I am willing to pay what you want. I am not here to argue their innocence.'

She had no facts to support her statement. She believed that it was so and determined that she was right. The girl was only insistent that her mother-in-law had to be eliminated and that she was willingly to pay any price for it.

Rhea felt that the girl was not open to any discussions or reasoning, though she seemed well educated, so Rhea asked her to leave. The girl should have substantial reason to make such a grievous allegation and the solution she was looking for was not comprehensible.

'It seems you know nothing about Tantra Rhea ji,' the girl accused Rhea and left in a scurry. Rhea had found something critically amiss in her conduct and accusation.

A couple of months later, Rhea was astonished by the girl's determination once again to see her. After all, this girl had passed her verdict already, but this time she revealed her identity that her name was Niharika.

'Rhea ji, I finally found a Tantric to conduct a ritual on my mother-in-law. However, he said that she had already got a protection done on herself. I told you I was right, as the

Tantric confirmed my suspicion that my mother-in-law had got Vashikaran (control of someone through Tantrividya) on her son. Therefore, to conduct a bigger ritual, he required very rare herbs and materials, which are expensive. Even then, I am going ahead with it, whatever it may cost.

'At times, I hear voices telling me that my husband is in a relationship with his mother. Rhea, it is God's will that I got to know and that I must do something about this immoral act,' said Niharika.

Rhea was quiet. The woman had been fooled by this so-called 'Tantric' who was exploiting her fears. He only reaffirmed and rephrased what Niharika was desperate to hear.

To try a placebo effect, Rhea took her to the temple and hoped her anxiety may die down and she may look at reality rather than hallucinate. At the temple, Rhea investigated the source of the voices Niharika heard, but there were no such vibrations perceptible; it was all just Niharika's hallucinations.

Rhea got her back from the temple and it was time for Niharika to hear the truth. Rhea wanted to be as gentle as possible with her, as she was sure of what was happening to her.

Rhea told her, 'Look Niharika, it is simple and straight, but what I am about to tell you is something you will have to listen, as I will only say it once and if you are sensible you will understand and take the corrective actions.'

Niharika nodded as if in acceptance, then Rhea went on, 'The person claiming to be a Tantric has merely played with your fears, he is in the business to make money off you. I am recommending to you, Niharika, that you see a good psychiatrist, as it is crucial for your well-being and mental health. If you want me to explain to any of your family members, I am willing to explain it to them. In my opinion, if you fail to see a good doctor, it will be disastrous for you and your family. Niharika, you require medical treatment, you are suffering from a mental disorder.'

Niharika was furious. 'Are you calling me mad? I am insulted coming to you, I thought you knew better, but now I am sure that you have no knowledge and you are an imposter. My intention was to tell you that you were wrong, but instead you are making absurd suggestions. It was a waste of time for me as you know absolutely nothing.'

A few months later, Rhea had heard from Chander that Niharika had passed away, as he had read an article and seen her picture in the obituary section of the newspaper. She had been married in a family of professionals, practising medicine and had been herself pursuing a PhD.

23

THERE REMAINED NO sadhak, there remained no ritual, nor was there any deity—all had merged into a singular identity. There comes a point in sadhana when a sadhak finds himself so deep in his ritual, so as to unite with the deity, that the worshipper, the worshipped and the prayer all seem to merge into one. Satya recognized that the time he had been waiting for had arrived. In the true sense, Rhea had come to bear the mantle. His assessment had been correct that she was the one.

As a culmination of his teachings, Satya gave Rhea the final diksha on Guru Poornima. After that day, he did not need to sit for his rituals for the upkeep of the kavacha (armour) with which he protected Rhea.

The world we live in, which is the visible world, is greatly influenced by the forces in the subtle realm. We remain unaware of our constant participation in the subtle realm, but Tantrics are aware of such forces.

At the initial stage of sadhana, some of the forces are disruptive and interfere with the sadhana. As the sadhana advances, a Tantra sadhak tunes into those forces, which are conducive to his growth as a sadhak. Radiating vibrations surround a Tantric, forming a shield, which are a result of his sadhana and are impervious. The strength of the protective shield is dependent on the advancement of his sadhana.

Tantra says that nature, which includes the human body, is made of three gunas (qualities)—sattwa (harmony, clarity, light), rajas (passion and dynamism) and tamas (ignorance, darkness and inertia). In the word Aum, A is equivalent to tamas, U to rajas and M to sattwa. The silence after Om symbolizes the state of trigunatita (tri–three and atita–beyond, meaning beyond the three gunas) that which is pure consciousness.

◆

It had been eight years since Krishnam had left. Neel called the phone number in the US, which he managed to get through a friend, which was supposedly Krishnam's. His heart was pounding loudly as the phone rang.

'Hi, could I please speak to Krishnam?' asked Neel.

'I am sorry, he is asleep, it is past midnight here. Who is this?' came a sleepy woman's voice.

'I am a friend of Krishnam's calling from India. Could you please give me his mobile number? It is urgent.'

'Could you leave your name and number and I will have him call you back?'

Neel gave his details.

'May I know who I am speaking with?' he asked.

'This is Rachel,' she answered and then cut the call.

◆

Today, Rhea was sitting in her office and trying to go through some files, which she hated.

'Rhea, places like Shaktidham are not just run on sadhana,' said Satya.

'An ashram must be financially independent, not be dependent on donations.' Satya had made sure that Shaktidham was financially independent. A Tantric should have the liberty to do what he wills and not be driven by financial need.

Satya was extremely leisurely and choosy in accepting to pray ritualistically for anyone. A procedural ritual of a Tantric prayer is a discipline that requires immense energy, rare ingredients, and precision. The person and the cause have to be worthy of it as each action has its consequences, even for the Tantric. Nobody came to Shaktidham without a problem. Donations were given as some believed that a part of their earnings went to charity, it would bring about further prosperity.

Rhea was supposed to go through a case file, which was a priority. She just could not get herself to concentrate. She left the file on the table and started sobbing.

Satya came through the door of her study. 'Rhea, I wish crying could help in attaining a favourable verdict. You will have to study it and do it by yourself, as no one else will.'

'I know that, Baba, but this was supposed to be done by Krishnam, was it not?' said Rhea spontaneously amidst her sobs.

Satya maintained his composure. 'Everything happens in time, and you have to be patient.'

'Baba, it has been eight years…' she said, looking at him.

'Rhea, you must understand, he is my son too,' said Satya with a smile.

Rhea hugged him and cried, 'Baba, when will he come back?'

Satya was silent…

Rhea walked to the sadhanasthal, where she sat numb for a while to find her composure. There was just one word in her mind—'Krishnam'.

But there was a lot of work to be prepared; Rhea preferred

going to the lawyer's office for all the consultations, as long meetings with the lawyer had become a regular feature. That particular evening, Mr Somnath Chakraborty, the counsel, a middle-aged gentleman on the other side of fifty, seemed to be preoccupied and lacked focus. She closed the file and looked at Mr Chakraborty, he in turn gestured to his assistant to leave. Mr Chakraborty had a friendly disposition and was considered one of the finest in the city of Varanasi.

'Rhea ji, it is no more a legal fight,' he said.

Rhea looked at him with a puzzled expression. 'What does that mean, Mr Chakraborty?'

'Rhea ji, this is serious,' his voice was almost a whisper. 'I got information today that money has been paid to a guy, who is a notorious criminal, to eliminate you. Mehta has really stooped low.'

Rhea was taken aback for a moment but she remained undeterred. 'Did you speak to Baba ji about it?' she questioned.

'Yes, I told him this morning.'

'What did he say?'

'He said that I should let you know when you visit.'

Rhea was quiet, trying to fathom what she had just heard. Her throat was suddenly dry.

'Give me a couple of days, I will come back to you on this,' said Rhea and left.

As Chander drove her back, she thought of how she could be killed—a gunshot, an accident, or some other ghastly way. Earlier that afternoon, before Rhea had left, Satya had gone into a maun-vrat for the next fifteen days. He would not be seen or heard by anyone for this duration, as he had broken complete contact with the outside world. Rhea could disturb him, but that would mean accepting defeat. To be alive is to be vulnerable.

'How can one give up without even a fight? I still have to live a life with Krish. One has to fight at least, to emerge as a winner or loser,' thought Rhea. 'Fear has to be faced to be defeated and I fear death as I have not lived. The meaning of my life is to be able to spend it with Krishnam and grow to achieve what I am supposed to.'

She went and sat quietly in the sadhanasthal, reconciling and absorbing the events of the evening. She touched Goddess Kali's feet and said aloud with conviction, 'I know you are there for me, I know that I will get through it and that you will find a way for me to come out of it. Bless me with courage and please guide me, Ma, I leave it all in your hands. I promise to leave no stone unturned but I know that finally it is only your blessings that will work. I don't want to die, I want to live with Krishnam.' She came out. She had no fear. Satya had always taught her to be prepared for the worst.

In the morning, she instructed Chander to call Devraj and request him to visit Shaktidham.

Devraj left immediately for Shaktidham on getting Rhea's call. It had to be something really important, as Rhea had never summoned him earlier. The last they had met was at an officer's house, during Dhrona's engagement ceremony, about a year ago. Devraj was now in active politics and was sure to get a ticket to contest elections this time again. However, he had lost in the earlier elections.

She then called the lawyer, Mr Chakraborty. 'Kindly have the affidavits for the land ready, I need them by this evening.'

Rhea and Devraj's meeting lasted for about an hour.

'Rhea, leave it to me. I respect the fact that no one should be physically hurt,' said Devraj.

Dhrona was presently posted in Varanasi and was the senior superintendent of police. He had been a bright student from a humble background; his education had been funded by the ashram because his family could not support the expense of his education. He had a reputation of being a tough officer, but he had a soft corner for Shaktidham. It was this place that had given him the opportunity to pursue his dreams to become a police officer and attain a respectable status in society. Except for Satya, no one knew that he was the child of a sex worker. His mother had passed away while he was in school and Shaktidham had borne his entire expenses till he became financially independent.

Since the past year of his posting in Varanasi, he frequented Shaktidham often to seek Satya's blessings. Dhrona believed that acknowledging a good turn was as great as doing it.

Rhea made a phone call and requested Dhrona to meet her at Shaktidham early next morning. It was unusual, therefore he knew that it would be something extremely important. Dhrona came early next morning with a garland of roses to be offered to Goddess Kali, in the temple, before he met Rhea.

The meeting was brief; he heard her out and said, 'It is my call and I will take it. Just avoid going out for two days.'

Three days later, the local newspaper carried an article about this dreaded criminal who had been killed the previous night in an encounter with the police.

Next day, Chander announced the arrival of Mr Chakraborthy to Rhea late in the evening, which was rather unexpected.

'Escort him to the veranda,' she told Chander.

'It's late and he didn't even call,' thought Rhea.

As Mr Chakraborty saw Rhea, he broke into a smile.

'I have some good and interesting news, Rhea ji.' He sounded cheerful.

Rhea asked the reason why he had come in a rush.

'Mr Mehta called me some time ago. I told him that I had heard through some sources that his son had been kidnapped after school for ransom. He brushed it aside as a rumour and insisted that his son was away at his aunt's house in Nagpur for a few days. I think he has kept the police away to deal independently with them and it seems like a well-guarded secret.'

Rhea sat listening intently, without a word.

'Anyway, the good news is that he confirmed to me that he was ready to return our land, which he had encroached upon. He further wishes to donate his adjacent land to Shaktidham too. He feels that Shaktidham's cause to build an orphanage is better than his resort project. He sent a message that he would feel blessed and honoured if we agreed. He would like to finish all the legal formalities as soon as possible. I am extremely surprised at the change of heart that he has had.'

'Please get all the necessary paperwork done without any delay. Also we are not interested in accepting his land, we have enough,' replied Rhea.

The day after, Rhea placed all the papers in front of Goddess Kali in the sadhanasthal.

Yes, Shaktidham was not run on rituals and prayers alone.

The next day, Satya broke his maun-vrat and called Rhea to the sadhanasthal. He blessed her, and handed the land papers over to her. He placed his hand on her head and his eyes were moist.

Standing in the sadhanasthal he said, 'Ask whatever you wish for and it will be yours.'

She looked at him and said, 'Baba, you know.'

She touched his feet and left. Satya stood still for a long time in the sadhanasthal without moving. That night after dinner, Rhea told Satya the sequence of events that had transpired while he was in seclusion. She also told him that she feared death.

After she finished, Satya said, 'Rhea, meditate on your death, visualize yourself dying regularly. It will keep you grounded and in touch with the reality of life, which is fragile. Life must be valued and lived fully while you have it. If you have lived, dying no more remains a fear.'

'I will meditate, Baba, but I will still fear death until I have not lived my life with Krishnam,' replied Rhea.

Devraj came to meet Rhea.

That day, Rhea made her first promise. 'Devraj, it is my promise that you will become a minister.'

Devraj looked at her and said, 'Rhea ji, I must win this time, I have experienced the pain of losing.'

'Come and take Devima's blessings the day you start your canvassing.' She had decided to perform a ritual to help him win.

24

IT WAS THE night of Puranmashi and Rhea was sitting in the sadhanasthal conducting the ritualistic Tantra prayers. She stepped out of the sadhanasthal after the symbolic sacrifice of a coconut and sat watching the moon, drenching herself in the silvery moonlight. The wind blew in her hair; she could hear the rustle of the trees.

Love is the energy behind all creation. The search for love never ends, yet it is all around us, for us to experience…

She drifted into the night with Krishnam, nearly nine years ago. As she lay beside him, his hands reached out to her. God, how she loved his hands. They moved on her body, gently, softly and removing all that came between them.

He kissed her, passionate and deep; his moist lips were on hers. She was moaning softly as he licked and kissed her breasts passionately, her nipples erect under his touch. He moved down to her belly. His hands touched her in places that no man ever had.

She felt an insatiable fire rising within her. 'Baby, you are mine,' said Krishnam softly.

They had had all the time in the world to explore each other; they broke all inhibitions. Both were learning and experiencing each other's sensuality. She could hear him moan, as her tongue moved down his spine. He turned around and pulled her to him.

He got on her, kissed her eyelids as if seeking permission and Rhea's hands moved through his hair, as if in agreement. He entered her slowly; she was already craving for him as much as he was for her. She was completely ready for him, wet even before he had entered her. She had been yearning for him to take her; this was her first time.

Her eyelids half shut as he moved inside he. She could hear him moaning; she felt his breath on her and could sense his heart throbbing. Her hands ran all over his back, clutching him.

He paused for a moment. His fingers moved on Rhea's face and he whispered tenderly, 'Open your eyes.' She did and their eyes met; she felt so complete with him in her.

As he resumed, she only sensed him, she could feel nothing other than him. At that moment in time, she let herself go, she was not there anymore and had lost herself completely. Her universe seemed to move with him.

She could feel the entire creation pulsating with them. She was soaked in his sweat. She whispered, pausing to catch her breath, 'Krishnam, I am yours,' her hands firmly holding his.

That night, they slept intertwined without a cover in each other's arms. That night it became clear to her what the saints meant by saying, 'Love is the first glimpse of eternity'.

It had been a physical union, which fulfilled the yearning of their souls. It was a moment where there was no space or time, just them. It was in the realm of eternity and the bliss of oneness. The experience was deep and simultaneously transcendent. It was like losing oneself in a way that was enriching.

Rhea opened her eyes laden with tears. 'I miss you,' she said softly.

She had frequently relived this night at the sadhanasthal, where Krishnam had made love to her the first time. It was after this union that she understood—she was a Goddess to him, to whom he had surrendered entirely. This union had made them step into this new world together; it united them in a way that they became one.

One night Rhea was lying on the floor, outside the sadhanasthal after her rituals, her eyes were closed. Bhairava attempted to strike her with vibrations, but as a result of her sadhana, an energy shield had formed around her that was impregnable and protected her. The vibrations dissipated as they struck the shield. Bhairava had failed to comprehend the extent of Rhea's sadhana.

Unaffected, she got up and went back inside the sadhanasthal; she sat and rested her head on Devima's feet in silence. She lay there in contemplation, as she was capable of returning vibrations of a much higher magnitude, thereby killing Bhairava instantly, or she could let him be.

'Actions and consequences' is an indisputable law of nature.

Action means karma. Simplified, it means that our karma entails every thought that goes through our mind, each word spoken, every expression and every physical act done with respect to its intent. Consequences are the effects, the results, or the outcome of our karma. The result of our actions, with respect to the intent, may directly affect the person responsible for the action and his surroundings.

Rhea came out of the sadhanasthal after a couple of hours; she lay the floor again. She looked up at the stars in the night sky and imagined the infinite vastness of the universe. Our earth is one of the few dots revolving around a speck within these innumerable galaxies. It has various life forms and the human race exists as a part of it, a race that has little reverence for the planet it inhabits. The ultimate power to create or destroy resides in nature. One can only adapt to nature or protect oneself; else perish. Nature has the power to eliminate all life forms, in the blink of an eye. It is perceived that the greatest power human beings have is their ability to think. However, there is another significant aspect, which is the capacity to elevate oneself spiritually.

This spiritual elevation is the elevation of human consciousness, which not only leads to self-understanding, but also a realization of the miniscule significance that we hold in respect to the universe.

Satya's teachings echoed in her mind, 'Adversity can be faced by most. If you wish to judge a person, give him power. The wisdom of a person lies in using it the least.' She went back in after she was convinced by her thought process and slept peacefully through the night.

Rhea woke up when she felt Satya's hand on her head.

'I am proud to be your guru and a proud father today. Now you are worthy to carry the lineage and protect the royal path of Tantra. I have passed my test. May Devima give you all that you wish!' Satya pronounced.

She got up and touched his feet; he blessed her with both hands on her head. She felt a strong current flow through her entire body.

'Rhea, you were like an empty bowl when you came to me. I have given you all I could. This path is now for you to walk independently. You are a master of the vidya, but remember, perfection is an ever-forward moving goal. The time has come when you know the rules well enough to break them or modify them according to your wisdom. And never forget that consequences follow actions.'

In a week's time, Rhea decided to visit Guwahati and boarded a flight with Chander. One learns the most from an opponent who can beat you. The ultimate test of wisdom is how one deals with his opponent or enemy. It is the test of your character, according to Satya.

In Guwahati, she went with Chander to visit the holy shrine of Shakti at Kamakhya temple first, and from there she went to visit the village where four Tantrics lived. The road beyond a point was not motorable and they had to walk through a jungle area to reach their destination.

They were all aware that she was coming. She went to visit all the four great Tantrics individually and seek their blessings. When one sets out to achieve the unattainable, there is no middle ground. Negotiation is not a way of the powerful, and consequences had to be borne by Bhairava. She was the youngest sadhak and the only woman in the field of Tantra. Not the Tantra that people wrote about, not the Tantra that the media and imposters exploited, but the uncontaminated Tantra, which was the prerogative of these six sadhaks, that had been handed down to them by the gurus of their lineage.

The path of Tantra is such that power is merely a by-product of the sadhana. In Tantra, how the power is used is most crucial. The accumulated power of all of them put together would be unimaginable.

Rhea went to the four sadhaks; Bhairava was the last. She touched everyone's feet with deep reverence. They all blessed her.

However, the meeting with Bhairava was different. He repented, 'No one can be more pitiable than a Tantra sadhak gone wrong. I lost my vision of sadhana and did what a sadhak should never do. And today, as a consequence, I sit in front of a sadhak who is old enough to be my daughter and ask her for her forgiveness. Will you find it in yourself to forgive this person who attempted to take your life twice?'

Rhea looked at him and said, 'The first time you were nearly successful, but Baba, had you not attempted what you did, I would not have reached where I am today. It all worked out fine in the larger picture. So I beg you not to seek my forgiveness, as I had taken that episode to exalt myself. You, therefore, are my teacher. However, Baba, don't we pay a price as severely for our victories as we do for our defeats?'

Bhairava blessed Rhea. He took out his necklace made of

rudraksh beads with a gold pendant, which had the image of Kali and Shiva inscribed on it, and put it around Rhea's neck.

'Rhea, wear it as a reminder that we sadhaks are as frail and susceptible to degeneration as anyone else. Earthly battles are fought with wit and brains. Never use your vidya for that, even when you are losing. I know your Guru Satya has given you the best, but then we all are human beings and we all have normal human emotions. I bless you with all that I can to make up all that you lost. You have travelled all the way to me and made me realize the one and the only truth—that my entire life has been a waste.'

She touched his feet to seek his blessings. He asked her to join him for the meal, where they sat together and ate in silence. She walked out from his cottage without turning her back towards him. Rhea touched the pendant and then touched the entrance of Bhairava's cottage with both her hands, then touched her forehead with her fingertips.

As she turned, she stopped in her path as a little boy touched her feet; she stepped back and looked at him. He seemed about nine years of age.

'What is your name?' she asked him.

'He is my son and my shishya, Rudra,' replied Bhairava, who followed Rhea out.

Rhea was quiet for a moment and then said, 'Vidya is passed on to one who is worthy of it.'

He signalled his son to go inside.

'My child has your fire.'

'Yes Baba, I can see that, but fire needs to be channelized; else it can cause great destruction.'

She walked away with Chander, who was waiting at some distance.

25

GENERAL ELECTIONS HAD been announced and were to be held in May 2004. Devraj was to start his election campaign and came to Shaktidham, as Rhea had instructed. Rhea put a red tika of Devima's sindoor on Devraj's forehead in the sadhanasthal. 'May Devima bless you with the power and success that you always desired. I hope and pray that you remain worthy of all that you are asking.'

'I will, Rhea ji,' said Devraj, with conviction.

'It's too early to say that, Devraj,' replied Rhea.

After Devraj left, Rhea sat in the temple and focused her entire thoughts on Krishnam. 'Krishnam, come back, I am waiting.'

Krishnam was in a meeting with a client when suddenly his concentration broke and he heard Rhea's voice. He excused himself saying he had an emergency that needed to be take care of.

On his drive back home, he heard Rhea again. 'Krishnam, come back.'

He was perspiring profusely as he entered the temple of his house. He looked at Satya's photograph and sat in front of Devima. Yes, it was time to go back home, he thought with a radiant smile. It had been almost nine years and Rhea wanted him back.

◆

Post the elections, Devraj had been given an important ministry and he came to Shaktidham with sweets to seek blessings from Satya.

'Baba, it will be a struggle for him to be able to handle success and power, though I hope it isn't,' said Rhea, after Devraj had left.

'Roots, Rhea, roots. If only he could hold on to them. The road of success and power sucks you in and as you go further and further in, your roots get severed. If he fails, it will prove that he was not worthy of this position.'

'Baba, he will lose it. I know, I saw it in his eyes,' said Rhea.

'The recipient should be worthy of what is given to him, else it is unfortunate for the giver,' replied Satya, looking straight into Rhea's eyes.

◆

A few weeks later, a sixteen-year-old girl was brought into Shaktidham by her parents. They had come to seek Rhea after all their efforts to comprehend the girl's problem had failed. She would get up in the middle of the night, night-after-night with the same nightmare, in which she was drowning in a river of blood and gasping for breath.

The girl's mother stated, 'Maharaj, this is my daughter Payal. She has a lot of problems, she refuses to act her age and interact with other children. Her regression happened gradually with time.'

The father intervened and said, 'Maharaj, she was brilliant in her younger days; teachers appreciated her performance as an all-rounder. Slowly, she started slipping in her academics and became a loner over time.'

Her mother continued, 'She just does not respond and always has a spaced-out look; when we met her teachers they also shared a similar view. She then failed the same class twice; we had to withdraw her, because her school refused to continue to have her as a student and no new school has accepted her. Now she is preparing to appear privately for her board exams.'

She turned her eyes slightly towards her husband, seeking approval, and said, 'We have taken her to various doctors and psychiatrists, but that has been futile, as she refuses to talk.'

Finally, on the verge of breaking down, she said, 'Maharaj, her psychiatrist told us that he has given up after trying his best. She seems to be possessed by an evil spirit and she needs elaborate rituals to free her from her agony. We came after much contemplation, with the hope that you will help us.'

In desperate moments, people adopt any means that can give them respite from their problems.

Payal averted her eyes as Rhea looked straight into them and said, 'I can only help if she wants my help. Please take her home, and let her think over it.'

She told Payal, 'If you want, you can come tomorrow morning, and yes, I want to talk to you alone.'

Payal came in the morning. Her resistance needed to be broken and Rhea took her to the session room, especially built for conducting one-on-one sessions. The room could be darkened completely, it had an audio player, on which she played soft instrumental music and lit some candles. A thick mat was on the floor for a person to lie on.

Rhea made her squat on the mat. She sat on her asana placed next to the mat, held Payal's hand and said, 'You will be safe here. You can trust me and talk about anything you want.

'Payal, I cannot help you, if you do not cooperate with me.

'Your future lies in your hands. You have to make the choice between light or darkness, for the life you shall live...'

'Do you believe in God, Payal?'

'Yes, Didi,' she broke her silence.

'Then trust God, he will take care of his child.'

Rhea made Payal do few yogic breathing exercises, to relax her mind and bring her to a receptive state, after which she made her lie down on the mat.

Rhea folded her hands and prayed to Goddess Kali to help the girl.

She made suggestions to relax her physically, mentally and emotionally. The girl was responding well and going into a state of deep meditation, but was still alert to Rhea's suggestions. She entered a state of hypnotic trance.

'Payal, go back to your childhood, when you were six years of age and tell me about your most eventful day that year.'

'I am at home, playing Ludo with my parents. I got my report card and I stood first in class. I love my school.'

'Now let's go to the next year,' said Rhea.

'I am in a zoo, having loads of fun with my parents. My mother has prepared a picnic basket and my father has taken the day off from his work. This is due to my insistence to visit the zoo on a school holiday. We go by each enclosure looking at different animals. Some are lazy and sleepy, while the monkeys are jumping around and playing in their enclosure. I am having the time of my life watching the monkeys. To end the day, Papa gets me two ice creams on our way back home. What a day!'

Rhea examines Payal for any signs of discomfort. 'Right, let's now move on to when you are eight years old,' suggested Rhea softly.

'Mummy and Papa are extremely happy today, we had gone to the hospital, and they told me I will have a sibling soon. They are overly excited...'

Rhea is contemplating and says, 'Let's move to the next year.'

'It is my winter vacation, my younger brother starts to cry in his cot while my mother is taking a bath. I pay no attention and keep reading my storybook. Suddenly, Mother comes, snatches the book and slaps me many times. She screams at me, "Could you not hear your brother crying, why did you not leave your book and give him milk?"

'I cry all night. Since he was born, I have been made to sleep in the other room and he sleeps with my parents. Their entire attention is on him and it feels as if my existence has been reduced to a shadow in the house.'

She paused as if she was stopping herself from saying something, then in a heavier voice, 'I hated him, from that day on, even more.'

'Yes, Payal, I want you to tell me about the day, which has burdened you, the burden of which you are carrying with you even today.'

A few drops of perspiration appeared on her forehead. She clenched her fist for a split second, as if fighting her resistance. 'That afternoon, Mother was sitting in the drawing room with a friend from the neighbourhood. I sneaked into my parents' room to his cot. I removed a pillow from his cot, covered his face with it and pressed hard. I didn't let go until…there was no more movement. I dropped the pillow back in its place and quietly exited their room.

'Nobody knew what happened to him… I know that I killed him, I killed my own brother. I killed him… I hate myself for it.'

Rhea stood quietly for a while. Slowly, she helped Payal come back to the present and be aware of her surroundings.

After she came to her conscious state, Payal was crying profusely. She had finally vented her dark secret, something which made her close herself, without even realizing that this was what she had been hiding in her subconscious.

Rhea held her hand; she placed her hand on Payal's chest, to assure her that she was with her. Payal was uncontrollable. Her emotional state went through guilt, relief and shame, simultaneously, her tears didn't seem to stop. She had had a lot of pent-up emotions since that day; the period while she was in her shell was dark, long, lonely and full of unknown fear. She had spent her formative years nursing a pain, which she had neither realized nor shared with anyone. She now despised herself for the crime she had committed.

'What has been done cannot be undone, Payal. You were a child and had the undivided attention of your parents. I can understand the confusion you had about your place in your parents' life, after the arrival of your brother.'

'If I tell my parents, Didi, I know they will hate me for the rest of my life.'

'Digging up the past will only bring trouble,' said Rhea.

'Payal, you were just nine years old then. Your ability to understand the situation was limited. What you did was a consequence of that. The act you committed was not because of your failure as a human being, but it was a conclusion of an emotionally hurt and a deluded child. You did something in retribution, as your feeling towards your brother was that he occupied your space in your parents' life. You had no rationale in taking his life, but it did happen. Now it is even more crucial for you to give your parents so much love and affection that they overcome their grief of losing their son. Your leading a normal life will be the first step in relieving your parents from some of their agony.

'Your remorse has to be channelized into positive actions; in this state, you are neither helping them nor yourself. Remember, at the moment they are dealing with two sorrows, one being your state and the other the loss of your brother.

'Nothing can erase the past and living it will only lead to self-destruction. You will have to learn to live with this truth, without burdening anyone with it. You have to move ahead as an individual by putting an end to your guilt, by forgiving yourself. This you can achieve with regular meditation. If you wish to, I could introduce you to meditation and I am sure you will come out of it,' Rhea said, giving her a tight hug.

Payal gathered herself, she had realized the gravity of her transgression; she deliberated for a while to bring herself to accept this new perspective.

Taking Rhea's blessings, she left without saying much, only trying to absorb what has just transpired in the past few hours. She promised Rhea she would be back the next day again to meditate.

Rhea settled herself back in the room, feeling drained but full of gratitude to Devima for helping her get through to Payal, a girl who had already punished herself so severely in solitary confinement. She lay down to close her eyes for a brief moment and then left to meet Satya.

'Were you able to get through to the girl?' asked Satya.

'Yes, Baba, she revealed what had been troubling her. She was dwelling on a guilt, due to which she had shut herself off. She had isolated herself from this world,' replied Rhea.

'Was she right or wrong, Rhea?'

'Baba, truth is neither right nor wrong. It just is.'

Satya smiled. 'Yes, it could be stranger than fiction. My child, you are learning.' He blessed her, as she touched his feet.

26

THE SUN WAS rising and a soft glow had filled the room. Rhea stood at one end of the hall and addressed the first group of students wanting to know 'Who am I'.

'The prerequisite to attend the sessions starting from tomorrow is that you have to come cleansed from all that you have read or heard or practised earlier. I assume that you are here to learn from these sessions. However, these sessions will only be able to give something to those who come with an empty bowl. Anyone who already knows is not the ideal student. Ask questions that arise from within. Don't ask questions relating to what you have heard or read. Feel it within you and then ask.

'I cannot answer the question "Who am I?" for anyone. It is a path to be traversed alone, and answers would be revealed to earnest seekers. Practices are simply tools that aid, the results of which will not be achieved overnight. The moment you are able to experience beyond the tools, you will have the answer to "Who am I",' Rhea paused.

'It also helps to remember at all times, that death of this body is inevitable, but this body is also the door to all your answers.

Revere your body like a sacred temple, for it holds all the mysteries of the universe. However, it will all seem paradoxical until you move beyond your body to understand "Who am I". The session will start from tomorrow at sunrise. Today, I would only request all of you to maintain silence, keep your eyes closed and sit here until sunset. Light meals will be served after the sunset, post which you may kindly retire to your rooms. Everyone must maintain pin-drop silence. Do not converse externally with anyone as it's forbidden. You will have enough to talk to yourself.'

At the break of dawn, Rhea was back with the group; she looked fresh and was ready to get this session underway. The entire group had been organized into rows with adequate space between them to lie down and practise the techniques of this session.

'Good morning everyone, how are we feeling today? Fresh and relaxed, I hope. Today, I will introduce you to the basics of energies in our body and their relationship,' said Rhea.

'Quantum physics states that the universe fundamentally exists as energy. The nature of the universe is different from what we perceive and the matter as we see is just energy at the quantum level. Considering the human body in the light of physics, we are energy beings. It is, therefore, interesting to note that Tantra saw a human body as energy and the entire creation as the manifestation of divine energy. It further saw the entire creation as interwoven and interconnected,' explained Rhea.

She remembered the first time she had learnt to experience that energy.

'Make the gesture like you are ready to slap someone with your left hand. Now point the fingers of your right hand towards the palm of your left hand. Keep the fingertips less than one inch away from the palm. Now slowly move the right forearm in an up and down motion so that the fingertips pass across the left palm without touching the palm. However, if anyone is left-handed, he should reverse the process. Your right hand is dominant if you are right-handed and your left hand is dominant if you are left-handed. This is the energy that one emits and is the energy that is also visible through Kirlian photography. From the dominant hand flows the energy that makes things happen. The secondary hand is used to receive energy,' Rhea explained to the group.

Some in the group felt strong sensations and some low. A student, Dr Vishnukant, was enjoying doing it, as he felt a strong sensation. 'What is this energy called, Rhea ji?' he asked.

'Some call it prana or the life force, some call it the force and some consciousness,' she replied to Dr Vishnukant.

'The two most important energy channels within the human body are Ida and Pingala. The perfect balance of the two leads to the complete activation of Sushmna, which is the central energy channel. Its activation and the free flow of this energy channel would lead to the balancing of the grounding and the liberation.

'Sushmna, the central energy channel, connects the chakras. Kundalini is a condensed, dormant form of energy concentrated at the base of the spine. It represents the primal force. Symbolically, it is illustrated by a snake lying coiled three-and-a-half times around the base chakra called the Muladhara. When Kundalini is evoked, it unfolds and climbs moving upwards, chakra after chakra.

'Chakra literally means wheel and circle in Sanskrit. However, in the Tantric context, it means a vortex of energy at specific areas, in the subtle human body. Physiologically, these chakras correspond to the seven major nerve ganglia or plexus that emanate from the spinal cord of our physical body. There are seven basic chakras. Chakra could be defined as a centre for receiving, assimilating and then transmitting the life force,' Rhea said to the group, as they listened intently.

They had a short break before they were introduced to breathing techniques, after which they had time until lunch. They were to maintain silence, keep their eyes closed and sit there.

The instructions post lunch were to stay silent and keep to

oneself until the sunset. The students could sit in any quiet area, without making groups and moving around too much. No one could lie down or take a backrest.

Later that evening after sunset, 'Rhea, have you studied biology?' asked Dr Vishnukant after the class.

'I did my post-graduation in physics,' she replied.

'Intriguing combination of science and spiritualism, reason and faith, very intriguing indeed. So can I say, that isn't faith something that can never be understood, similar to love?' inquired Dr Vishnukant.

'Love, like the world of mystics, can only be experienced. Words have serious limitations and the most beautiful and painful experiences in life can only be felt, they cannot be expressed or explained,' Rhea replied. 'Faith too to be understood has to be lived.'

Dr Vishnukant was visiting India and had come to Shaktidham to understand the world of mystics. A resident of United Kingdom, he was a rising star in the field of cardiology. Rhea had noticed his eyes fixated on her with utmost concentration. Eyes express it all to those that can understand their language. Eyes never lie even while the person does.

It was the second session and Rhea would today start explaining the seven chakras. As everyone settled in their places, she began, 'Today, I will start with Mooladhara—the root chakra.'

'Mooladhara is located at the perineum or the base of the spine, where the primal energy, the Kundalini Shakti dwells. This is the source from which emanates all forms of energy, be it mental, emotional, sexual, psychic or spiritual. This energy is one, but takes on different attributes depending on the centre through which it manifests.

'Kundalini Shakti traverses from Mooladhara through the chakras to meet the consciousness (Shiva) at Sahasrara or the crown chakra. This is the foundation on which the other chakras rest.

'Mooladhara is a chakra where consciousness manifests in

its most dense form, which is tangible and solid. Mooladhara or root chakras, it is known, brings about the stability and grounding essential for our survival at a material level. A balanced root chakra gives a sense of inner security. A strong foundation is mandatory for a strong structure. It relates to the element earth and is represented by the colour red. Red is the colour with the longest wavelength and lowest vibration in the visible spectrum.'

'Rhea ji, what plexus does it correspond to?' asked Dr Vishnukant.

'It corresponds to the coccygeal plexus. The glands affected are adrenals. Some texts say that the first chakra is related to gonads because they are physically closer. Whenever our survival is threatened the adrenal glands are triggered, resulting to a flight or fight syndrome,' replied Rhea.

'What is flight or fight syndrome?' another student asked.

In the most basic sense, it is that in case of a perception of threat of survival or attack it is a physiological reaction, which creates a boost of energy, enabling us either to fight or run away.'

'Most spiritual texts say that the entire material world is an impediment to spiritual growth,' asked Dr Vishnukant.

'You have read a lot, Doctor,' said Rhea with a smile. 'Matter is a truth that cannot be denied. Denial means denying the beauty of life all around you. Your physical body is material; you would be dead without it. Matter without spirit is a corpse and spirit without matter is a ghost, in the words of Marion Woodman. Both refer to something that is dead. Matter and spirit are intertwined in creation at this plane of existence and both are non-existent without each other. To live one, the other has to be lived. It is the obsessive attachment to the material world, which is seen as an impediment when one can see nothing beyond it. Doctor, can you live without the material?'

'No, I cannot.'

'Let us work on pragmatism then, which is possible in the

space that we live in,' replied Rhea.

'Coming back to our subject of today; being in touch with the earth brings a sense of grounding. It gives us a feeling of being alive and present. It is the test of our thoughts, ideas and beliefs, as it is at this plane that the materialization of the abstract occurs.'

To experience the grounding to the earth, Rhea made the entire class walk barefoot on the soft grass outside the hall. They felt Mother Earth nourishing them and holding them, as they were aware now. They were then made to lie on the grass with eyes closed, their attention focused to the earth.

'Take a deep breath in, feel the energy from Mother Earth entering through your feet and filling your entire body up to your head. As you breathe out, feel the energy being released into the earth through your feet. Now feel this constant exchange and flow of energy with Mother Earth. With every breath, breathe in abundance and well-being. With every exhalation, find your roots and peace in connection with the earth.'

The sessions went on and Rhea came into Dr Vishnukant's life in a way that neither could comprehend at that time. Rhea could often sense his eyes totally focused on her. He had no time to feel. But he had the capacity to feel deeply and intensely like most of us. He asked her intelligent and stimulating questions.

She encouraged them to attend to their world within, to meet, and know the self. Rhea did not teach; she learned through her sessions.

She said, 'Know yourself and if you can do that, you will know all that is worth knowing. It is a personal journey for every individual. The path is shown; it has to be walked.'

Rhea requested all the participants to wake up before sunrise the next day as they would go and take a dip in the River Ganga. River Ganga is a symbol of purity and is prayed to as Mother Goddess Ganga by millions of devout Hindus.

'Good morning to everyone, I hope everyone is well rested

today. So this morning we will start understanding about Swadhisthan or the second chakra, as it is known. Swadhisthan is located in the area of lower abdomen. Now we will all enter the Ganges for a dip, where I will give some suggestions. Please remain close to me, so that everyone can hear me,' Rhea told the participants.

After they entered the water, she said, 'Observe the movement of the river, its flow. Then feel the water cleansing you. Feel the soft earth under your feet.' She waited for everyone to be able to observe, as a person doing this for the first time would need some time before they could focus on the observation.

'Now, close your eyes and become aware of your body, feel the blood flow to every cell of your body. Now start to become aware of the continuous flow of blood inside you. Observe that every moment there is a movement.'

'Now, I want you to visualize the colour orange in the area of your lower abdomen. Feel the presence of the second chakra, the element of which is water,' she told the participants.

The dip lasted a little over twenty minutes, after which they all went back to Shaktidham. They took a shower and regrouped in the hall in an hour.

'So, can anyone tell me, how did it feel?' asked Rhea in the hall.

'Very good' ;'Great' ;'Excellent' ; 'I feel fresh and rejuvenated' were some of the answers. Then came the answer, which Rhea wanted to really hear.

'It gave me a sense of freedom, which was different from the grounding experienced yesterday,' replied Dr Vishnukant. 'Yesterday, it felt like holding on and today it felt like flowing.'

Dr Vishnukant felt attracted to a woman after a long time. He had probably been too busy to notice that it had been a few years since he had had any sort of relationship with a woman. In fact, with no one since his wife had passed away, a few years ago.

'Swadhisthan corresponds to the sacral plexus and is the

point of sexuality. It relates to emotions, pleasures, sensations and nurturance,' continued Rhea.

'Rhea, some systems claim that indulging in the senses leads one away from spiritual growth,' asked a student.

She replied, 'Every system works on its procedures and beliefs. However, I would say that if that is true, we should be born without sensory organs.

'The second chakra has to be balanced. Denying pleasures is equally detrimental as being overly attached. Using all the senses heightens the pleasure of anything pleasurable.'

Rhea could feel Dr Vishnukant's gaze. Rhea asked all her participants to rise early the next day to experience the beauty of the rising sun.

After the session, Dr Vishnukant came to Rhea and asked her if he could experience the beauty of the rising sun with her the next day. The day was special to him, as he did not remember when he had last enjoyed the beauty of the rising sun with awareness.

His life consisted of rushing in and out of the hospital building, with patients, OPD, and cath. lab. He was caught in a concrete jungle and he needed some fresh air. He wanted to share this experience with her. Rhea had informed him that all the students would be doing that together.

After Rhea had finished for the day, she sat with Satya and told him, 'Baba, the doctor asks intelligent questions.'

That day the session was scheduled to start with dawn. The group walked silently to watch the sky, with its beautiful changing hues. The world seemed to have come alive with the rising sun.

'Good morning everyone, we start with chakra three or Manipur today. Manipur is located at the solar plexus above the adrenal glands. The element is fire here.

'Close your eyes and feel the warmth of the rising sun. Feel the same glow and warmth at your solar plexus and feel it spread into every cell of your body. Feel the power of this energy within you and absorb the energy from the sun and feel it within you. It is this fire that glows in every action you take to meet challenges,' Rhea said.

'From earth or grounding or matter, we moved to water or flow or movement, and now we are at fire or energy. It all happens when matter and movement come together and a third state is created—energy or fire,' Rhea told the class.

'In our bodies, it relates to our metabolism. Fire burns upwards. It transforms matter to create heat and light. Similarly, the third chakra is the point of transformation. The fire, in this chakra, ignites and propels us to move upward through all the chakras,' explained Rhea.

Later they dispersed for the day.

Rhea asked everyone after dinner to spend some time observing an individual fire. It was a beautiful sight at night. All had to light their own fires and observe it until the entire wood burnt out, and then retire to their rooms. Twenty fires were created and a rug had been placed for each one to sit.

The next day Rhea asked, 'So, what were your observations?'

'Initially, I struggled to light the fire and it took time and effort, but then it was smooth,' replied Dr Vishnukant.

'Does anyone think it symbolizes anything?' asked Rhea addressing the group. A few hands went up and she pointed towards one to speak.

'Yes, I think it symbolizes that the beginning is the toughest and once it starts, things start to flow more smoothly and easily,' one of the students named Manju replied.

'Remarkable observation,' she replied.

'It is the power of our will that helps us take our journey upwards. It is this will that meets all our challenges and gives us the power to stretch ourselves and meet our goals. This whole process is a route that transforms us. It is this fire that pulls us upwards towards our goals, our freedom. Once the flame is lit, there is heat and a glow,' added Rhea.

Dr Vishnukant asked Rhea if she would walk with him. After a short walk, they stood under a tree. Dr Vishnukant spoke and Rhea listened. He was not generally a person who talked much. He started to speak to her about his life. He had done his medicine from Johns Hopkins University in the US. He was an interventional cardiologist and currently working in London. He did not speak of his personal life beyond that. He spoke about his hectic life, his patients, and cath. lab. Rhea could see that he was very ambitious and his only focus in life was his work.

He informed her that he had come to visit his parents in Varanasi and came to know of Rhea's session through a friend, who was a devotee of Satya. Dr Vishnukant believed in God and chanted the Gayatri mantra each day. He had read various interpretations of the Bhagavad Gita. There was a deep-rooted restlessness, which was unaddressed in Dr Vishnukant, observed Rhea.

That night Rhea was mumbling in her sleep, 'Krishnam...'

'I am waiting for you,' she heard him say clearly. She got up from her sleep.

Next morning, Rhea was a little groggy, as she had difficulty in going back to sleep after she heard Krishnam's voice. She addressed the group in the same vivacious manner as she did each day, 'Good morning to everyone, hope all are well-rested? That's good. So today, we will go on to the fourth chakra or the Anahata, which is located at our hearts. This is called the heart centre, corresponding to the cardiac plexus, and the element of this chakra is air.

'It corresponds to the thymus gland,' said Rhea, looking at Dr Vishnukant.

'This is the centre of our chakra system, uniting the forces above to the forces below. It is the centre of love and integrates matter with spirit. This love is not the kind of love that is person-centric, as in chakra two. This love radiates all around us and is experienced within our being. As the field of this love grows, everything coming within it is blessed by it. At this point, Shiva and Shakti bond together and hold the structure of life. The balance of the heart chakra leads to the balance, between the mind and body, which results in a relationship with the self. This in turn forms our relationship with others around us.

'Air, the element of this chakra, is the lightest element until now from the base chakras. Air is associated with dispersing, lightness, and softness. Air represents breath, the vital process, which keeps us alive. Breath awareness is an essential part of the meditation process too.

'Our emotional states are reflected clearly in our breathing patterns. When we are shocked or surprised, we may hold our breath, when we are stressed, our breathing process becomes shallow and rapid. We all understand that breathing is most vital to our existence, but ironically we pay very little attention to it.

'Breathing influences the activities of every cell and most importantly, it is directly linked with the performance of our brain. Human beings breathe approximately fifteen to sixteen times per minute and approximately 21,600 times, in a day. Other than influencing the quality of life, the length of our life is also influenced by our rhythm of respiration.

'Most of us have poor breathing patterns that create stress and disturb us both physically and emotionally. Some of the poor breathing habits are shallow breathing, irregular breathing, uneven inhalation or exhalation cycles, frequent pauses, holding the flow of breath, breathing from your mouth and chest-breathing (thoracic breathing), which are most common.

'However, with a little consistent effort, we can re-establish breathing patterns, which are conducive to our well-being. Diaphragmatic breathing is the body's natural breathing method and allows the most efficient exchange of air within the lungs with minimal energy,' Rhea explained.

Rhea made the participants lie and relax their whole body. She asked them to simply become aware of their natural breathing process and eliminate jerks and pauses while breathing.

'What is love?' asked Dr Vishnukant.

'I would say it is an energy that binds creation. It allows growth, but retains coherence at its core,' replied Rhea.

'How do we get love in our life?' asked a student.

'By giving it—love is self-perpetuating,' said Rhea.

'So, are you saying that love means forming a connection?' asked Dr Vishnukant.

'Well, I would put it like this—love is the awareness that you are already connected with everything, it is the understanding that we are all interdependent and interconnected,' replied Rhea.

Dr Vishnukant was drawn towards her.

'Rhea, why do we use the word "chemistry" in human relationships?' asked a student.

'Human bonding is apparently similar to chemical bonding. Many a times when a person has something in his or her energy field,which we desire or require, we are drawn to the person. If he or she requires something back from you too, we may form a bond. Essentially it is the need to balance, to grow beyond, and to expand. What we seek is seeking us too.'

'Is the movement always towards fulfilment of some deficit only?' asked Dr Vishnukant.

'Well, not exactly. It could also be a comfort where one shares a lot in common, forms a bond too. Hence, it's the chemistry at work,' said Rhea smiling.

'Further, when we look towards fulfilling some deficit, we end up in disastrous relationships too. In the end it's all about self. No one can complete us except ourselves,' added Rhea.

Rhea asked them to lie down, bring their attention to the heart and become aware of the heartbeat. She suggested that they visualize a dot of light symbolizing love in the centre of the heart and let this dot of light beat with the rhythm of the heart.

She then suggested that they expand this light filling their body, engulfing them and then engulfing the room, the city and beyond. She asked them to visualize the entire earth, full of love, which was emanating from the dot of light in their own heart and moving beyond into infinite space, slowly filling it completely.

Dr Vishnukant visualized a beam of light from his heart to Rhea's.

Rhea noticed that Dr Vishnukant was fair, well-built and had a slight paunch. He had straight hair and a bushy moustache. He wore spectacles that completed the look of a doctor and had a pleasant appearance.

◆

'Good morning to everyone, hope all of you had a good sleep?' Rhea addressed the group at the start of the session. 'So today we will go on to the fifth chakra or the Visuddha, which is located in the region of the throat.

'The meaning of the fifth chakra or Visuddha is purification. The fifth chakra affects the thyroid and parathyroid glands. This nerve centre is related to communication.

'Communication results in forming associations. The element of the fifth chakra or Visuddha is ether. Ether is known to exist because of the subtle vibrations in the universe. Sound is the medium through which you enter into the world of vibrations and is the bridge between the abstract and manifested physical world.

'Cymatics has established that soundwaves when projected into different mediums of matter create patterns and forms; these forms are astonishingly similar to nature. A vibration is characterized by a repeated and regular pattern of movement through time and space. Rhythm is, therefore, the basic feature of all life forms. Mantras have been seen to affect the cellular and the atomic structure. In Hinduism, it states that "Om" denotes the vibration on which creation rests. Different frequencies result in different pitches.'

'Rhea ji, many a time one feels that his thoughts have travelled to the person concerned,' remarked Dr Vishnukant.

'Yes, thoughts too are like things in the subtle world,' said Rhea.

'It is also not uncommon that, just when you are thinking of someone, you hear from him or her,' she continued.

She pointed towards a raised hand in the group to speak. 'I have experienced a strange phenomenon often, Rhea ji, that whenever some calamity is approaching, I just know that something bad is about to occur. One of the instances was when my mother passed away in a car accident and I had been extremely restless a week before that. I was sure that a calamity was about to strike at me. A week later when the phone rang, I knew that bell would change things for me forever. It was the news about my mother,' said the participant.

'Yes, certain things are difficult to explain but they are there. Telepathic communication is not really an alien phenomenon and in small ways we all do encounter it. Thoughts are vibrations, which when strong enough, travel through ether and reach the concerned person. It is important that the other person is receptive too. Telepathy indicates connectivity beyond the gross or physical world. A quiet mind is able to perceive the realm of vibrations,' said Rhea.

'When we operate from the fifth chakra, we become aware of all subtle vibrations around us and within us. We all affect and get affected by everything around us,' continued Rhea. She nodded at Dr Vishnukant's raised hand to speak.

'Yes, just the presence of someone can elate you,' said Dr Vishnukant, looking straight into Rhea's eyes.

'The vibrations emanating from a person largely depend on his thoughts, emotions, and actions. A person with positive vibrations will charge everything around him positively. A person with negative vibrations depletes his entire environment,' said Rhea.

'There are times, Rhea, when we think negatively and one does not know how to control that,' said a participant.

'One important aspect to understand is that at a given moment, the mind can either think positively or negatively. Mind cannot have parallel positive and negative thoughts. The moment a negative thought comes in, one must immediately substitute it with positive thoughts. Mind needs to be disciplined,' replied Rhea. 'The mind serves well, but makes a bad master,' she added.

The group chanted 'Om', which resonated in the hall for an hour and the session for the day ended with a very positive vibration. Everyone seemed to be humbled with the experience of chanting 'Om' in a group.

That night again, as Rhea slept, she dreamt of Krishnam and that she was interlocked in a tight embrace with him. She could hear his heartbeat. Both of them were in long black coats.

She got up as the dream ended and sprinted down. It was dark and she knocked on Satya's door.

He opened the door, Rhea was grinning and hugged him tightly. 'Baba, Krish is coming back soon.'

'Yes, my child, it's nearly time.'

The next morning, Rhea was very happy; Satya had said it was time for Krishnam to be back. She was starting with the sixth chakra today. Rhea addressed the group in the hall, 'Good morning, and how is everyone today? Our session for today is on the Ajna chakra—the third eye or the sixth chakra.

'The Ajna chakra or the sixth chakra is situated in the midbrain and is the intuitive centre. It is what we call the seat of wisdom. At this point the two energy channels, Ida and Pingala, converge along with Sushmana. Ajna chakra corresponds with our pineal gland, which is a photosensitive organ and regulates our sleepwake patterns. This is also the centre of perception, imagination, awareness, and insight. The sixth chakra brings us to a higher vibration than sound, which is light and which essentially is an electromagnetic energy. We are only able to perceive our world of sight through light. Colours are light, which are vibrating at different frequencies. We see only certain frequencies of light as various colours. Each chakra in its balanced state is represented by a specific colour,' Rhea explained.

'Rhea ji, I have heard many a time, that colours have healing powers? Is it correct?' asked an elderly female student.

'Light as a source of healing is an established fact. Recent studies have concluded the fact that colours have a definite effect on our body and mind. All creation is made of electrons and photons. As they vibrate they create electromagnetic fields, which we also call radiation or light. The frequency of visible light is referred to as colour. The amount of energy in a light wave is proportionally linked to its frequency. High-frequency light has high energy and low frequency light has low energy. Violet has the maximum energy and red the least in the light that is visible to the human eye.

'Ajna chakra is represented by the colour indigo and transcends time, as light is the fastest observed fact. Visible light occupies a small part in the electromagnetic spectrum. X-rays, ultraviolet, infrared, optical and radio waves are a few of examples of light which are not visible to the eyes.

'We are able to, therefore, help our healing process as the colours can balance our energies be it physical, emotional, mental and spiritual at a psychological level,' replied Rhea.

'Rhea, what does a balanced Ajna chakra result in?' came another question from the group.

'A balanced Ajna chakra evokes further development of intuition and results in quick perception of events and situations. It further results in extreme mental clarity. It is a centre of "I see". One can develop an insight into certain future events and get a valuable understanding from the past. It helps you to develop a strong visualization of positive events in your life. A strong visual imagination acts as a magnet to draw the visualized into reality,' replied Rhea.

Rhea introduced to the group a new exercise, where she asked them to sit with their spine straight, close their eyes, inhale and exhale ten times deeply and evenly.

She continued to suggest, 'Now concentrate at the centre of your forehead. Keep your eyes closed and draw both your eyes towards this centre point of third eye. With your eyes closed, simply look upwards to your forehead. Now start your chant of "Om". As you do it, keep your eyes concentrated towards the third eye.'

'Rhea ji, I felt a strain, a strong sensation at the centre of the forehead,' said one of them.

'That is natural, as you will need to practise to get over it. Do it only as long as you are comfortable,' replied Rhea.

That night, Dr Vishnukant was lying in bed. He was going over the day's session, when his thought went towards Rhea and fixated on her voice. It was simply captivating. In that brief moment, he moved from the meditation hall to his home in London, in his imagination he saw Rhea. She was in his arms with him in bed. He felt blissful.

'Good morning and how is everyone today, I hope well-rested? Our session for today is on Sahasrara or the seventh chakra, which is also commonly known as the Crown Chakra.

'Sahasrara is also known as the lotus with a thousand petals and is approximately located four fingers' width above the crown of the head. The crown of the head is the position where a crown would be worn.

'There are thousands of nerves here, which is evident on examining a transverse section of the human brain. It exhibits a structure with an arresting resemblance to a lotus with a thousand petals. This is the centre where Shiva and Shakti merge together, where matter and energy merge with consciousness.

'The individual at Sahasrara merges with its source, which is the universal consciousness, creating a state of bliss. It is a point where our consciousness moves to the higher consciousness, from our bonding with the earth, through the elements of each chakra, being water, fire, air, sound and light, reaching its source. At each chakra or level, we arrive at a further elevated state of understanding and liberty.

'Sahasrara is represented by the element thought. As we observe our thoughts, it brings a meaning to the experiences and we create our life. Our life is an interpretation of what we make from our thoughts.

'Thus, the seventh chakra is the master chakra, which relates to the master gland, the pituitary gland. Everything begins in the mind and goes downwards to be manifested as matter, which is a representation of the Mother Goddess Shakti. Whereas Shiva is represented by consciousness, which is the seed of all that is created,' Rhea explained.

Dr Vishnukant had a question as usual and asked, 'Why this is called the chakra that liberates?'

'Dr Vishnukant, what you asked is a very relevant question. Let me put it as follows; a thought is the opposite of matter, which is constrictive and limited. It is thought that transcends time and space. There are no barriers to our thoughts, we can be anywhere beyond the geographical constructs and limitations of time in an instant. It is this enormous power that lets us live and create. Thought is the ability that ascertains our meaning of life. Therefore, we choose the quality of our life by giving meaning to it. Our life at every step is determined by the meaning, which we interpret from the situations we encounter. Equipped with the meaning, we act to materialize it in our world of matter. Thus we see that we have the power to be liberated, the power to manifest and the cosmic dance of Shiva and Shakti. That is why this is called the chakra that liberates,' explained Rhea.

'The ascending current culminates into liberation and descends into manifestation. In Tantra, both are equally important. Human life oscillates as a balance between being and not being,' she said and then added, 'as we chant "Om", with every "Om" we visualize the coiled energy starting from the Muladhara and traveling up to Sahasrara, after which it descends again reaching the Muladhara.'

Rhea then summed up the final session of the programme 'Know thyself' and explained to the participants, 'You now know the tools, use them to understand and experience yourself.'

'I have enjoyed the sessions, they were very relaxing, and have given me a new perspective towards life. I will be leaving for London tomorrow. Would you like to come and work with me in London, with my patients? It would be interesting! Your well-being and interests will be taken care of; I have a wing in my house that is vacant, fully furnished, and independent. You are most welcome to stay there,' proposed Vishnu to Rhea.

'I need some time to think,' she replied.

'The sessions will have to be modified for the benefit of hypertensive and cardiac patients. Do give a serious thought to it and we could work well together. If you don't like it there, you can always come back,' he said.

'Though I will ensure that you like it there,' he said with a smile.

A week later, on Monday morning, 'Didi, your friend Nethra has come and wants to meet you,' said Chander, as Rhea was sitting and browsing through the newspaper with her morning coffee.

'Send her in,' said Rhea.

'Good morning Rhea, how are you?' wished Nethra, as she came in and sat across Rhea near the swing.

'Thank you for meeting me,' Nethra said.

'What brings you here, after so many years?' asked Rhea, without indulging in any polite conversation.

'Whatever had happened was rather unfortunate, or should I say, it was immaturity on my part. I should have known better then.'

'That is the past, Nethra. I have moved on and it is unimportant in today's context. My question remains the same. What brings you here, after so many years?'

'Rhea, I am here to seek an answer from you for the dilemma I am in. I am married to a doctor; we had an arranged marriage and have a lovely daughter. The marriage by all standards would be considered good.'

Rhea was looking at her. Nethra became quiet.

'Yes, I am with you, Nethra,' said Rhea gently. Rhea could sense her discomfort in wanting to reveal her problem and sat quietly.

After a considerable silence, she said, 'Rhea, I am in a relationship outside marriage. There is something special I share with him, which I cannot explain. I would also not like to break my marriage.'

Rhea's face showed no expression.

'He fills a vacuum in my life, which remains in spite of my being married. Please tell me if I am wrong, Rhea. It is gnawing me from inside and I am confused.'

Rhea sat quietly for some time, thinking how to explain this to her.

'Nethra, I am not qualified to answer this question, as coming from where I come, there are actions and consequences. If conviction to act is strong, one must be able to bear its consequences with the same conviction.'

Nethra looked at Rhea. 'Rhea, your words give me no comfort.'

'Truth is not always reassuring or soothing,' she replied.

'Do you hate me, for what I did?'

Rhea looked into her eyes and said, 'No, I don't hate you Nethra.'

'Then can we start afresh?' asked Nethra, expecting Rhea to relent.

'Nethra, the past that we shared cannot be recreated. What you know of me is only memories,' replied Rhea.

27

SIX MONTHS LATER, Rhea disembarked from her flight at Heathrow airport. This was her first trip abroad and she did not know for how long. It had been a tough decision, but one has to adapt to the ever-changing nature of life. From her childhood, her life had revolved within Shaktidham; for her to leave its bounds was to enter the unknown. But there was a world outside, which also needed to be felt, understood and experienced; without which she would never grow completely. She needed to step out of the confines and protection of Shaktidham and Satya, to learn, to make the right choices and decisions and gain meaningful experiences in the world outside. This for her was a breach of security and a tough decision. Security lies only in adapting to the ever-changing nature of life.

Dr Vishnukant had written various emails and made numerous calls asking Rhea to visit and work with him. If only Dr Vishnukant had realized that Rhea was not a person who could be possessed, as it was only Krishnam who possessed her by giving her complete freedom. Dr Vishnukant was a person, who came into her life to be an instrument of transformation, to contribute to her growth as an individual.

◆

It was late evening and Dr Vishnukant was waiting to receive Rhea at the airport. He was wearing a grey suit that made him look older than his forty years. He had a twinkle in his eyes as he saw her; he greeted her with a lot of warmth. They just shook hands to greet each other.

'How was your flight, Rhea?' he asked.

'The flight was good, but I am really tired, as I could not sleep on the flight,' replied Rhea.

During the drive back from the airport to Dr Vishnukant's home, Rhea looked at the different cars on the highway, the greenery around and the general cleanliness. The architecture completely changed as they entered the city of London and she loved the beautiful architecture, the organized traffic and the layout of the city.

They arrived at Dr Vishnukant's house at Baker Street; the drive from the airport was an hour and a half. The house looked beautiful from the outside, as they parked. The house had a small, manicured garden out at the front. Dr Vishnukant got her luggage from the car and rang the doorbell. An elderly-looking gentleman, who had white hair, opened the door with a warm smile. 'Rhea, this is Raju kaka, he's been with me since my childhood, his dad too worked at my parental house back home. Raju kaka, Rhea memsaab; she will stay with us as I told you and you have to look after her as you look after me,' said the doctor.

It was evident that Raju kaka seemed very pleased to have another person in the house.

'Bitti, come, I will show you your room.'

He took her luggage upstairs. The stairs ended at a small landing with just one door. He opened the door and took her through a small passage that led to a sitting room. The sitting room was tastefully done in white, with an intricately carved mantel and a cosy fireplace. To the right was a small study through a door, with a table, chair and a bookshelf with about twenty-five books. Rhea noticed that the books seemed new. The table was placed in front of a window; a tree just outside the window covered it with its branches partially. Opposite the study was a small pantry, with a table for four.

'Bitti, if you ever wish to cook something for yourself, the pantry is functional and stocked with almost everything that you may require. My cooking is not bad, so you may not need to use this pantry. I can cook a few different kinds of food other than Indian. Half of the time Bhaiya misses his meals. With you around, I will get a chance to cook something,' he said with a smile. They came out of the pantry and to its left opened the door, which led into the bedroom.

'This is your bedroom,' said Raju, as he put Rhea's luggage in her room. The room was spacious and pleasing. Opposite the bed was a double window, Rhea looked out the window. Though it was dark, she could faintly see a small rear garden, which was lit with blooming flowers. The garden was immaculately kept; a wooden bench and some statues were set at places.

'Raju kaka, what is that?' asked Rhea, as her attention had been drawn to a door in the bedroom.

'That is a gym, which has never been used, so far Bhaiya has never used it.' He addressed Dr Vishnukant as Bhaiya.

The room was cosy and comfortable. On the wall above the bed hung a painting of a woman taking a bath, a sensual semi-nude painting. The bedroom had an attached bathroom with a small dressing area.

'Bitti, call for me, if you need anything. I am going to make tea for Bhaiya and you. Would you like to have it downstairs or here?' Raju asked Rhea.

'Wherever you serve it, Kaka,' said Rhea, with a smile.

Raju served tea in the back garden, which overlooked Rhea's bedroom.

Dr Vishnukant was waiting for her. 'Rhea, I hope you liked your place. Please feel comfortable to tell Raju kaka if you require anything. The phone in your room is an extension of the phone downstairs. Please feel free to call up India as and when you feel like.'

'Doc, I really liked the place and thank you for the pains you have taken to make it so comfortable and cosy.'

'Rhea, can you please call me Vishnu, I have a name.'

Rhea laughed. 'Okay, Doc.'

'I have to see a patient, so I will have to go to the hospital for a bit. Why don't you have your dinner and get some rest and I'll be back in a jiffy? I can't thank you enough for coming; I am so looking forward to working with you.'

The doctor stood up to leave.

'What about your dinner?' questioned Rhea.

'I will have it on my return. You must be tired with the travel, so you relax and make yourself comfortable in the new surroundings. We can start work after a week, so that you can see London during the next week.'

Rhea went up and unpacked her bags; she took a quick shower and had a sumptuous meal. She went back up to her bedroom, but before she slept she placed the statue of Goddess Kali on her bedside table.

Satya had given it to her before she left, saying, 'May Devima take care of you.'

'If you want privacy, lock the door of the sitting room, which leads to the stairs,' Raju kaka had told her. She latched her bedroom door. She felt comfortable in her new surroundings. Raju kaka stayed in the house; he had a room on the ground floor next to the kitchen.

When Rhea woke up, she had no idea for how long she had slept and opened the window curtains. The sun was up and it was nearing midday. She saw the time, it was past 11.00 a.m. She was still sleepy and went straight back to bed.

She dreamt again about Krishnam, she saw herself and Krishnam in the sadhanasthal lighting a lamp. She was mumbling, 'Krishnam.'

It was noon as she opened her eyes again. She took a bath and went downstairs. There was no one around, but the table for lunch had been laid. She spoke to Satya and Neel, and told them briefly about her journey along with the details of where she was staying.

She was excited to go around London. She inquired from Raju if there was a park around; he told her that Regent's Park was close by. She took directions and went for a long walk to the park in the evening. She always liked to follow her routine of going for a walk in the evenings. She had liked walking in natural surroundings since childhood. It energized and relaxed her simultaneously.

After she returned, she saw Vishnu's car pull up in front of the house.

'Hi Doc,' Rhea said cheerfully.

Vishnu smiled and said, 'Hi, so how was your day? I am sorry I got caught up with a couple of critical patients and forgot to send you the car and driver.'

He was unshaven and looked really tired, it seemed he hadn't slept.

'Did you come home last night at all, after you left?'

'I couldn't make it back last night, but tomorrow you can come with me, drop me off and I will tell Sam the places to show you around in London.'

At night, both had dinner and spoke about where she would like to go visiting the following day, before they retired to their bedrooms.

The next day, she visited some historical monuments and museums. She liked the feel of London and found it vibrant and pulsating with life. Vishnu did not come in until late that evening; it took Rhea a couple of days before she understood that she should have her own routine, independent of Vishnu. She was not expected to wait for him at dinner and even if she did, it was pointless.

She spent the next six days exploring the city of London. She liked the idea of working in the city. It was a Sunday. The entire week she had barely met Vishnu; he would come in late after she had slept and would be sleeping when she left.

Time passes like a wink of an eye when all is going well and seems like eternity when the going gets tough. It seemed like eternity for Rhea since Krishnam had left. There was not a moment when she was free from Krishnam and she knew neither was he. She came downstairs to have tea that Sunday morning. Vishnu was sitting and reading the newspaper with a tired look, but was pleased to see Rhea.

'So, madam, how are you?' he asked.

'Good, and how are you, Doc?'

'I am tired. Were you able to cover most of the places?'

'Mostly I did. I saw Madame Tussauds, the Big Ben, the Natural History Museum, London Eye, the Thames. I also went to Harrods and Selfridges; it was great.'

From Monday, Rhea was going to start working at the hospital. She began as an observer with Dr Vishnukant; while he attended to his patients, she wanted to understand the background and assess the issues people had here. His patients came with hypertension, diabetes and cardiac problems.

In a span of two weeks, Rhea concluded that some of the major culprits were sedentary lifestyles, wrong dietary habits and stress. Genes too played a role, but the precipitation was due to lack of self-care and it was not always about what one ate, but also about what ate one. We are a race so unaware of the fact that we are being consumed largely by inner turmoil. We are all just running a race to no end and even a simple 'why' is not addressed by us.

In the two weeks which had passed, she noticed that Dr Vishnukant himself had an erratic lifestyle, similar to his patients', without any time for food, no physical exercise and hardly any water intake. He would survive on some biscuits, chips, with an overdose of caffeine and aerated beverages to top it all. A large bottle of antacid ornamented his table at all times, which he would take swigs of, as if it were fruit juice.

All that learning at Shaktidham had been a sheer waste of time, thought Rhea. He was a good doctor, but overly ambitious. He loved the adulation he got from his patients and thrived on it. Humility was not a virtue he lived by. There was an underlying restlessness that was clearly evident in his demeanour, which she had noticed during the workshop as well. There was some dilemma somewhere, an inner chaos that was reflected in his outer life.

28

DR VISHNUKANT WAS sitting, surrounded by an ocean of small pebbles, pleading for water. He seemed to be in a lot of pain—his voice was feeble, his lips were dry and he was going on asking for water. Rhea woke up; she was in her world of dreams. It was 6 a.m., time for her to rise.

Quickly, she got into the shower. She did her deep breathing exercises and meditated as per her regular routine. She needed these forty-five minutes to an hour every morning to herself. She missed her sadhanasthal and the rituals, however.

The last thing she wanted was to tell Dr Vishnukant her dream, as he wouldn't understand. She sat, smiling, thinking that if she had been in Shaktidham, she would have narrated everything to Satya, as she woke up.

She had a knot in her stomach as she did not like the idea of Dr Vishnukant in pain. She had to find a way to communicate this to him, that he was going wrong. Vishnu was, in the end, an arrogant man; he too was chasing something unknown. We pay as severely for our victories as for our defeat—she wanted him to understand this. The price paid for success may be so high that it takes away the pleasure of triumph. One thing was certain—Dr

Vishnukant would have a problem, which could be averted only if he drank adequate water.

She decided to pen down her thoughts, which had to be introspective and not instructive to Dr Vishnukant. Can anyone actually save anyone? Well, one could at least give it a try, as it largely depended on the person if he was willing to be saved.

Rhea wrote a letter to Vishnu.

Dear Me,

At the beginning of my life, I had a vision of how I wanted my life to be. But did the vision, along with professional and material accomplishments, include the quality of life?

Maybe, but I never really introspected on it and today, the reality that is staring me in my face is that I have totally lost myself. With all my professional progress and material luxuries, do I have time for myself?

Am I human or a machine?

Machines too need to be tended to with regular maintenance or care; else they will have a major breakdown. Am I moving fast towards a burnout? Or is it easier for me to play the blame game?

'Circumstances led me to this state', I may end up saying.

Am I responsible for my life?

Probably if I think deeper I will realize that it was solely in my hands to restructure my life. The truth is that I am accountable for myself.

Do I need to ask myself, 'Where am I going? What do I want? And who am I?'

To understand myself, I first have to understand what all I had to give up in order to attain success. A price has to be paid and health is not the price I would like to pay. Therefore, I need to balance my work and my personal life.

Though I love my work, better health and a healthier

lifestyle will only increase my efficiency as life is like a rainbow, with various colours, like various aspects. Therefore, all aspects need to be balanced for harmony and fulfilment in life.

There is no doubt that ambition is a great force, but if the price paid is greater than the achievement, it may bring only regret in times to come. I need time for contemplation and to make certain choices, which will enrich the quality of my life.

From myself

'It's personal, Doc, kindly read it in peace,' Rhea handed the letter to Dr Vishnukant in the hospital.

That night, Vishnu came back after Rhea had slept. He instructed Raju to pack his lunch every day along with Rhea's.

Sunday morning was Rhea's first workshop in the hospital for cardiac patients. Everything had been organized the previous day. Dr Vishnukant was still asleep when Rhea left the house, as the workshop was scheduled for early morning.

She would introduce patients to a lifestyle that would help them feel fitter and healthier within their given limitations due to ailments. While the workshop was in progress, Rhea saw Dr Vishnukant peep through the door, smiling. The workshop was received very well. The patients appreciated Dr Vishnukant's efforts to adopt a holistic approach towards the treatment. The workshop included physical exercises suited for the patients, breathing techniques to balance their nervous systems and methods to harness the power of mind to heal oneself.

Rhea explained to the patients that the power of our mind is unlimited. Our belief and will to heal is important, along with the treatment. Maintaining a positive approach with modifications in their lifestyle would help them live without anxiety. She explained that emotional well-being was as important for their healthy hearts. Repressed emotions, negative thoughts create stress and are enemies of their hearts. Love and joy are the two greatest friends of our heart.

'Life is unpredictable and made of small things. Enjoy all the small things it offers. Love with abandonment and do things that give you joy.' Rhea knew that even if we knew what life had in store for us, it would not make much of a difference. Most would still move towards disaster, thinking that they were invincible.

Human nature is such that no one ever believes that his or her life is fragile. Rhea was not saying anything new—we all know this, but apply it only after we are hit. We all know that we will die, but look at our lives, do they reflect that? She repeated what Satya had explained to her, 'Death is inevitable, it comes to anyone and everyone, the rich, the famous, the good, the bad, beautiful, ugly, intelligent, even a moron. It's all about the quality and meaning that you lend to your life. Live, do not just exist.'

Dr Vishnukant got very positive feedback after the session and Rhea was satisfied with what she delivered. The smile on the face of the patients made her feel exhilarated. An elderly gentleman came to her and blessed her with his hands on her head for what she gave.

'May God bless you,' he said. 'You are doing noble work.'

A thirty-year-old came up and said, 'After what you said, I am confident that I will be able to lead a better and normal life. Thank you so much.'

An old woman hugged her saying, 'The workshop was wonderful, and so were you. I will try and practise everything and come see you next month.'

Rhea would always wear white for the workshop. It was a colour that signified peace and was soothing to the eye.

That night, she thought of the words Krishnam had said to her a long time ago, 'You will make a good teacher.'

'Rhea, next Sunday I too will attend the workshop,' said Vishnu. After reading Rhea's letter, he was trying to make efforts to bring about a change in his hectic life.

Dr Vishnukant started waking up on time—mostly—he started going to the gym and after that they would leave for the hospital together. He also started to meditate with Rhea, and at times, they would exercise together too. On Saturdays, he joined her for a walk to Regent's Park.

One Saturday Dr Vishnukant asked Rhea, 'Would you like to go out for dinner tonight?'

'Yes, why not?' replied Rhea.

'We will try and dine out every Saturday,' said Vishnu enthusiastically.

'Let's first make it possible tonight,' she said, laughing.

It was past seven in the evening already.

'I am sending Sam, he will bring you to the hospital. Meanwhile, I will attend to the emergency and will be free by the time you get here.'

29

THEY ENTERED WHAT was a classic English boutique restaurant. The place was softly lit with music in the background. Candlelight glimmered on the table. Rhea had made efforts to dress; she wore a short, black, body-hugging dress with black leggings and high boots. She had even applied light make-up.

'Wish you were here, Krishnam,' she thought. Every time he returned from the US he brought stuff for her and he always said, 'Nobody has said or can ever say that a sadhak cannot enjoy other aspects of their life.' He made her wear those dresses and then took them off to make love to her. Rhea was so engrossed in her thoughts that she did not realize that Dr Vishnukant had already finished ordering.

'You are looking gorgeous this evening,' he said to nudge her out of her thoughts. She had only ever heard this statement from Krishnam. She smiled; this was unlike Dr Vishnukant, and he was probably trying to cover up for her having to pick him up from the hospital. He was usually not vocal or gave lavish compliments. She noticed Vishnu unabashedly staring at her and it made her slightly uncomfortable.

'You are staring at me,' she stated and added humorously, 'am I looking that good?

'Yes, you are,' replied Dr Vishnukant. 'You always do, and I am sure you know that you are very beautiful,' he said looking straight into her eyes this time.

Rhea closed her eyes and said, 'Thank you!'

Her attention was drawn to the piano that had started playing and memories flooded her thoughts. *Krishnam pulled her nose. He was running after her and then caught her tight at the waist. 'You can never run away from me, I will catch you,' he said. 'Your place is in my arms.' He kissed her gently on her neck.*

'Have you gone off to sleep or are you in your dream world?' asked Dr Vishnukant, patting her hand. She opened her eyes and became aware of Dr Vishnukant's hand.

On Sunday morning the week after, participants in the workshop had increased; Rhea would need to conduct a second workshop on Saturday too. Vishnu somehow had not been able to attend any of the workshops.

On Saturday, she took up another new group for a session.

One of the participants asked, 'Does praying to God help us solve our problems?'

'Yes, praying gives us strength. It depends on the faith you have in God and your prayers, as God is as powerful as we make him. The stronger our faith, the greater is the strength of God to help you. For prayers to be effective, your thoughts must be focused and with intent,' replied Rhea.

'Rhea, can you tell us a way to pray?' asked the participant.

'Pray the way you like, but with faith, and believe in your prayers. I will tell you the way I pray and it works well for me. First, we have to realize that while praying we are dealing with great power, which resides within us. Any and all techniques which enable us to direct our flow of this power can be applied.'

She explained further, 'The first step is communication with God, whatever is your concept of God. Each day, take time out alone to spend with your deity and understand that your deity is with you all the time. Form a habit of communication with your deity each day and whenever you're faced with a problem, tell your God about it and seek His grace. Ask Him with faith to show you the way through the problem. Remember at all times that when God is with you, there is nothing to fear.'

Rhea went on, 'Do not make it just a problem-solving technique but practise it every day of your life. The second step, after having communicated your problem, is to start visualizing the desired outcome with intensity. Let us say, your work is going through a difficult period, you start visualizing with intensity, the way you would want your work to flourish. Like, you could visualize an office full of employees reporting to you, or picture in your mind a flourishing office with clients walking in and out to see you.

'A successful person assumes that he is successful. A healthy person assumes a healthy state and works to attain it. By doing so, you are applying a mechanism of vibrations to send a message of your intentions to God. These vibrations bring back in your life what you desire, as vibrations end at the point of source,' she explained.

'The third step is to always thank God for granting you what you want in life, even before you have it. As you acknowledge the presence of what you desire and thank God for his grace in advance, it also helps you negate the origin of any negative thought process. The entire process has to be followed with a positive attitude and faith. Work and prayer must to go hand-in-hand. Pray as if all depends on God and work as if all depends on you,' she emphasized.

'Pray for good health, also; in the meantime, do all that is in your power to attain it. Eat well, exercise well, think positive and sleep well. God helps all those who help themselves, so leave no stone unturned in your actions,' explained Rhea.

'What if our prayers are not answered?' asked a participant.

'If you trust God, learn to trust His will too. If He is not granting your desire, trust that He may be protecting you by not granting your desires. Or maybe He wants you to learn from a situation. Even if you are persistent with your prayers, He may not grant you your desire because it may not be good for you. God's intention is to make us the kind of person He wants us to be. Praying to God is not tantamount in any way to God resolving our lives to our desires. Praying only denotes that God will be with us in our trials and tribulations and give us the strength to make ourselves better individuals, by passing every phase of life with dignity,' Rhea answered.

'Rhea,' a young woman said, 'if I do not believe there is any God, as it's only a consolation we give to ourselves, how should I face an unfavourable situation?'

'Okay, if you do not believe in God then you do not have to pray to God. Use the power of your thoughts and act upon them to make things happen in your life the way you desire. You can invigorate your life with the power of constructive visualization and act towards achieving your goals and desires. Visualization means applying your imagination with your faith; in your case you need to have faith in yourself,' replied Rhea.

'I went to church every Sunday, I was regular with my prayers, why am I suffering then and why did God let me down?' someone questioned Rhea, seeking an answer to his dilemma.

'We don't come with an invincible body; a physical body experiences its pains and pleasures, which is a natural aspect. It has little to do with our faith in God and it cannot be construed that a person with faith will not suffer. It is simple—he who has faith will not see this as suffering, but as an aspect of life, which is natural and part of his growth process. Hence, it ceases to be construed as suffering. The truth is that in any situation, our attitude is always in our control and we have the power to choose our attitude. Degeneration and illness of our body is natural, but still we need to nurture it and take care of it, as we carry it until the last breath. Negligence towards our body often invites diseases. We can also choose not to indulge in self-pity and keep blaming circumstances around us or God.'

The hospital was talking about Dr Vishnukant's endeavour at introducing something exceptionally different to enhance a patient's response to recovery and better living. People were talking about Rhea's work. A newspaper ran an article with the heading 'Spiritualism meets Science' covering the workshops and had photographs of Rhea and Dr Vishnukant. 'There comes a point where science and spiritualism converge,' went one of the headlines.

After the workshop, Vishnu would be waiting in his chamber for her. She would discuss the details of the workshop with him, the questions asked, the answers given.

◆

Rhea couldn't lose another moment. She had to call Satya; she did so from Dr Vishnukant's mobile. 'Baba, the response was wonderful. I enjoy working here, but I am missing home. Please come to London, you will love it. You will feel proud of my work,' Rhea told Satya.

'Rhea, my blessings are always with you, keep up the good work,' Satya replied.

'Yes Baba, I will and I also know that you are not coming here!' Satya laughed. Rhea went on to tell him some of the details of the workshop.

Three days later was Puranmashi and she was missing the sadhanasthal. Satya must be conducting his ritual prayer today, thought Rhea. It was a different world altogether. Though Rhea was missing Shaktidham, she was also enjoying what she was doing in London.

As she was on the treadmill that evening, music blaring loudly in the background, Vishnu entered in his jumpsuit. Rhea noticed that since his regular exercising he had really toned up and was looking better. She watched him walk to the exercise bicycle and his posture seemed to have transformed. Rhea looked at him appreciatively and did not avert her eyes, even when he noticed Rhea looking at him.

Rhea said, 'You are looking much better,' and made a thumbs up gesture. Her face was already pink with forty-five minutes of exercise. Vishnu gestured to turn off the music.

'Rhea, it seems that you have forgotten that we have to go for the twenty-fifth wedding anniversary of Sara and Thomas. Sara called just to remind me today and insisted that you come too. Would you be ready and downstairs by 7.00 p.m.?' asked Vishnu.

Thomas had survived a massive heart attack six months ago. He was Dr Vishnukant's patient and had attended Rhea's workshop too. The team of doctors had said that it was pointless; he would not make it, his chances of survival were negligible. Dr Vishnukant conducted a rescue angioplasty, propagating his belief that they must to do their best to save a life and not give up. It was a complicated procedure and Thomas survived, but was very low on self-confidence and fearful of living after the angioplasty. Dr Vishnukant had suggested to Sara that she get Thomas for Rhea's rehabilitation workshops.

After the workshop concluded, Sara had hugged and blessed Rhea. The week after she came again to thank her, 'My darling, may God bless you. Though Dr Vishnukant surely did save his life, it was you who gave me Thomas back,' she cried, hugging Rhea.

Today was their twenty-fifth wedding anniversary, which they were celebrating and it was a very special evening for them.

Rhea looked at herself in the mirror. 'Not bad,' she thought, 'rather, quite impressive,' she concluded.

Krish would have said, 'Ah, my princess, you look lovely.' She smiled at the thought. She wore a blood-red evening gown, which she had bought last week. It was off-shoulder, fitted till the waist and then flowed from the waist covering her stilettos. Her curls fell until her waist; she complemented her look with ruby and diamond jewellery, which Satya had given her on her twenty-first birthday.

She knocked on Dr Vishnukant's bedroom door. He answered, 'Who is it?'

'Rhea. I am ready.'

'Come in, I am ready too.'

She entered as he was wearing his necktie. 'I never get it right the first time,' he said.

She looked at Dr Vishnukant. He was wearing a white shirt with black trousers, which fitted him well, and was struggling with his necktie.

After about five tries, he got the knot to his satisfaction and turned to pick up his jacket from the bed. He laid his eyes on Rhea and she made no effort to turn away from his look. Rhea looked back at him nervously and raised her eyebrows, questioning him. He just took a deep breath, nodded and wore his coat. He seemed to be in some dilemma, since they did not talk much in the forty-five-minute drive.

Thomas and Sara were extremely happy to see them. Thomas handed them a glass each of celebration champagne. Vishnu looked at Rhea, confused; she winked at him and sipped the champagne.

Vishnu and Rhea had a glass of wine each afterwards.

Krishnam's favourite song came over the loudspeaker, 'Nothing's gonna change my love for you' by Glenn Medeiros. 'I love dancing, Doc, would you care to dance? The number that is playing is one of my favourites.'

'I can't dance,' said Vishnu.

'Never mind, how about doing something that you don't know and have never done it before? Try it, it's fun,' she replied. She felt like letting her hair down after the wine. Dr Vishnukant put his hand on her waist and gently pulled her close. He held her firmly as they danced. His touch was gentle and she felt comfortable and put her head on his shoulders. She was enjoying this evening.

Rhea had another glass of wine and danced comfortably with Dr Vishnukant. Neither wanted to leave the dance floor.

'I had a great time tonight,' said Rhea on the way back.

'Every moment I spend with you is beautiful,' replied Vishnu. Rhea was silent.

Rhea could not sleep; she missed Krishnam and his touch, which always said, 'Welcome back home'. Lying on her bed, memories of Krishnam flooded her mind.

Rhea wandered back in time to the sadhanasthal, where Krishnam was gripping her hand as she held a coconut. It had been the first time she felt different when he held her hand.

'Yes, now,' he told her. They broke the coconut into two equal halves, as an offering in front of Goddess Kali.

'Perfect bali,' said Krishnam.

Rhea smiled and said, 'Don't you know I am just perfect?'

Krishnam laughed, 'Perfect for me,' and lightly nudged her nose.

Another time, she remembered how both were running in mustard fields and he caught her by her waist and they came to a halt. He looked down at her, still holding her waist from behind, then bent over and kissed her at the nape of her neck. He turned her around to face him and caressed her face with the back of his hand.

Rhea always had an underlying paranoia about Krishnam leaving; his going away to study had impacted her in a strange way. One day, after he had returned from the US for good, there at the sadhanasthal she said to Krishnam, as they finished meditation, 'Touch Devima's feet and promise me never to leave again,' said Rhea.

'Never ever,' said Krishnam and was about to touch Devima's feet, when Satya said something pertinent, 'Life is unpredictable. The words "always" and "never ever" cannot be uttered by mortals like us,' he said and walked away.

Both Krishnam and Rhea looked at each other, as Krishnam withdrew his hand.

'You have tears in your eyes, Rhea,' said Krishnam.

'Baba never says anything without a reason,' said Rhea.

While Rhea thought about Krishnam, in New York that evening Krishnam was uneasy and restless. He could do nothing, as nothing held his concentration. He even tried to go for a walk to change his mood, but came right back home.

Early next morning, Rhea was pale and her eyes were swollen after crying last night and due to lack of sleep. Rhea called Satya. 'Baba, I am missing Krishnam and it's getting worse.'

'Concentrate on your work and leave everything to Devima,' said Satya. 'It's good to be patient.'

'I want Krish back, Baba,' Rhea said adamantly.

There was a long silence from the other end, then a deep sigh and Satya said, 'Did you ever let him go? Did he ever go away?'

Rhea got dressed and came down for breakfast. 'Rhea, you seem to be preoccupied today, everything is well I hope?' asked Dr Vishnukant, looking concerned. 'Are you missing home? Do you want to go back?'

'No, I am good,' she replied.

'I will take a day off tomorrow and we will go to the countryside and walk in the woods,' suggested Dr Vishnukant.

Rhea's face remained impassive. She did not reply. They went to the hospital and came back without much interaction with each other.

The next morning, Rhea heard a knock at her door. She was surprised to find Dr Vishnukant carrying coffee for her instead of Raju and said, 'You didn't have to, I could have made one for myself, if Raju kaka wasn't around.'

'Good morning, I thought as I am up I will do the honours today,' said Dr Vishnukant. Rhea smiled and took the coffee.

After the coffee Rhea rushed in to shower, finished her meditation and got dressed for the hospital. She came down to find Dr Vishnukant ready and waiting for her for breakfast. He looked puzzled. 'I thought we had planned to go for a walk in the woods, your footwear...' he said smiling and looking at her.

'Oh.' She turned around to go back upstairs.

'Rhea, your shoes are in the living room. Keep something warm too, as the weather is unpredictable.'

Dr Vishnukant was wearing a pair of denims with a red t-shirt; he looked relaxed and fresh. As she sat in the car, he held her hand and asked gently, 'Are you feeling better today?'

'Yes,' she replied and withdrew her hand. They headed north, drove towards Milton Keynes, taking the M1, and then exited towards Bedfordshire for the Millbrook Golf Club. It was a relaxing and fun-filled day. Rhea had never seen Vishnu so utterly easy and peaceful in the almost four months since she had come to London.

They ate lunch at the Millbrook Golf Club, in Bedfordshire. He ordered the same dish as Rhea; he drank what Rhea had to drink. The countryside was full of shades of green. It was breathtakingly beautiful and a bright and sunny day. Behind the golf course was a wooded area where they went after lunch. While walking in the woods, they raced to a tree and back. It suddenly started to drizzle without warning.

'Where is your jacket, Rhea?'

'I left it in the car.'

They were nearly soaked by the time they could get back to where they had parked and Rhea was sneezing. It was a long drive back home and would take almost an hour and a half, if the motorway weren't clogged.

Rhea closed her eyes and drifted to the night when Krishnam had pulled her out of the bed while it rained cats and dogs. They had snuck out into the fields and had a blast in the rain.

Both Vishnu and Rhea were still wet when they reached home. Vishnu instructed Raju to prepare soup for them. Rhea took a quick hot shower, changed and came down.

'Doc, I will fall ill tonight,' she said spontaneously, without thinking.

'Rhea, I also got wet.'

'Yeah, but you will be fine,' and then suddenly she was quiet. Dr Vishnukant frowned and shrugged his shoulders with a puzzled look.

Rhea's body was aching; she was burning with temperature the next morning. Raju gave her coffee, but she just went back to sleep. She somehow finally coaxed herself out of bed and went downstairs; Vishnu had already left for the hospital. She asked Raju for a bowl of cereal and took a paracetamol to bring down her temperature and went off to sleep.

The fever came down slightly for a while and then shot up again. Vishnu called as Rhea had not come to the hospital and Raju told him that she was not well and sleeping; she hadn't even eaten lunch.

It was late evening when Dr Vishnukant returned home and went upstairs to look Rhea up. There was no response as he knocked on her bedroom door twice. He went in and saw she was fast asleep.

Rhea felt a hand on her forehead and she mumbled, 'Krish, is that you?'

'Kaka, get the thermometer. Why didn't you call me and tell me that she had such high temperature? I thought she is probably down with a slight cold,' said Dr Vishnukant to Raju.

He took her temperature. It was 105 degrees.

Rhea tried opening her eyes, but she couldn't. She felt an ice-cold sponge on her head and feet. Dr Vishnukant gave her some medication. Rhea was in a hazy and dreamlike state, unable to comprehend what was happening.

Dr Vishnukant heard her mumble, 'Come back Krish, I am waiting,' and she repeated herself.

Rhea was reliving the day Krishnam had left Shaktidham and she was sitting in front of Goddess Kali in a state of shock. When some things break there is no sound.

It was late at night and her temperature was not dropping. 'Krish, can you hear me, I am waiting for you,' Rhea screamed.

Dr Vishnukant, who was constantly monitoring her, got up from the recliner and checked her forehead and pulse.

'Rhea, I did not know you were so unwell. I am back now.'

'Krish, Krish,' Rhea called out.

'Rhea, relax, I am here,' said Dr Vishnukant.

Vishnu called up a colleague and friend and requested him to take a look at Rhea, as her fever was not breaking. Dr Vishnukant told him that she got wet in the rain yesterday and was in a state of delirium.

The doctor arrived in a short time and till then advised Dr Vishnukant to start cold compression. He gave her an injection and some oral medication, which he brought with him. He wrote a prescription for Rhea and gave it to Dr Vishnukant to administer.

Meanwhile, Satya was sitting in Varanasi in the sadhanasthal in front of Goddess Kali, praying for Rhea.

'Ma, take care of Rhea. I have never intervened in what you wanted for us, but I cannot see her like this. She is my daughter.'

Intense chants with the waning moon and sweet aroma filled the sadhanasthal.

'Rhea, you have to get well, you have to come out of it. Rhea, you are a sadhak, receive my vibrations. Have faith in Devima.

She will send Krishnam back when you are ready.' Satya tried to connect with Rhea and give her instructions telepathically.

Satya heard Rhea's cry, 'Baba!'

'Rhea, you are here, in London, once you are fine you can talk to Baba,' Dr Vishnukant said, looking at her helplessly.

Dr Vishnukant didn't leave her alone. He slept on the recliner, and he kept a watch over her through the night.

On the other side of the Pacific Ocean was Krishnam, who was again restless and walking up and down in his house. Finally, he sat himself down and focused his thoughts on Rhea. He was afraid that Rhea now seemed to be crossing her threshold.

'Rhea, now listen to me and listen carefully. You have to be brave; I will be with you soon and don't make it more difficult for me. There isn't a lot of time left, do not scatter yourself like this. Take a hold of yourself now. Stop it and come out of this state.'

Dr Vishnukant heard her mumble another time, 'Yes, Krish.'

After a while, Rhea settled down and slept soundly.

Satya finished praying for Rhea and came out of the sadhanasthal.

Krishnam sat quietly, lost in his thoughts.

Vishnu got up and saw Rhea was sleeping peacefully. He touched her forehead to check her temperature, and she felt normal. Vishnu heaved a sigh of relief.

'Rhea, who is Krish?' asked Dr Vishnukant, after he finished examining her the next morning.

Rhea looked at Dr Vishnukant, startled by this most unexpected question.

'Who, did you say, Doc?' she asked, hoping that she heard the question incorrectly.

'Who is Krish?' he repeated.

'Why did you ask me that?' she asked, taken aback completely.

'You were repeating his name continuously in delirium last night.'

'Must have been a painful delirium, I guess,' replied Rhea laughing, without giving any answer to his question.

'That was not an answer,' said Vishnu with a very serious expression.

'Some questions are better left unanswered,' replied Rhea firmly, emphasizing that she owed him no explanation.

'How are you feeling Rhea?' asked Satya.

'I am good now.'

Rhea took a week to recover and was back to work thereafter. Satya from that day on called every day to speak with her.

'My blessings are with you, be strong and everything will be good,' he said.

They had just finished discussing about a patient and were sitting across a table. Dr Vishnukant told Rhea that a few days later he was to go on a trip to attend a conference in Edinburgh. He asked Rhea to go along with him, as it would be a good opportunity for her to see Scotland.

Rhea agreed readily and was looking forward to her visit to Scotland. Dr Vishnukant informed her that they would reach on Wednesday; on Thursday and Friday he would be busy during the day. On Saturday he would be free to show Rhea around and they would return on Sunday. Vishnu had been to Edinburgh numerous times and told her about some of the places she must visit.

30

THEY CHECKED INTO a luxury hotel on Princess Road; they had adjoining rooms. The rooms were contemporary while retaining the charm of Scottish heritage. Rhea spent Thursday taking a city tour. She first went to the Edinburgh Castle, which stood above the city and offered a magnificent sight of the city below. Rhea had taken a guided walking group tour of the castle. The 'Witches Well' got her attention, as women who practised witchcraft had been burnt there alive. Witchcraft is the alleged use of magical powers and historically believed to be used to cause harm to people. The modern term given to witchcraft is Wicca.

Rhea's knowledge of Wicca was limited and she knew that a practising Wiccan was called a witch. Some of its principles are similar to that of Tantra, as it saw the whole creation as sacred and worshipped nature. Wiccans used spells and rituals to pray for divine help. Their rules said that actions taken should harm nobody; they believed that any action taken comes back three folds to the witch, be it good or bad.

Between the fourteenth and the sixteenth centuries, many persons were prosecuted, imprisoned, burnt alive and stoned on charges of practising witchcraft. Most of them were women. The ambivalence remains to date; they are considered to have powers that can harm or heal. The same status is shared by Tantra. Everything in nature or manmade can be utilized for good or can cause havoc. A vaccine made from the same virus can be used either as prevention for disease or a biological weapon. How to use a resource is of prime significance.

She then went on to Castle Hill and took 'The Scotch Whisky' tour.

Rhea came back to the hotel tired from her excursion. She had a cup of coffee and decided to get a massage at the spa. She later took a bubble bath with aromatic oils, and as she came out, she felt lighter. She changed into an evening dress and waited for Dr Vishnukant.

Finally after a long wait, Dr Vishnukant knocked at her door; he looked tired and asked if she would like to join him in his room in fifteen minutes.

She knocked and Dr Vishnukant opened the door promptly, 'I am watching a very interesting interview. The guy is a lawyer of Indian origin, extremely charismatic and speaks amazingly well.

He has recently won a very controversial case against the state of Texas,' said Vishnu.

The person being interviewed on screen was saying, 'Perfection may not be attainable, but if you chase it, you do catch excellence.'

'But why is perfection unattainable?' asked the host.

'Perfection is attained only when there is nothing left to take, but does that ever happen?' he redirected the question back at the host.

The host smiled. 'No,' he replied.

'What does excellence mean to you?'

'I would say paying attention to every detail.' He stopped and then added further, 'Excellence is an attitude, not a skill.'

Rhea stood frozen like a statue, watching the interview.

'Do you believe that luck has played a part in your winning this case?'

'I give it my best, then leave it up to God and only ask for His blessings. I have observed that the harder I work, the luckier I get, and God's blessings seem to work more.'

'Damn, he is too good!' exclaimed Dr Vishnukant without moving an eyelid.

'With all your excellence, do you understand emotion and have you ever found time for love?' the host got a wee bit sarcastic in his last question.

'Whatever I understand, I understand because I love,' he replied with a smile.

Dr Vishnukant switched off the television as the interview got over and stated, 'He is a deadly combination of substance and an imposing persona. His body language is a mix of understated arrogance and simplicity.

'I am so tired, my neck and shoulders are hurting,' said Dr Vishnukant after a while, when Rhea did not react.

Rhea was still staring at the television screen.

'Rhea, what happened?'

'Nothing, I will be back in a bit.'

She did not return for quite some time. Dr Vishnukant went to her room.

'You are looking pale, are you okay?' he asked her. 'Rhea, I just don't understand you beyond a point. I had a long day and now I have to struggle with your unexplained behaviour.'

Rhea was quiet and unresponsive. He shook her lightly. 'Are you okay?'

Suddenly, as if nothing had happened she said, 'Doc, why don't you make yourself comfortable on the chair, I will give you a light massage.'

Dr Vishnukant looked at her vaguely, wondering, but didn't say anything and sat in the chair.

Rhea massaged his neck and shoulders; he nearly dozed off in the chair.

'Why don't you lie on the bed and let me give you a back massage?'

Dr Vishnukant was tired and didn't mind getting his back massaged; he lay on his belly. Rhea pressed his back gently, the way Krishnam had massaged her.

After a while, Rhea asked, 'Doc, are you feeling better?'

Dr Vishnukant had slipped into sound sleep. There was no reply. Rhea went to the washroom, changed into her nightdress and lay down on the bed next to Dr Vishnukant. Sleep eluded her. She kept tossing and turning for a long time but slept. She woke up and glanced at the watch eventually. It was past 11 a.m. She found a folded note on the pillow, where Dr Vishnukant had slept.

'Thanks, slept really well after long. See you around five.'

That day, she went to Saint Giles Cathedral, which had a collection of stained-glass windows. It was a Parish church named after the patron Saint Giles, a hermit who lived in the seventh century. She also went to Mary King's Close situated under

Edinburgh's city chambers, which is infamous for paranormal activity and is considered a haunted place. The guide mentioned noises heard and ghosts seen by visitors at various times.

Much to Rhea's surprise the bell rang dot on time at five. She answered the doorbell to find a refreshed-looking Dr Vishnukant. He asked Rhea to accompany him to his room; he swung the door open and Rhea was stunned, as the room was lit with a couple of candles on the table and a bottle of wine placed on it. As she sat, Dr Vishnukant handed her a small box and asked her to open it. It was a brooch with the most exquisite red crystal rose and a delicate stem and two leaves.

'Rhea, I slept like a log last night and I feel infused with energy. You have magic in your hands.'

'But you need to take care of yourself, I will not be there always,' said Rhea spontaneously.

'Why, where are you going?' asked Dr Vishnukant in a matter of fact manner.

Both were quiet for some time, realizing the enormity of the words he said. He looked intently at Rhea; she looked into his eyes. He could not comprehend the fact that Rhea would ever go away.

He poured the wine. He told Rhea about the conference and discussed all the places she had gone sightseeing. The first bottle of wine was over quick; he opened the second bottle.

After some time, Rhea was a little tipsy; he stood up and stretched out his hand towards her. Rhea took his hand and stood up too. He pulled her closer and said 'Rhea, don't leave me ever. I cannot imagine a life without you.' Rhea gently pulled away.

'Doctor, please,' said Rhea. The thought made her feel sick and she sat on the bed.

He ruffled her hair affectionately. Her head was spinning and the feeling of nausea gripped her. She got up from the bed and rushed into the washroom and threw up in the washbasin.

Her head was spinning and she was stumbling a bit. She got out of her top, as she had thrown up on it too and got into Dr Vishnukant's shirt, which was hanging in his washroom. Dr Vishnukant came in and saw her struggling with the buttons. He helped her button up, then took her back to the room and tucked her in bed. She fell asleep right away. He kept watching her sleep for a long time and then got in bed. He pulled her closer to himself and closed his eyes. His head was close to her bosom and he could hear her heartbeat. He fell into a deep slumber.

Rhea on the other hand went into her world of dreams. Krishnam and Dr Vishnukant were both telling her, 'Don't leave me. I cannot imagine my life without you'. She saw herself fading away in a cloud of mist.

The telephone ring broke her dream. Wrong time, thought Rhea. She was irritated as her dream was incomplete. It had never happened before. There had never been any disturbance at home, which interrupted her dream. She would now have to wait; if and when the dream repeated, she would know more. As she stretched her hand to pick the phone, she realized Dr Vishnukant was on the other side of the bed. It took her a second to recollect the events of last night. The ring woke up Dr Vishnukant too. The cab driver had arrived for the day as per the booking. He ruffled Rhea's hair as she jumped out of bed and into the washroom, wore his bathrobe, and went to her room.

They were about to get in the cab when Rhea saw the driver. Rhea looked at Dr Vishnukant and said, 'I don't want to take this taxi.'

'But why, Rhea?'

'I am not comfortable.'

'Why? What is the problem? It's a comfortable car, then why are you not comfortable?'

'I will not take this cab, please call for another one,' she insisted.

Dr Vishnukant was exasperated and apologized to the driver. He was obviously both stunned and irritated with the incident. He found Rhea's behaviour rather erratic. He asked the concierge to arrange for another car.

'Rhea, at times I don't understand your bizarre behaviour.'

Rhea kept quiet and maintained a straight face.

'Rhea, I need an explanation for what you did right now.'

Rhea's lips were sealed, though she looked at him as if saying, 'Never ask me for an explanation, because there are times when even I do not know why I do what I do. With time, I will know and so will you.'

Her unresponsiveness irked Dr Vishnukant, but he chose not to probe any further and left it at that. They went out of the city to see the countryside. The countryside looked like a beautiful painting created from an artist's imagination. Rhea was chirpy once again as nature was something she loved and related to. Vishnu was observing her reactions more than anything. They came back to Edinburgh to shop and eat. Once they were out of the hotel, the day went well.

On their return to the hotel, they saw a crowd at the reception. Three tourists had met with an accident. Their friends who were travelling together were in the crowd. The cab driver and two of the tourists died on the spot and one was battling for his life in the hospital. It was the same cab which Rhea had refused to board.

The driver was detected to be under the influence of drugs and had lost control of the cab. Dr Vishnukant turned to look at Rhea but she was gone. He knocked at her door; he hugged her as she opened her door and kept stroking her hair. Rhea was quiet; Dr Vishnukant was completely stunned with this episode. He realized he was in love with a woman with faculties that were difficult to understand logically.

31

A FEW DAYS back into their routine, Dr Vishnukant went to the library to do some research.

Clair simply means 'clear' in French and voyant means 'seeing'. Some people have more highly developed senses than what we call normal. Clairvoyance or 'clear seeing' is the paranormal ability to see things which cannot be seen through normal vision. It is one's ability to see or perceive persons or events, which are distant in time or space. An example of dream clairvoyance would be, if you were to dream about something that is either not known by anyone else or hasn't happened yet and it later turns out to be true.

Clairaudience or 'clear hearing' is the ability to hear sounds and things, which are not perceivable by the human ears. Example, one who can hear voices, sounds, bells, or music that are otherwise inaudible.

'This sounds like schizophrenia,' thought Vishnu aloud, while he read the text.

Clairsentience or 'clear feeling' means an extra-sensory perception. Such persons have the ability to feel what others feel and as intensely as the actual person going through it.

Clairalience is being able to smell odours that have no physical source. The source could be in some other space and time.

Clairgustance is the ability to taste something that isn't there in one's mouth. For example, something cooked by someone in some other space and time could give the same taste to the person gifted with this ability, as if he or she was tasting it in the present time and space.

'This is eerie,' Dr Vishnukant muttered.

The fact is that all of us are gifted with these faculties in different proportions. At some point, we have experienced it and called it coincidence. Vishnu folded the notes and kept the paper in his pocket.

Rhea went to visit the patients at the hospital every day. Most of them would vent out their traumas and pain to her. There were some who wanted to be heard, some would just lie holding Rhea's hand. There were people who felt victimized by life and circumstances, especially their loved ones. There were also some who felt that God was a traitor, because in spite of their regular prayers and belief in God, they were suffering. Both Dr Vishnukant and Rhea were engrossed in work individually, but the truth remained that every night Rhea searched for Krishnam's arm and Dr Vishnukant slept imagining his head close to Rhea's bosom, hearing her heartbeat. Every morning, they got up to an emptiness that never seemed to dissipate from their life. Rhea's disrupted dream was still a cause of irritation for her.

◆

Neel had confirmed a week ago about his trip to London to see her, as he had some work in Birmingham. He was coming in before the weekend to spend time with Rhea and she was looking forward to it. She was supposed to pick Neel up at the airport, but couldn't as she had to be with a patient in the cath. lab.

Sam came in to inform that he was back after dropping Neel home, so she could leave when she wanted. She called her assistant and updated him with the status of all patients, as she would be off this weekend.

'I too will come back with you, if you can wait for another half hour. I will finish for the day by then,' said Dr Vishnukant.

As they entered the house, Raju knocked at the guest room door on the ground floor. Neel came out and picked up Rhea. 'How is my friend?'

She was giggling.

'Good, in fact great after seeing you,' Rhea said.

Dr Vishnukant watched them, as if scrutinizing their relationship. She introduced Neel to Dr Vishnukant. Neel thanked

Dr Vishnukant for having him at his home, as he had insisted earlier that he would stay in a hotel nearby. Dr Vishnukant was not talking much; he was simply watching them together. Neel and Rhea were busy chatting about Varanasi and his work. Rhea was aware of the fact that Dr Vishnukant was observing them.

Neel and Rhea were out in London all of next day. When Dr Vishnukant came back at night, they were still chatting in Neel's room and he could hear them laugh. Rhea heard him enter the house and asked him to join them, but he told her that he was tired and would like to have an early supper and sleep.

Neel winked as she entered the room. 'Your Doc seems to be disturbed.'

She threw a pillow at him and he hit her back with it. That started a round of pillow fight. The decibel of squeals and laughter was high.

'Reminds me of the old times,' said Neel and then nearly bit his tongue.

Rhea looked at him, but did not show any reaction. Neel suggested that they all go out for dinner. Rhea knocked at Dr Vishnukant's door. 'Why do you need to knock the door, you can just walk in,' he said with irritation in his voice.

'We are going out for dinner. Would you like to join us?'

'Rhea, I told you I am exhausted,' replied Dr Vishnukant.

Rhea was in a playful mood; she picked up a pillow and threw it at Dr Vishnukant. 'Come on, Doc! Stop being a bore.'

Dr Vishnukant caught the pillow and said, 'I am not Neel, Rhea.'

Rhea looked up, startled. His tone was sarcastic. She left the room without saying a word.

'What happened, Rhea?' inquired Neel.

Rhea said nothing. Neel gave her a tight hug. 'Let's get ready quickly and go.'

She went up to change and as they were about to leave, Dr Vishnukant came out dressed to join them.

The next day Neel and Rhea were out roaming around London. By late evening, they were standing by the River Thames watching the sunset.

'Rhea, I think the doctor is a good guy and he seems to be in love with you. Give yourself a chance. Too much time has passed, eleven years is a long time. There is a world beyond Krishnam.'

'Neel, please, have you come here to talk about this?' she said, looking straight into his eyes. He turned his face away.

'Neel, our definitions of love are different.'

'What is your definition, Rhea, hanging on to the ghosts of the past?'

'There are no ghosts and there is no past. Krish was my past, is my present, and will remain my future,' said Rhea and started walking. Neel followed her with a deep sigh.

The week passed like an elongated party. Dr Vishnukant and Neel had struck a comfortable chord. It was Neel's last night in London and he was leaving the next day. Neel and Rhea had tequila shots that night until both got drunk.

'This is like old times, only Krish is missing,' said Neel spontaneously.

'Krish is a name I've often heard without knowing who he is,' said Dr Vishnukant suddenly, attentive on hearing Krish's name from Neel.

There was a long awkward silence.

'Yes, Neel, the past doesn't let go of us. We try and live our present, with one foot in the past,' said Dr Vishnukant to break the silence. His voice had an obvious sarcasm.

'Past can be very painful,' he added rather contemplatively.

'Or very beautiful,' replied Rhea.

'Either way, it holds us tight in its grip,' said Dr Vishnukant.

'Rhea, why do we hold tightly to memories?' asked Neel, slightly slurring.

'They are the only things that do not change,' she said,

laughing a hollow laugh.

There was an uneasy silence for some time.

'Doctor, you know my friend, she is very strong,' said Neel.

Small talk carried on for a while until Neel fell asleep on the couch. Dr Vishnukant helped him to his room and Rhea retired to her room.

The next day Rhea went to see Neel off. Neel hugged Rhea to say goodbye and whispered softly in her ear, 'Rhea, move on.'

Rhea whispered back, 'Krishnam is coming back soon.'

Her reply left Neel flabbergasted and he looked at her in disbelief.

'I wonder which world you come from, Rhea,' said Neel.

He handed a neatly folded piece of paper to her and said, 'It's time you give it a reality check.'

She kept the paper, which had a number scribbled on it, in her coat pocket.

32

IT WAS THE beginning of December and London got cold. Rhea had been in London for nearly nine months now. Dr Vishnukant was perpetually overworked and chronically fatigued.

One particular night, he came back rather early complaining of a headache and refused to eat. Rhea went into his room and saw that the fireplace was burning; the room had a soft orange hue.

She loved fire as it reminded her of havans at the sadhanasthal, back home. It reminded her of the power which if left untamed could destroy, and if channelized positively could create. But then destruction of the old also paved the way for the new, she thought.

She saw Dr Vishnukant lying on the other side of bed with his hand on his head. Rhea sat beside him on the bed and put her hand on his forehead. He kept lying still without a stir. She waited for a while and got up to leave when he caught her hand. He pulled Rhea. She lost her balance and fell on him, her head on his chest. She heard his heartbeat, as both remained still for a moment.

He put both his arms around Rhea and rolled her to her side of the bed. He said softly, 'Rhea, I need to tell you something.' Rhea was quiet, but distanced herself and sat erect on the bed.

'Rhea, I was married and my wife committed suicide. She was pregnant at that time. We had had an arranged marriage. We were a normal couple; we had no serious grievances with each other. She did mention a couple of times about hearing some voices at night and that I spent way too much time with my mother. I attributed it to the initial adjustments and some to attention seeking measures. I wonder whether I was right,' said Dr Vishnukant with a heavy voice.

'She was five months pregnant when she took that extreme step. Ma and Daddy were home and I was at the nursing home. She was doing her doctorate in biochemistry. It still eats me up as to why she did what she did. She hung herself and I can neither forget that sight nor that feeling. I don't know what went wrong, or what happened. I really do not know if in that year that we were together, I knew her at all,' recounted Dr Vishnukant.

'I informed her parents about what had happened; in fact they drove down immediately and decided to cremate her body before things took an ugly turn. We eventually told everyone that her blood pressure shot up, which was the cause of her death. I left Varanasi to settle here. It's been years since and I still wonder why she did it. Our marriage was with each other's consent. She never really complained about anything. It will always remain a mystery.'

'What was your wife's name?' asked Rhea.

'Niharika,' he replied. Rhea was stunned, but sat staring blankly in space.

'It's better if some things remain a mystery. It's not always good to know everything,' Rhea said.

Dr Vishnukant was looking at her, her eyes closed and he ran his fingers on her face and neck. 'As usual you smell lovely, Rhea. Why do I love you so much?'

Rhea could not hear him. Her hands were locked in a tight fist. He kissed her softly on her forehead. Before his lips moved towards her lips, she opened her eyes and gently pushed Dr Vishnukant back. Rhea was calling out to Krishnam in her mind.

'No,' she said and separating herself from him, stood up.

'Rhea, what is it? Is something wrong? I desire you and I thought you desire me too. I do not understand why you are holding yourself back.'

'I am sorry, but I think you have misunderstood me,' she said.

'Rhea, I have missed you beside me since that night in Edinburgh. Every night my hands search for you beside me. Every morning I get up to a vacuum.'

She was quiet.

'What is it, Rhea? Be honest, do you not desire me?'

'I don't love you, the way you expect me to.' She walked away saying that.

Her life in Shaktidham was so different than her life now. Nobody had ever said things to her that made her uncomfortable. That night the dream came back to her. Krishnam and Dr Vishnukant calling out to her and she fading in a cloud of mist. A hand pulled her out from the mist; she came out and was in Krishnam's arms. Both Krishnam and Rhea were wearing black overcoats. In her dream, as she looked back, she saw Dr Vishnukant looking at them sadly. It was a dream that gave her a sense of happiness and sadness.

◆

Rhea came out of her workshop and found a patient waiting for her outside her chamber. She called him in and was quietly listening to him.

Dr Vishnukant knocked and came in. 'Sorry to disturb, Rhea. How long will you take? I am going home.'

'About half an hour, Doc,' she replied.

Dr Vishnukant went out without replying.

'The most important aspect of any relationship is respect and if it lacks respect then everything else is a farce,' Rhea was telling the patient.

'Rhea, I can drop you back. Would you like to have a cup of coffee?' asked the patient.

'No, Doc is waiting. I have to go back. It is late.'

Rhea came out and walked to Dr Vishnukant's chamber, but it was locked. Rhea enquired at the reception, but found out that he had left forty-five minutes ago.

'Kaka, where is Bhaiya?' she enquired on reaching the house.

'He has slept as he was tired. He did not even eat.'

Rhea knocked at Dr Vishnukant's door a few times. She tried opening the door too, but it was bolted from inside.

The next morning, Dr Vishnukant had left before Rhea woke up and came downstairs. She got ready and went to the hospital. That evening, she went to Dr Vishnukant's office and sat facing Dr Vishnukant across his table, updating him about the patients. His expression revealed nothing in relation to the previous night.

Dr D'Souza, a senior surgeon and the head of the oncology department walked into the chamber. 'Good evening, Vishnu.'

'Good evening.'

'How is the little angel? I have come to meet my little angel and have a chat with her,' said Dr D'Souza, looking at Rhea.

'Have a seat,' said Dr Vishnukant vacating his chair.

'Rhea, I would like you to conduct workshops for my patients too.'

Rhea looked at Dr Vishnukant, but he looked away.

'Please carry on with your conversation. I have to attend to something,' said Dr Vishnukant and left.

Rhea knew he had nothing to attend to as it was time to leave. Instead, he went home and sent the car back for her.

'Bitti, Bhaiya is in his room and said that he would not like to be disturbed. Is there some problem?' asked Raju.

'It seems so,' she replied.

Vishnu was not interacting with Rhea beyond work. He was curt and spoke little. Rhea was unable to reach out to him. She was not used to this, as Satya, Krishnam or Neel had never been like this. Rhea noticed that the lack of exercise and his erratic lifestyle was taking its toll on Dr Vishnukant. He looked tired and overworked. She had not seen him smile in days.

Her work with cancer patients was making her popular amongst the patients and doctors of the department. Treatable patients were encouraged to bravely fight their situation. Terminal patients were motivated to accept and lend quality to whatever life was left.

'Death is not to be feared, it is to be taken as a change. If you have lived today, tomorrow shouldn't be feared. Live every day as if it's the last. In any case, no one has ever seen tomorrow,' said Rhea.

Rhea was watching Dr Vishnukant as a spectator; it seemed he had closed her out of his life. Professionally, he was climbing the ladder and was a renowned doctor. Success can be demanding. However, the definition of success is different for different people.

One night, Rhea and Dr Vishnukant were sitting in the living area after dinner.

'Each one is responsible for their lives without an exception. You, in any case, have cut me totally from your life,' said Rhea.

Dr Vishnukant looked at her tenderly.

'Even if I want to, I cannot cut you away. The truth is that you have never been able to accept me,' replied Dr Vishnukant.

'Deeper the relationship, more tending it needs. The person we love the most is the one who has the power to hurt us the most. One cannot afford to be careless in relationships which are precious. One needs to be even more sensitive as so much is at stake. Precious things have to be looked after, as there may be no replacement for it,' said Dr Vishnukant, looking at Rhea.

'Doc, I do not see us together in the way you do,' said Rhea sadly.

'Not a single moment in my life is without you; don't you see, Rhea, that I love you?'

'Just because I don't love you the way you want, doesn't mean that you are not important to me,' she replied.

He stood up and pulled her towards himself and kissed her hard. She tried pushing him, but he was aggressive.

'Be mine, Rhea,' he said.

'No, I can't be yours the way you want me,' said Rhea and gently moved away.

'Please, don't force me like this in future. It upsets me,' she said, annoyed.

She started to open the gift given to her by one of her patients. Dr Vishnukant pulled it from her and threw it on the sofa.

'I am talking to you, damn it, and you choose to behave indifferent,' he said, screaming at her.

'Certain things can never be talked about, they have to be felt,' replied Rhea, maintaining calm in her voice which infuriated him further.

'It has to do with your past, isn't it? Honestly, I do not wish to know your fucking past, Rhea,' his voice was even louder now.

'No, Vishnu, it is about my present and future too.' She did not lose her composure and replied in a matter-of-fact manner. Vishnu held her and shook her violently.

'Leave me now, Vishnu,' said Rhea, in a low-pitched, ice-cold voice. Her eyes were blazing and her anger unconcealed. Raju came out of the kitchen, hearing the commotion, and Dr Vishnukant left her as he entered. She picked up the gift and walked up to her room.

These kinds of emotional outbursts were alien to her and anger had to be controlled. She could never let Dr Vishnukant be a target of her anger. She held her small statue of Goddess Kali in her hand and took deep breaths, until she felt normal.

Yes, love had overcome anger. As she unwrapped the gift, she looked at it, stupefied. It was a beautiful black overcoat, the same overcoat that she had seen herself wearing in the dream. Rhea sat holding the overcoat, dumbstruck.

So the time was nearing to be with Krishnam. The euphoric feeling wiped away all traces of unpleasantness from her altercation with Dr Vishnukant. She tried on the overcoat and it fitted her beautifully. She put her hand in the pocket, checking out the fit and admiring it in front of the mirror, when she felt a small box in the pocket. It had an exquisite pair of diamond earrings and a delicate necklace, with a pear-shaped diamond on it.

'Oh my God, Krish would have bought me something exactly like this,' she thought.

She kept looking at the necklace and smiling.

◆

The next day, Rhea went to see Gagan, who had given her the gift. Rhea took his address from the patients' record and went to his office. The office was housed in a three-storied building and his cabin was on the third floor, which was restricted. The entrance to the floor was locked and an access swipe card was required to enter. There were just three chambers on the third floor and his cabin was the last. Rhea went back to the reception and insisted that Gagan at least be told about her visit. Gagan came to receive her. In his wildest of dreams, he had not expected Rhea to visit him, that too at his workplace. Rhea brought the box back with its contents.

'Gagan, I cannot take this,' she said, while handing it over to him.

'Why, did you not like it?' inquired Gagan.

'It is beautiful, but it does not behove me to take such a gift from you.'

'Rhea, it's too small a token for what you have given me. I can never do anything to repay you,' said Gagan.

'But, I did not give you anything, Gagan; I was just doing my work. Not everything can be repaid, one must leave it at that,' said Rhea.

'Rhea, please try looking at it beyond the material aspect. It is an expression of my thoughts and feelings. They are not merely precious stones; I have invested them truly with my feelings, affection, and immense respect for you. Please don't make it an issue. It's not for you, Rhea, it's for myself. I went numerous times to find something, which you may like. Finally, I went with a friend visiting me and he selected it on my behalf.'

'I must say your friend has excellent taste.'

Rhea came back with the box; Gagan was persistent. The next day she went and bought a pair of diamond-studded cufflinks for Gagan as a gift.

Rhea felt better as Dr Vishnukant apologized for his outburst and it seemed all would be well again between them.

She called up Satya. 'Baba, I am missing home, I am missing my pujas and I am missing you.'

Satya was laughing on the phone.

'Then come back, Rhea.'

'Baba, I am enjoying my work here too, but I will return with Krishnam soon.'

'Then enjoy. It's natural to miss home and yes I am making preparations to welcome you both back home,' said Satya.

◆

'There is no perfect human being, there is no perfect life. Life, as we perceive it, is the time spent between birth and death. Is it fulfilling in the deeper sense? Did one follow his destiny? Did one live fully in a way that one could say, "Yes, I was born for this and if death was to come anytime, I have neither grievance nor any regret." Such a person could be someone who has lived his life perfectly and fully. Many live, yet are not alive. Many are alive, but do not get a chance to live,' said Rhea.

The workshop was for the cancer patients, undergoing chemotherapy and radiation, some after their surgery and some without surgery. The chemotherapy treatment was painful and had its side effects.

Amongst them was a young girl, Merrill. She had been experiencing severe headaches and nausea. After investigations, the diagnosis was that she had glioma in her brain. After craniotomy had been conducted, the pathology confirmed 'glioblastoma multiformes' in the parietal lobe. It is the most belligerent form of glioma, a malignancy that could not be cured. The reoccurrence was expected anytime. Her expected survival was put at few months; for how long, it could not be determined. All questions don't have answers. Merrill was twenty years old and wanted to live.

She came up to Rhea after the workshop and clung to her, weeping.

'I want to live, Rhea. Save me,' she pleaded.

Rhea held her as she went on, 'Why did it happen to me? How come so many old people are living? I have yet to live my life. I don't want to go away from my parents, my family and my boyfriend. It's difficult to comprehend that anytime I will leave this world and the world will go on as if nothing happened!'

'Rhea, why is God so cruel, ask him? Ask him, he is your God...' she wept.

Rhea had no answers, she just held on to her until her sobs subsided.

'Yes, Merrill, whoever said that life was fair?'

There is no consolation, except the fact that 'this is life'. It was senseless to say it must be God's will. It was senseless to even say 'I know how you feel' and it would be pointless to say 'you must be strong'.

Rhea knew there was nothing she could say to diminish Merrill's pain. Merrill did not need any clichés. She had to find meaning and appreciate whatever time was left. Rhea had to shed light and show her the way.

'Rhea, your eyes seem swollen,' said Dr Vishnukant, while at the dinner table.

'Were you crying today?' he probed further, when she did not respond.

She was quiet and fiddling with her fork and not eating. Dr Vishnukant left his meal and sat beside her.

'What is it? Something is extremely disturbing.'

Rhea narrated the entire incident of Merrill's pain.

'I understand that it's tough on you.'

'Yes, Doc, at such times one realizes how fragile life is. We get caught up in so many petty issues that we forget we have the greatest gift called "life". It's only in this moment that we live, the rest is so uncertain. Time and again, I am reminded of this truth, which we seem to forget while we live our lives.'

'Rhea, you are right. Who knows what tomorrow holds or if it will come.'

They finished their meal in silence. She never wasted any food on her plate, once she took it; it had to be eaten however miserable she was. Food was a source of energy and one had to be thankful to God for it being provided.

Rhea got into the Jacuzzi and closed her eyes, but she just could not push Merrill away from her thoughts. She stopped trying; instead she tried to feel her pain.

The pain of losing all her loved ones! The pain of knowing that none of her dreams would be fulfilled; the pain of knowing that the world would go on without her! The pain of knowing that she would be only a photograph in a frame!

The pain of knowing that you are slowly dying, but you want to live. The thought of all this pain was overwhelming.

It was fearful not to know what awaited after death. Tears were flowing from Rhea's eyes. She heard knocks at her bedroom door.

'It's me, Rhea,' said Dr Vishnukant. 'Open the door.'

'Yes, just a moment. I am changing.'

'Come downstairs to my room, Rhea. The fireplace is lit.'

Rhea wore her pyjamas and went down to Vishnu's room.

'How are you feeling now?'

She gave a feeble smile.

'I can see my woman is not in her element.'

His mobile phone rang and he had to rush immediately as it was an emergency call.

He returned home late the next night, exhausted. Rhea had seen him in the hospital while taking rounds. He had been busy with patients. She came downstairs, as she heard the car pull up in the drive.

She opened the door for Dr Vishnukant since it was after midnight. Raju laid out the dinner, while Dr Vishnukant went in for a bath. Rhea waited for him at the dinner table. Almost an hour passed by, but no sign of him. Rhea knocked on his bedroom door a couple of times, but there wasn't any response. She opened the door to find that he was fast asleep. He was still unshaven and in the same clothes in which he had returned. Rhea asked Raju to clear the table and go to sleep. She went in Dr Vishnukant's bedroom, bolted the bedroom door from inside and quietly slid into the quilt beside him. She slowly stroked his forehead and watched him sleep. He looked like a baby while sleeping. She kissed him on the forehead and closed her eyes as she lay beside him. He turned over and his arm came across and held her. After a while, she gently removed it.

'You have a bad habit of moving around in the bed,' Krishnam always told her, as she frequently tossed and turned, changing her sleeping posture while she did not fall asleep. She would think about everything she did the entire day while in bed. She would try and analyse if that day her life had been fruitful, if she had learned anything from that day, about the places where she had messed up and where she could do better. It was Satya who inculcated this in her. He had made her write these answers every night as a child.

'It is important to take stock of your life,' he would say.

Some rituals are important until one can naturally penetrate them and understand the reason behind them. Sometimes, the key to its significance lies in what seems most insignificant. The writing had gone, but mentally she would go through it every night. She went through the entire day in her mind's eye, shifting postures, until she finally lay quietly. Sleep was eluding her, as thoughts of Merrill filled her. Dr Vishnukant slept through the night like a log.

In the morning, as Rhea turned to leave the bed, Dr Vishnukant said, 'Don't go, I want to sleep' and held her.

'Doc, I have work at the oncology department, some patients are coming to meet me.'

'Will you only call me Vishnu when you are angry with me?' he questioned, without opening his eyes.

She laughed and said, 'Vishnu, rest well.'

She came back from the hospital late that afternoon. Dr Vishnukant was still sleeping and his mobile phone was switched off. Rhea was exhausted—every day she had patients who cried, and everyone came with problems.

33

IT WAS CHRISTMAS next week and then the new year would set in. It was extremely cold and the skies were mostly grey. Dr

Vishnukant and Rhea were both busy with work. Christmas passed with Rhea at home and Dr Vishnukant at the hospital.

We all run after things we don't have. Love may not be the primary want in everyone's life. It may come after name, fame, and wealth. Only when you have experienced it all can you realize that life is all hollow and meaningless.

For Rhea, it had always been Satya and Krishnam, but then she'd never had to struggle for anything. All material aspects were placed on a platter in front of her since her childhood. Her struggle had been different; eleven years was the price Krishnam and she had to pay for her to be what and where she was today.

'Rhea, where is my light blue shirt? Have you seen it?' shouted Dr Vishnukant.

'Kaka accidently burnt the other one while ironing,' he said.

Rhea was in the shower.

'I am wearing the navy blue suit, have to attend a doctors' luncheon being organized by the British Medical Council,' Dr Vishnukant was shouting out to her, through her bathroom door.

'I will take time. It is in my cupboard; you can take it out.'

Rhea had developed a habit with Krishnam; he insisted that she wear his shirts and sleep. When Dr Vishnukant's, shirts were not to be found, he knew they would be hung in Rhea's closet, smelling of her. He loved wearing those shirts. She never realized when she once wore Vishnu's shirt in Edinburgh and then she started sleeping in them most of the nights.

Satya always said, 'Don't be casual about things that should be taken seriously. Know the difference.'

Dr Vishnukant opened her cupboard. Four of his shirts were hanging, washed and ironed amidst Rhea's endless clothes. As he was taking out his blue shirt, his attention was caught by a beautiful small black box. He opened the box out of curiosity. A pair of diamond-studded cufflinks shone brilliantly in the box. He took his shirt and shut Rhea's cupboard.

◆

'Hi Rhea,' said Gagan on the phone.

'How are you, Gagan?'

'Good, angel. What are you doing for New Year's Eve?'

'Well, nothing really,' she replied.

'How about dinner with me?'

'I will ask Dr Vishnukant if he would like it that way.'

Gagan burst out laughing, 'Angel, I asked you only.'

'I told you what I had to,' she said, giggling.

Both started laughing.

'Aha, angels have wit too,' said Gagan affectionately.

'Come out with me on the first then.'

'Sure.'

'Will pick you up at seven.'

New Year's Eve went past like any other day. Rhea had picked up some red wine and a chocolate cake to welcome the new year with Dr Vishnukant. She had asked Raju to prepare a couple of salads for dinner. She had called Dr Vishnukant several times, but his phone went unanswered. She spoke to Satya, wished him a happy new year and took his blessings. She also had a long chat with Neel. She put on some music, had half a bottle of wine, had her dinner and slept off, as there was no trace of Dr Vishnukant.

Dr Vishnukant came back the next morning. Rhea came down and peeped into his room and saw him sleeping. In the afternoon, she tickled his feet to wake him up.

'Happy new year, Doc.'

'Happy new year. Sorry about last night, I had an emergency. Let's go out for dinner tonight,' suggested Dr Vishnukant.

'I am going out for dinner with Gagan. He had asked me for yesterday, but I said I'll meet him today.'

Dr Vishnukant remained silent.

◆

'Black looks good on you, Rhea,' said Gagan, as Rhea got in the car that evening.

Rhea took a deep breath. 'I like the fragrance you are wearing.'

'Thanks, angel.'

'So, where would you like to eat?'

'Gagan, don't give me the jitters, have you not made reservations?'

He smiled and showed off his dimples. 'We will go wherever the lady wishes. Don't bother about anything, when I am with you.'

Rhea laughed aloud. 'Yes, Sir.'

He took her to an awarded restaurant with a choice of a few cuisines. Rhea had read about the place a couple of months ago in a magazine. It catered to the glitterati visiting London from all over the world. It was a must-visit restaurant while in London. Gagan had booked a private corner for them. He asked her about her work and how she got into it. Rhea told him that she loved it and she got into it quite by chance.

'I am from Shaktidham, an ashram in Varanasi. My father is my guru too. I started taking classes at the ashram and that is how it all started.'

Gagan ordered for a Lebanese platter and a Mexican platter as starters and chose a rose wine from their wine list.

'I was taking sessions for spiritual aspirants and Dr Vishnukant came to attend it. He opened the doors for me that led me to where I am presently.'

'What exactly is spiritualism, Rhea?'

'Well, to sum it up in a line, it is simply knowing yourself.'

'Ah, that is the simplest definition that I have heard.'

'Rhea, your work is appreciated a lot, I feel honoured sharing these moments with you.'

'Thanks, Gagan. It's not work for me; it's something I truly love to do. It gives me a deep sense of fulfilment. Every smile that comes from to my students brightens my day.'

'So, you like calling them students and not patients?'

'We all are students, students of life,' she said.

They had their dinner over some lighter conversations. He drove her back to Dr Vishnukant's house.

'Thanks, Rhea,' he hugged her, as she got out of the car.

She hugged him back, 'May this year bring you all the good things and relieve you of all the baggage you are carrying.'

◆

Dr Vishnukant opened the door.

'You are back early, Doc?' asked Rhea, with a smile.

'No, Madam, you are late,' he said with sarcasm in his voice.

It was past midnight.

'The fireplace is lit. Would you like to have coffee downstairs?' asked Vishnu.

'I will change and come.'

Dr Vishnukant was lying and watching television, when she came in the room. The fire burnt brilliantly. She sat in the duvet opposite him and sipped on her steaming coffee, which he handed to her.

'It seems you had a good evening.'

'Yes, it was fun,' Rhea replied and went on to narrate where they had gone and what they had eaten.

'So, Gagan mentioned that people are appreciating your work; he is a lawyer.'

'Doc, it's our work and I am here because of you. So I guess the credit actually goes to you.'

Dr Vishnukant laughingly said, 'Rhea, lawyers are liars.'

Something in Vishnu's voice was alarming, thought Rhea, and so was what he said.

'Maybe they are, but I know that he was not lying,' said Rhea, as she got up and walked out of his room.

◆

Merrill was waiting for Rhea in her chamber. Looking at her even now, it wasn't difficult to judge that she must have been a very pretty young girl. Radiotherapy had resulted in darkening of the skin and she had developed freckles on her face and hands; her hair was slowly growing back though. There was puffiness on her face and she had gained weight due to the steroids that she was prescribed.

'Rhea, it has reoccurred, it is showing in the scan. Rhea, what would you have done if you were in my place?' asked Merrill. 'I know I am dying. The treatment makes it worse.'

She then nearly screamed, 'Your God cheated on me, at least you should be honest.'

'Yes, it is difficult to accept that one's faith does not protect one in this way. It does not change the fact that life is the way it is. Our faith, if it's faith at all, will give us the strength to face it,' said Rhea, looking at her.

This was a tough one; she had to place herself totally in Merrill's shoes. It was definitely not easy and not completely possible. Rhea asked her to meet her the next day. She went to visit her referring doctor, Dr Beck.

'Medically, we are only trying to prolong her life as much as we can. We have our limitations, but we are not giving up. We have to keep trying, keep fighting until her last breath. The scan revealed reoccurrence. The treatment would be symptomatic.'

'So then, I assume it's not about fighting anymore, it is about acceptance at this stage,' asked Rhea.

'Well, you could say so, but as a doctor I have to follow the protocol of treatment. Denying the treatment could lead to instant death,' said Dr Beck.

Then, most unexpectedly, Dr Beck added softly, 'Rhea, this is medicine. If I were you, I would go ahead with what I believed in.

There is a whole world beyond medicine.'

Rhea suggested to Merrill the next day when she came to see her, 'Merrill, had I been in your place I would not go ahead with any further treatment. I would like to make my living moments as wonderful as I could.'

'You have beautiful eyes, they have so much tenderness,' she said, looking at Rhea. 'I am scared of dying. Help me, Rhea.'

Rhea took her hand. 'Yes, death is scary but nevertheless a reality which we all have to accept. Do you believe in God, Merrill?' she asked.

'Yes, I am a Catholic.'

'Merrill, God has set before you, life and death. Choose life while you are alive.

'Can you give me some time alone? Every day, starting from tomorrow, you can come to me at 10 a.m., barring Saturday and Sunday as I take workshops,' asked Rhea.

'Rhea, this will be taxing on you,' said Dr Vishnukant, after he heard from Rhea about Merrill's one-on-one sessions.

'I know, Doc, but I cannot say no to a dying person.'

'You are starting a trend that will sap you. I will have to find a solution,' he said.

Rhea's secretary Joey made a call to Merrill, stating the fees for individual sessions by Rhea. Joey had clear instructions from Dr Vishnukant that in future he had to make calls informing the patient of the fee for any individual sessions that Rhea decided to take. The fee was high enough to act as a deterrent. Only a person desperately and genuinely in need would take it.

Two days later, Merrill sat across Rhea in her chamber.

'Rhea, I have finally decided not to go ahead with any medical treatment,' announced Merrill.

'You are worth more than your illness, Merrill,' said Rhea.

She instructed Joey not to let anyone disturb them and made Merrill lie down on her back. All lights except the night lamp that glowed discreetly in the corner were switched off and a soft blue tint spread across the room. Rhea played soft instrumental music in the background.

Rhea then made suggestions to Merrill. 'Focus your attention on your breath. If thoughts come, gently draw your attention back to your breath…

'Observe your body in your mind's eye, from head…to toe… back from toe…to head…Now, observe your body from the inside in your mind's eye, from head…to toe…and then toe…to head…

'Now slowly, by paying attention to every part, every sensation, within your physical self, visualize a body of golden light. Feel that body of light, detaching itself from your physical self. You are now the body of light.

'Now, stand out and observe your physical body; your physical body is dead. Observe your dead body as a detached spectator. Your identity transcends the physical body.'

Rhea could sense her restlessness.

'Merrill, feel and observe… Bring to your mind's eye, the images of all your near and dear ones surrounding your body; their reactions as they surround your lifeless body.'

Tears were streaming down Merrill's closed eyes.

'Your body is being placed in a coffin. Now, visualize your funeral procession, the priest is reading out the funeral oration… You are now observing the coffin with your body being lowered into the grave… The earth covers the coffin and people are going back…

'The body that you thought was you is no more, but you are still there observing everything. Your journey back home begins now.

'Observe, you are lighter, calm and relaxed…You are moving upwards, slowly drifting, and enjoying the freedom and lightness. You find yourself standing in front of a golden gate; step in… the entire place is washed in golden light. You have now entered the dimension of divine light… You now feel a deep sense of belonging… This is the dimension of pure love and wisdom.

'You now become a part of that light. You are love, light and wisdom. Feel the oneness with the only one…

'Merrill, you were unique before your body was declared ill, you had interests and you had a personality that set you apart from everyone else. All that still remains, even after your illness. Keep that going.'

We all are fearful of the unknown and death is unknown.

34

THE SATURDAY MORNING session with the cardiac patients was in full swing. Normally, no one would be allowed to enter mid-session. Rhea saw a tall, elderly person entering. He was fair and balding and wore spectacles. He sat down quietly in the last row. Rhea had just started a relaxation technique, which he learnt quickly. After the completion of the session, he went up to Rhea and extended his hand with a warm smile.

'Dr Bryan. I am a cardiac surgeon from New York.'

Rhea had heard of him. He was one of the stalwarts of cardiac surgery.

'I am organizing a meet of cardiologists in New York, approximately two months from now and would like to give you a slot for a talk on stress management.'

'Dr Bryan, I don't think that talking about something that all the cardiologists already know is a grand idea to me. Yes, I could walk you through an experiential relaxation technique.'

'That's an awesome idea. Could I have your business card? I will finalize your slot and send you all the details on your email.'

'I do not have a card, you could communicate with Dr Vishnukant.'

'Oh, you work with Vishnu, is it? Great, he would be there to attend the conference too. Rhea, it was a pleasure meeting you and I don't have to elaborate on how good I felt while attending the last bit of your session. Had I not been taking the return flight tonight, I would have loved to attend the complete workshop tomorrow. However, I will look forward to your session in New York. What kind of slot would be comfortable for you?'

'I think half an hour would suffice,' said Rhea.

'Oh, considering the venue and the large number of participants, it will not be possible to organize this kind of lying-down arrangement,' said Dr Bryan, pondering. 'Anyway, Rhea, once I have organized it, I will get back to you and discuss the finer details.'

That evening, Rhea was sitting with Dr Vishnukant and mentioned her meeting with Dr Bryan.

'I wonder if he will remember the conversation tomorrow,' said Dr Vishnukant with a smirk.

'He seemed quite interested, rather he was sure that he wanted a session for the cardiologists at the conference,' replied Rhea adamantly.

◆

Merrill's sessions were regular—at times she was angry and cursed her fate, at times she was full of laughter. Today, Merrill decided to write a note to all those who meant something to her. In the note, she would thank each one of them for touching her life in their own special way, making a difference to her in their own unique way. She hugged Rhea and kissed her on her cheek and left.

'Rhea, I will drown myself in ice cream today,' she said, while walking out.

'Have my share too, darling,' replied Rhea.

Merrill's mother came to meet Rhea. 'Rhea, this is for you. I wanted to say thank you, so I baked a cake for everything you are doing for my daughter.'

'Smells great, thank you so much and I am simply doing my work,' she replied.

The next person Rhea encountered was Dr Beck. 'Can I have some of your precious time? I want to chat with you, beautiful,' he asked. The young, vibrant Dr Beck was known in the hospital for his volatile temper.

Rhea knew that was his way of talking. He was too busy to just sit for some polite conversation. She asked Joey to get them two coffees.

'So, Dr Beck, now tell me.'

'Nothing darling, was just missing you,' he said, winking at her.

Rhea winked back. 'Ah, if only it were true. I know you were not missing me.'

He smiled. 'I want to talk to you, personally, if you can spare some time?'

'Sure, please go ahead.'

'It's my anger. Do something please. I am in a bit of a hurry; I have a surgery lined up.'

Rhea laughed loudly and took out a small card, the size of a credit card. 'Doc, are you looking for a quick fix?' she said mockingly.

She made a smiling face and wrote 'STOP' in capitals, with a red felt pen, on the card. She also wrote 'weak people get angry and I am not weak' and gave it to him.

'Keep it in your wallet. This is for you; do not wave it in the face of the other person. Take this out and look at it before you decide to blow your top the next time. Dr Beck, have you heard of the famous man whose prayer to God was "God, give me patience, but give it to me now"?' she asked.

Dr Beck gave Rhea a hug and left.

As he was coming out of the chamber, he bumped into Dr Vishnukant.

'Hey Vishnu, how are you?'

'Good, Beck. You look happy!'

'Yes, Rhea has that effect on me,' he said, winking at him.

Dr Vishnukant smiled and entered Rhea's chamber.

'What's with Beck, Rhea?'

She laughed, 'He wanted a quick fix.'

'Quick fix, meaning?'

'Forget it, Doc. It was work-related.'

Rhea did not talk about anything personal discussed by anyone. It was about the trust placed on her. Moreover, why burden anyone with issues not related with them? As it is we carry enough baggage of our own.

Gagan had an appointment with Dr Vishnukant the next day.

'Your Gagan is coming tomorrow for a check-up,' said Dr Vishnukant jokingly.

'I know, he has asked me out for coffee after that. I am sure all will be well,' said Rhea.

'Is it the coffee that interests you or is it Gagan?'

Rhea looked at him, winked, and said, 'Both.' She assumed that Dr Vishnukant would understand that she was joking.

Post the examination the next day, Dr Vishnukant said, 'Gagan, you are doing good, nothing out of place.'

Suddenly, Dr Vishnukant's attention was caught by the cufflinks Gagan was wearing. The diamond-studded cufflinks shone brilliantly. He recalled seeing them earlier in Rhea's cupboard. His expression changed suddenly and dramatically.

'Is something the matter, Dr Vishnukant? You look upset.'

'No, you can leave now,' replied Dr Vishnukant curtly.

35

MERRILL HAD COME for a session after the weekend. 'Rhea, I asked my parents to drive me to the countryside and I watched the sunrise. It was a beautiful sight. Daniel gave me lots of comedy DVDs, which I intend to start watching from today.'

Daniel was her boyfriend. Rhea had taken his number from Merrill's mother and called him up last week. She had suggested that he should try to think of ways to make Merrill's living moments as beautiful as he could.

'Don't treat her as if she is dying. She does not need pity, she needs compassion. I hope you will treat her as if she is as alive as all of us,' Rhea had told her parents.

'Rhea... Rhea, Dr Vishnukant has been taken to the emergency,' said Joey nervously, as he rushed into her chamber.

'Emergency, for what?' she asked alarmed.

'He had excruciating pain in his lower abdomen.'

Rhea rushed immediately to be with Dr Vishnukant. The ultrasound revealed kidney stones. He was given medication and told to drink as much water as he could. If all went well the stones would pass out automatically. One was less than six millimetres and the other was about five millimetres. An ESWL would be required, if the stones did not pass through the urinary tract. Rhea listened quietly and so did Dr Vishnukant, as the consultant explained the situation to them.

A few weeks later, at the dinner table, Dr Vishnukant said, 'Rhea, I have to leave for a conference in New York next week.'

'Is it the same conference, the one that Dr Bryan was organizing?' she asked.

'Yes,' he replied, engrossed in his thoughts.

'He did not invite me as he promised,' said Rhea with dejection.

There was no reply from Dr Vishnukant.

'Can I come along too, and see New York? After the conference, we can go visit other cities?'

'No, I will be busy there and I have to return as soon as possible.'

'Okay then, I will only see New York and come back with you,' insisted Rhea.

'No, Rhea, you are not going with me,' replied Vishnu, irritated.

She looked at him in disbelief; he was looking at his platter and eating food.

'I will be on a very tight schedule and I do not see any scope of going out anywhere.'

She finished her food in silence.

'Rhea, you have your patients too and do you think it is possible for you to leave them and go away for so many days?' said Dr Vishnukant, the next morning at the breakfast table.

Rhea just looked at him and said, 'Well, I don't have emergency cases like you and I can go around myself, if you are busy. In any case I will not go now.'

◆

A week later, Gagan called up Rhea. 'Hey Rhea, how are you doing?'

'I am good, Gagan.'

'How about dinner tomorrow? It's a Saturday. I thought I would invite Dr Vishnukant too.'

'He is away in New York,' replied Rhea.

'Awesome, I will have the undivided attention of my angel. Rhea, how about if I prepare food for you and you spend the evening at my place?'

Rhea was quiet for a second, then said, 'Yes, sounds good Gagan.'

The evening was beautiful. Gagan had prepared Indian food for Rhea. Rhea was licking her fingers, after eating rice and rajma.

'This reminds me of home; rajma was cooked quite often,' she said.

Gagan had made paneer with capsicum along with the rajma and rice. There was Indian mango pickle served as well. Rhea kept aside the fork and ate the food with her hands. She smiled when she saw the fork and knife. Krishnam always insisted that she learnt the proper use of a knife and fork. She had complained once to Satya that Krishnam was spoiling the fun of eating food. Satya had told Krishnam to let her be and she had teased Krishnam with her tongue out.

After dinner, Gagan showed his house to Rhea. The house had a very modern, minimalistic look. It was understated but stylish. Each and every artefact placed was exquisite. It reflected the fact that the buyer had an eye for good things and the means to buy them. A lot of steel had been used instead of wood. It was cosy, yet could be extremely formal depending on the mood of the host.

After he showed her around the house, Gagan put on some music and showed Rhea photo albums of his family in New York, and college. Coincidentally, he had graduated from the same college as Krishnam.

'Rhea, tell me about your family.'

'I have only two people in my family. My father is also my guru. He is not my biological father; yet, he is my father, my mother and my teacher. My biological parents passed away in an accident.'

'And the other?'

'Krishnam.'

'Who is Krishnam?' he asked.

'The core that remains stable within me, in spite of any peripheral movement. Some people, whether they are there or not, are still a part of you. A part that lives until you are alive. He left but still he never left. An effortless saint, who is content, steadfast in every situation and loves me the way no one can. He is the man who possesses me in every way, without possessing me physically. There are no maps to navigate the unknown, so I did what I thought was best for us. I asked him to leave us and stay away until I was ready for him. He complied with my wishes but will come back soon. We have waited for eleven long years.'

Rhea had a distant look in her eyes.

'Eleven years in this time and age! My God, that seems like love from a fairy tale.'

'When you give eleven years of your precious life to be with someone you can imagine his worth. Every step I took was to be with him. Are fairy tales so painful?' she asked with a smile.

'They do have a happy ending though,' replied Gagan with a smile.

◆

'Rhea,' said Dr Beck, as he entered her chamber the next morning at the hospital. 'Merrill has just been admitted. She had a paralytic attack and has lost her speech.'

'But she was fine yesterday, she attended her session.'

The moment she uttered these words, she knew they were unnecessary. This is life. Things change in a split second, most unexpectedly, and with Merrill it was expected anytime.

'How long, Doc?' asked Rhea with a sigh.

'She will not go back home now, earlier the better,' replied Dr Beck.

Rhea went to meet Merrill. She placed her hand on Merrill's forehead. Merrill opened her eyes and seemed to register Rhea's presence. On seeing her, she attempted to speak, but the words did not come out; it was just garbled sound. Rhea just sat beside her for some time. Merrill had pipes coming out from her nose. She seemed semi-conscious and her breath was heavy.

At night, Rhea sat to meditate and pray.

'Devima, make it easy for her. Please take her.'

Early in the morning, she got a call from the hospital that Merrill was having severe breathing problems and her blood pressure was falling. By the time Rhea reached, Merrill's breathing had stabilized, but she was now in a coma. Merrill's parents were distraught. Daniel too was with them. The day passed with her breathing becoming heavy and uneven and then stabilizing.

'Dr Beck, why can't you make it easier for her?'

'It is illegal, Rhea.'

The next morning, while Rhea was in her chamber, Dr Beck came in.

'Rhea, talk to Merrill,' he said. Rhea looked at him, astonished.

Dr Beck was a hardcore medical man. Abstraction or metaphysics had no place in his life, but he had always shown an understanding towards the unknown.

'Dr Beck, do you think a patient can hear while in a coma?'

'I don't know, Rhea, but I think you can be heard even by the dead,' he said, with a weak smile.

'Merrill is not letting go,' he said.

Rhea and Dr Beck went into Merrill's room. Her breath was irregular and she was gasping. Rhea sat beside her and put her hand on her forehead.

'Merrill, go. Christ is waiting for you with open arms, fear nothing. A beautiful world awaits you,' whispered Rhea into her ears.

Tears were flowing down Rhea's eyes as she repeated, 'Go darling, the light is waiting to take you in its cover. Move Merrill, move, let go. Step out of your body.'

Merrill struggled to take a few shallow breaths. Then her mouth was left open. Rhea had pulled the ventilator tube. Dr Beck looked on in space, as if he had seen nothing and heard nothing.

36

DR VISHNUKANT RETURNED from his trip to New York and Rhea went to pick him up at the airport with Sam. His stomach ache returned while they were driving back home. He was perspiring profusely and his lips were dry.

'Rhea, it is hurting a lot.'

He took a tablet and Rhea put his head on her lap and asked him to place her hand where his stomach hurt, as Sam drove back.

That day on, Dr Vishnukant seemed to drown himself in his work. Most of the nights, he would return after Rhea had retired to her room. The pain never came back after Rhea had placed her hand on his stomach. Later tests revealed that his stones had disappeared.

As Rhea slept, she had a dream. Krishnam was going away in a cloud of mist. She called out to him, 'Krishnam, where are you going?'

'Rhea, I am waiting and I am beside you.' She got up with a start.

There was a knock on her bedroom door. As she opened it Dr Vishnukant literally pushed his way in and bolted the door from the inside. 'Why do you need to do that?' asked Rhea, edgy.

He did not reply.

'You have alcohol on your breath,' she said and was extremely perturbed.

'Yes, it was an official dinner with colleagues and I had a couple of drinks. I hardly know what is going on in your life, but I think it's time for you to know what is going on in my life,' replied Dr Vishnukant, with disdain.

'What is it, Doc?' asked Rhea, totally shaken by his tone. She started walking towards the door to unbolt it when he pulled her back and pushed her onto the bed. Rhea was totally astounded. Her attempt to balance herself and get up was negated by Dr Vishnukant, who threw himself on her, crushing her.

'Rhea, I really wonder if you are so dumb and blind that you can't see the obvious. I love you and desire you. Every night, I sleep with you in my thoughts. Every day, I am haunted by you.'

Then he whispered, 'Rhea, I want you,' bringing his mouth

very close to hers.

Before she could say anything, he kissed her. She tried to push him with both her hands, but he caught them with his left hand and held them tight over her head. With his right hand, he pulled down her pyjamas roughly. His hand moved gently, caressing her right thigh. He looked at her, held her face with his right hand, and moved her face towards his. 'Look here Rhea, look at me. I want you now. I have never desired any woman like this before.'

'No, Vishnu,' Rhea said softly, 'you are hurting me.' Tears trickled down the side of her eyes.

'Don't make this blunder,' she said.

His lips came on Rhea's and he forced his tongue to open her mouth. There was love, there was hunger, there was passion, and there was resentment. In her mind, Rhea was saying, 'I am not angry, I can't be. It is Dr Vishnukant. Devima, please help me with this situation.'

His grip over her hands was slowly loosening, as Rhea began to respond to his kiss. Slowly, his hands moved under her top to feel her body. He stopped kissing her and pulled her top off.

'My God, you are beautiful.'

'Vishnu, please stop,' Rhea said, pleading.

He looked into her eyes and Rhea looked into his. No, nothing could stop him tonight, except the fire in Rhea when she got angry.

Looking into her eyes, he said, 'Rhea, it's not easy for a man to sleep beside a woman he loves and desires and not react. How could you not see it or do you choose not to see the pain you have inflicted on me with every rejection? Rhea, even an angel like you can hurt someone so much.'

He was looking at her body with amazement, in the way we look at something that is beautiful and mysterious. Something which we have really wanted, but have been denied until now. Today, he finally broke all the rules to solve that mystery and he saw that it was worth it. His desire for her sought fulfilment at any cost.

'You are intoxicating, Rhea, and you are mine.'

When the truth is difficult to accept, we try and affirm things the way we want. We know deep inside that the truth is something else.

'Rhea, just be with me. I do not want to hurt you, but I will if I have to.' It was an aggressive plea. It was a plea that considered fulfilment as the only recourse.

'If you do not desire me then just say it.'

Rhea could only say 'Vishnu' and his lips came over hers again. Every touch of his was filled with passion.

She closed her eyes and focused her thoughts on Krishnam. Yes, in her mind she was with her Krishnam now and he was making love to her.

That night, Vishnu loved her with all his being. He would have probably never known that he was capable of so much passion, had it not been for her. He had never loved a woman this way. She stimulated his senses and stirred his soul equally.

Today, he wanted to tell her everything that he never had. He revealed his desire, at times, with aggression and at times, being gentle and caring like the Dr Vishnukant Rhea had known. At times, he caused her pain that had its own pleasure.

The room slowly filled with Rhea's moans. He took care of all her pleasures. As he entered her, he said, 'I am yours, Rhea.'

It was the truth. With every thrust, he watched her face. She did not want him to stop anymore. As she trembled under him with a moan, he saw what he would not forget until his last breath; it was the look on Rhea's face. He had never seen her look so incomparably beautiful. Radiant, eyes closed, mouth slightly opened, small drops of perspiration on her forehead, her open hair, and the expression which says 'bliss'. He let out a moan and was consumed in the ecstasy that he had neither experienced nor imagined before.

In his moan he did not hear Rhea whispering, 'Krishnam, it was beautiful.'

He covered her with a blanket and kept fondling her hair. He made love to her again, passionately; again and again until it was daylight and birds were chirping outside; until both were totally spent and fell asleep.

Lying in Dr Vishnukant's arms, she was dreaming. She saw Krishnam standing with open arms and saying, 'I will be with you soon; the time has come.'

She mumbled, 'I am so sorry, I am sorry.'

Dr Vishnukant kissed her on her forehead. 'It's fine, love. You made up for all the hurt, sleep tight.'

'Krishnam, I am waiting,' Rhea was mumbling and Dr Vishnukant put his hand on her mouth.

37

'RHEA, IS IT possible to meet you?' It was Gagan.

Rhea agreed. When they met up, without any preliminaries, Gagan rushed into what he had to say.

'Rhea, I am going through a divorce. My wife is involved with someone else. She asked for a divorce. I knew that someone else had come into her life all the while. I refused to accept it. It was a blow to my ego.

'I really do not know when we lost each other or if we had ever found each other. She wants to keep the custody of our children, without visitation rights. She is keeping the house in New York. She does not want the children to meet me until they are adults, as it will be difficult for them to adjust to their stepfather. I am not opposing that either. She is free to start afresh.

'It is tough for me Rhea, I love my kids. I knew the younger one is not mine. The to-be stepfather is the actual father. She thinks I am oblivious to that. One may spend an entire life with someone and still not know the person. My refusal for divorce was her greatest fear and all she had to do was ask me.'

Gagan spoke his heart out, as they looked at the water flowing, sitting beside the Thames.

'Life moves on,' said Rhea. 'Let's take a walk.'

They got up to go.

'Rhea, is your guru a Tantric?'

'Yes, Gagan, and I too am a student of Tantra and I practise Tantra.'

'Rhea, I did not know that Tantrics are so beautiful. I had a different picture of Tantrics,' said Gagan, with a naughty smile.

Rhea was laughing. 'Yes, the media and movies have done a great job of promoting that image.'

'You know, I was constantly denying the truth. At times, I would be angry, because I thought I was a good husband. I am not sure whether I put up with everything to save this marriage or it was my ego. When I came to London, I was very depressed. I have accepted the facts but yes, I am still bitter. I need healing,' said Gagan.

'The day you can genuinely wish her well, you will be healed. Let your forgiveness not be bitterness cloaked up in acceptance. You will have to truly forgive, to have a fresh start.'

They walked quietly for some distance.

'I offer my respect to your guru; I would be honoured to seek his blessings. He must be a great man to have a shishya like you.'

'He definitely is a great man and I am what I am because of him,' said Rhea.

'May God give you everything that you want,' Gagan said, with great tenderness.

'When is Krishnam coming back?' he asked.

'Very soon,' she replied cheerfully.

She came home after dinner with Gagan; Dr Vishnukant's phone was ringing continuously on the dining table. Rhea saw that the call was from Dr Bryan. She knocked at Dr Vishnukant's door. There was no reply. She opened the door and saw that he was fast asleep. There was a second call from Dr Bryan, it kept on ringing incessantly, so finally Rhea answered the call, assuming that it could be urgent. 'Dr Vishnukant is sleeping, Dr Bryan.'

'Whom am I speaking with? It's rather urgent.'

'Hi, it's Rhea.'

'Oh Rhea, how are you?'

'I am good, how are you doing?' asked Rhea.

'I am very well, Rhea, but I am upset with you for backing out from your commitment of coming to New York for the conference. I had organized a slot for forty-five minutes for you.'

'But Doctor, how would I know, you never communicated.'

'I had sent an email addressed to you at Vishnu's email id and you replied saying that you were too tied up with your patients. I called Vishnu later and he said that…' Dr Bryan stopped midway. He was quiet and so was Rhea.

'Oh my God, Rhea. Why did he do that?' Dr Bryan asked.

There was complete silence and no words came out from either end.

'Oh, Dr Bryan, I am so sorry. I remember I was tied up and Vishnu did mention it. I am sorry for the inconvenience you had to go through.'

'Rhea, take care of yourself. It was unprofessional of Vishnu.'

The next day, Rhea told Dr Vishnukant at the hospital that Dr Bryan had called. She then said, 'I want to go back to India. Please get my tickets done.'

He did not reply and walked out of his chamber without a word.

After Rhea finished her work, she went to meet Dr Vishnukant and saw his chamber locked.

She saw the driver near the reception. 'Sam, where is Doc?'

'I already dropped him home.'

'Oh, no,' said Rhea and went towards the car.

'Ma'am, is there a problem?'

'Not something that you can solve, Sam,' she replied smiling.

She reached home and was rushing upstairs, when Dr Vishnukant called out, 'Rhea, the passport is with me, you are not going anywhere.'

Rhea sank down on the stairs. Dr Vishnukant walked up to her. 'Rhea, you are the kind of person who can be loved effortlessly. But you are not the kind of person whom one will let go easily, without resistance. You mean the world to me and I am selfish enough to do everything in my power to save my world from destruction.'

He held her hand and sat beside her.

Rhea heaved a sigh. 'Vishnu, this is not my world and you know it.'

'Rhea, you really loved him.'

'No, Vishnu, I still love him.'

'Then where is he, Rhea?' he screamed. 'Call him; he will take you from here, if he loves you. Why the hell did he let you come here with a different man and work in a different country? What kind of a man is he?'

Rhea looked at Vishnu and said calmly, 'You will never be able to understand him.'

'No, tell me about him. I am rather eager to know why you are so obsessed with him. I am curious to know if he actually exists.'

'Vishnu, are you naïve enough to think that you can stop me from going? So far, I let you do what you did because you are important to me,' saying this she got up and walked into her room.

She entered the room and on the bed lay a small box with a note under it. The note read 'Marry me, Rhea' in Dr Vishnukant's writing.

She opened the box; a solitaire glistened in a ring. She sat on the bed, her head reeling. Her heart was racing. She took the neatly folded paper Neel had given her with a number on it and dialled the number. The phone was answered in two rings; the voice that answered was one that she had known forever.

◆

Dr Vishnukant came up later at night. Rhea's bedroom door was open and all her belongings lay scattered on the bed.

'What is this, Rhea? You have to go back to work. You will not go back.'

'I am packing and I will go, Vishnu.'

'I have brought chocolates for you,' said Dr Vishnukant, in a dismissive tone.

Rhea did not look at him, but continued to pack. He held her upper arm tightly and said, 'Stop it, Rhea, you know you can't go.'

Rhea looked at him and said, 'Vishnu, I will go, don't make it worse. You do mean a lot to me.'

He left the room.

The next day in the evening, Rhea was sitting dressed in black trousers and the black coat, with her packed suitcases and bag, when Dr Vishnukant entered the house.

'What is this, Rhea?'

'Vishnu, I am going.'

'Rhea, please let's settle this. I will not let you go now. Let's rethink in a few months.'

'Do you actually think you can make me do anything I do not wish to do? You know nothing about me or my life, do not make this ugly, I warn you.'

'Rhea, you are making it ugly. You know I love you.'

Rhea sprinted up the stairs without replying. She sat quietly in her room holding the statue of Devima that Satya had given her.

Dr Vishnukant walked up to her room.

'Rhea, please.'

She interrupted, 'Vishnu, please leave me alone. I am trying my best not to get angry.'

38

SHE FELT HIS presence. He was close, very close. The doorbell rang; Rhea rushed down, her heart was beating so loud, she felt the whole world could hear it. He had finally come after so many years. Raju opened the door and a gentleman asked for Rhea.

'Rhea, don't run like this, you will fall,' said Dr Vishnukant and came rushing behind her.

He saw Rhea run towards the visitor. They were locked in an embrace for what seemed like eternity.

Vishnu went ahead and asked the stranger, who was holding Rhea in a tight embrace with his eyes closed, 'Yes sir, what can I do for you?'

The stranger opened his eyes, naughty twinkling eyes, thick hair gelled and combed back without a parting. He seemed very familiar; he certainly was some celebrity. He could nearly place him, yes; he had seen his interview on television.

He held Rhea with his left hand and extended his right hand to Dr Vishnukant. 'I am Krishnam, glad to meet you Dr Vishnukant,' he said and turned to walk to the car.

Both Krishnam and Rhea were wearing black coats. Krishnam opened the door for Rhea. Rhea hugged Dr Vishnukant as she was about to get in the car.

'I love you, Rhea,' he said. Rhea smiled with tears in her eyes.

'Dr Vishnukant, Rhea loves you too. I am sure you understand that,' replied Krishnam.

Dr Vishnukant had not missed the tenderness in his voice.

For two days, Rhea and Krishnam were booked in a suite at a hotel. He had to meet all the concerned people to get her visa for the US done on priority. Gagan had brought few forms, which she was required to sign. Gagan was a senior partner in Krishnam's firm.

'So Rhea, he is your Krishnam?' Gagan asked, laughing.

'Come on, Gagan, you knew it,' Rhea said, smiling.

'Rhea, I got to know later, after I had a heart attack and survived. Krishnam had come to London to see me. I was telling him about the angel who saved my life. He had simply stated, "So you met Rhea" and his eyes said the rest. We had gone together and he was the one who selected your coat and jewellery.'

◆

'So Rhea, you are finally with me,' said Krishnam.

'I know,' Rhea replied, as she closed her eyes and reclined her seat in the aircraft. The last three days had sapped her energy. The steward came in to serve champagne before they took off.

'How is Baba?' asked Krishnam.

'Misses you a lot, Krish.'

Krishnam just watched Rhea while she slept soundly.

They drove into his huge mansion on the outskirts of New York.

'Krishnam, this is not a house, it's a palace,' said Rhea, as they drove into the driveway.

'It belongs to my princess,' said Krishnam.

The car stopped at the porch. He said, 'Close your eyes now,' and lifted her in his arms. He was walking up the stairs, going through doors. He put her down and held her hand. 'Now, open your eyes.'

There she was, standing in the temple. It was a replica of the sadhanasthal at Shaktidham. It had numerous pictures of Satya. On one side, she noticed, he had a framed picture of her. She rang the temple bell and both of them touched Devima's feet and held each other in a tight embrace. Rhea couldn't control her emotions anymore and cried aloud, letting her heart out. Tears flowed from Krishnam's eyes too. Eleven years is a long time. That night they slept intertwined in the temple.

When she opened her eyes, Krishnam was lying beside her looking at the ceiling with a smile on his face.

She watched him for some time. 'Krishnam, our world is so different from others. No one outside can comprehend it. Krishnam, let's live our lives.'

'I cannot lose you, Rhea, never. I can take no chances,' said Krishnam.

'Krishnam, I know nothing will happen to me. The lineage and the vidya must go on.'

'No, Rhea, you know it is not that simple; the woman I marry will die giving birth to the child. I can marry no one except you and I cannot let you die. Baba lost his mother at the time of his birth; he lost his wife, my mother, when I was born. Rhea, you know he loves you more than himself. He let me go, his only son, to protect you and let you grow.'

Rhea looked at the statue of Goddess Kali. The truth was that their lineage had been cursed.

Many generations ago a daughter had been born to a sadhak. His immense disillusionment could not be concealed, as he had wanted a son to whom he could pass on the knowledge of Tantra.

When she was eight years old, the girl went to her father, who was preparing for his ritualistic puja on a night of Puranmashi. She asked her father to initiate her as a shishya and be her guru to master the path of Tantra.

The father, shocked and livid at her audacity, refused. The girl was gifted with faculties beyond what we call normal. That night, in the temple of Goddess Kali, she had cursed her father, saying that she was leaving, but no woman would ever be born in the lineage. And that any woman the sadhak married would die giving birth to a male child. She claimed that the sadhak praying to Shakti had insulted Shakti in an unimaginable way and the price had to be paid. The girl left that night and no one knows where she disappeared.

That sadhak again had a child, a son; his wife died giving birth to the son. Since then, every sadhak who had married had lost his wife during childbirth. No girl was ever born and no one remarried.

It was said, after a few generations, a sadhak did immense sadhana to break this curse. It was known and passed on over the next generations that he had a revelation in his dream. Sometime in the future, the girl would come back into the lineage to seek her evolution, through Tantra. If then the sadhak recognized her and imparted his knowledge of Tantra as a guru, and if she married the son of her guru and gave birth to a child, then the curse would be broken. But if the sadhak did not recognize her, he would be the last of Tantra sadhaks of their lineage and Tantra would be lost in oblivion.

She would become the finest until now in this lineage of sadhaks. She would be the guru to the next successor. That generation would see in a her a sadhak who would redefine and modify the vidya for the coming generations.

No one knew in which generation it would happen. For all one knew, it may have been just a story. It could also be the truth. The curse was documented and given as a family inheritance in a box of gold to the next successor.

The revelation of breaking the curse was just heard, from one successor to the next. Krishnam was the thirteenth sadhak born in that lineage and twelve generations before the lineage had been cursed.

Neither Satya nor Krishnam had the courage to say yes to Rhea. They both loved her more than themselves.

This was the last of the lineage. Krishnam would not marry anyone else, or father a child. There would be no more sadhaks in the lineage after Krishnam.

'Krish, I am the sadhak of this generation. This generation is the changeover, from you to me and then our son will carry forward to the next generation. I know it and I know the curse breaks with me.'

Krishnam picked up Rhea in his arms and took her to a room.

'Rhea, this is our room.'

He gently put her feet on the floor and held her by the waist. There was a huge portrait of Rhea hanging on the wall facing the bed; below it was a beautifully carved mantel of the fireplace. The king-size bed had side tables with Krishnam's and Rhea's eleven-year-old photographs together. The colour theme of the room was white. On one side of the bed were two carved wooden chairs upholstered in a white fabric. On the far side of the room, an arch led into a small corridor which lead to their separate walk-in wardrobes and washrooms. As Krishnam led Rhea into her wardrobe, she exclaimed in delight. Her wardrobe was full of innumerable clothes and footwear.

'It will take a lifetime to wear all of this,' she said.

'I look forward to seeing you in them. You know I like to shop for you,' he said.

He opened her storage, which had a huge digital safe. Rhea saw lines of jewellery and watch boxes.

'You were always with me, my princess.'

Rhea called up Satya and asked, 'Baba, do you trust me?'

'What kind of question is that, Rhea?'

'Baba, you have to reply.'

'What is it, my child?' he asked.

'Baba, I want to marry Krishnam and give birth to his child and carry forward this lineage.'

'Rhea, you know everything. What can I say?' he said resignedly.

'I know that Devima will take care of us. I want to live my life too. Baba, either all of us live together or all perish separately. I want to live and I know the curse breaks with me, I am The One,' Rhea said steadily, with faith.

'Rhea, my child, I want you to live and live happily, so be it.'

'Yessssss Baba.'

After disconnecting the phone, she looked at Krishnam with a naughty smile, 'Krish, do you trust me?'

'I do, Rhea, I have always known that you are the one,' he said, pulling her nose.

39

THE NEXT DAY, Krishnam told Rhea that his ex-girlfriend, Rachel, wanted to meet her.

'It will not be easy,' Rhea said to Krishnam.

'Still, it has to be done. I owe her that,' replied Krishnam.

Rachel was a tall, extremely pleasant-looking woman. She had an almond face with shoulder-length blonde hair. Rhea noticed that she had a well-endowed, proportionate body. She looked pretty in her beige trousers and red jacket. Krishnam hugged her and so did Rhea. Rhea observed Rachel's discomfort in their hug. Krishnam introduced Rhea to her and left. As they sat in the sitting room, there was an awkward silence.

'Rachel, I cannot be in your place, but I can imagine it must be hurting,' said Rhea softly.

'Rhea, it's not about Krishnam actually, it's about me. You were always there and he never ever tried to camouflage anything. He was clear that for him, it was and it would always be Rhea. It's just that I fell in love with him. I gave myself to him, hoping that somewhere down the line he will be free from you. However much I tried, I just could not enter his world beyond a point. It seemed he did not have the ability to love anyone else or be loved by anyone else other than you.'

Rachel had been in a relationship with Krishnam for the past five years. She hoped that one day he would reciprocate and respect what she felt for him. Instead, Krishnam told Rachel that

Rhea was coming back, about six months ago.

'I had not bargained for your return, Rhea, and I felt vengeful. My heart was aching and I felt humiliated, betrayed and extremely angry. But then, I realized that I could not live my life in hurt and bitterness. It had been a tremendous sense of loss, but I told myself that I had a life before Krishnam too. I realized I had to stop blaming myself for not being able to get him to love me.

'It was never about me, as he would never be able to love any other woman, except you. What I went through is normal. It still hurts, but I had to meet Krishnam's Rhea. I wish you the very best, may the both of you have a beautiful life together. I am happy that I still have the ability to love and be loved.'

She handed a gift to Rhea. 'Your wedding gift, Rhea.'

◆

It was a foggy day in San Francisco, as they entered Krishnam's house. The butler greeted them with a warm smile. Rhea saw her pictures placed all along the mantel in the master bedroom. The house was situated in the suburbs and was just a five-minute walk from the beach. It was windy, but sunny later that day and they walked along the shore, holding hands.

'Krish, had you ever imagined that I would make it back to you?' asked Rhea.

'I knew you would,' he replied. 'I knew you would be the one to set the rules one day.'

The next day, Krishnam drove Rhea to Napa valley in his Ferrari. They visited some of the famous wineries. Rhea had never seen or had such a variety of wines or cheese.

As they were lying in bed talking, Rhea asked, 'Krish, how will you work this out? It is a different life and status that you enjoy here.'

'I have waited for us to be together, for Baba, you and me,' said Krishnam.

'With all the vidya, I still cannot leave everything and be a part of this life. Krishnam, your work is here. You are in the midst of all this luxury. Will you be all right just walking away?' she questioned.

'The only time it was ever tough for me, was when I had to walk away from Baba, Shaktidham and you. I was only waiting until you were ready for us. It was important for us, for you to reach where you are. I left, only to be together. I knew you had but one choice, to pursue your sadhana and reach a stature where you set the rules. You had to carry on the lineage. Rhea, I know our world; you either had to do it or die. And yes, Rhea, I will unflinchingly leave my life here completely and be back home with Baba and you,' he said, laughing.

'At times, I really wonder who is a sadhak, Krish, you or I?' questioned Rhea.

40

IT WAS A week before Deepawali. The sadhanasthal was brightly lit and Meena stood with a thal to welcome Rhea and Krishnam. Satya was waiting for them at the sadhanasthal. Rhea touched his feet and gave him a tight hug. Krishnam too touched Satya's feet and held him tight. Rhea embraced Devima after touching her feet. Krishnam followed suit and touched Devima's feet.

Satya suddenly stepped back. 'Rhea, what have you done?' His face was pale with fear. Krishnam or Rhea had never seen Satya with fear in his eyes.

'I know that Ma will take care of me and you will have a grandchild,' replied Rhea.

She took Satya's hand. 'Baba, trust your shishya. I love you, I love Krish and I love life. I will not throw it away for anything. Baba, I know Devima will take care of me.'

Krishnam stood quietly. Satya did not reply and sat quietly with his eyes closed in front of Goddess Kali's statue.

Rhea sat beside him quietly. 'Baba, don't spoil it for Krish. He has returned after eleven years.'

Satya did not open his eyes and Rhea was now in tears.

'Baba, I have come back after such a long time and I am crying.'

Satya took a deep sigh and opened his eyes and then he finally said, 'Yes, I do trust you Rhea.' He extended his other hand and embraced Krishnam.

◆

Dr Vishnukant's mobile kept on ringing without any response.

Rhea finally called up the home number. 'Raju kaka.'

'Ah Rhea bitti, how are you?'

'I am good, Kaka. Where is Bhaiya?'

'He is in the hospital and has not come back home for three days. He hardly returns home these days.'

'Please tell him I called,' said Rhea.

Deepawali, the festival of light and illumination, was on amavasya. Satya always said that darkness was simply an absence of light.

Shaktidham was lit up with hundreds of lamps and Satya, along with Rhea and Krishnam, conducted the Laxmipuja. Satya also did a ritualistic night-long Kalipuja. Goddess Kali on this night was prayed to as the destroyer of ego and all negative traits that led to severance from the whole. Rhea was dressed in a beautiful red lehenga, designed and gifted by Kritika. She wore an exquisite and elaborate diamond set with a maang tika. Her hands were adorned with diamond-studded bangles. She had mehendi on her hands and feet. That night, Krishnam and Rhea were wedded in the sadhanasthal in the presence of Rhea's Devima. Satya solemnized the wedding. On Rhea's insistence, Rhea's Devima performed a symbolic kanyadan.

Rhea was sitting in the sadhanasthal and meditating, after

the wedding. When she reached back into their room, it was dawn. While Rhea had been away, Satya had got a new room made for Krishnam and Rhea. Rhea was in her fourth month of pregnancy.

◆

'Didi, I got selected in the combined medical test and I am joining a medical college,' said Payal.

'I meditate every day and the dreams come no more. I will take up the profession of saving lives,' she said with her eyes down.

'Payal, look into my eyes and talk,' said Rhea.

As their eyes met, Rhea said, 'I am proud of you.'

Payal handed a packet to Rhea and said, 'My parents sent this for Shaktidham.' Rhea went and placed the packet in front of Devima.

Rhea was reading the newspaper a few days later. There was a news article on some ministers involved in a grave money scam. Devraj's name was mentioned too.

'Krish, I feel Rhea and you should be in New York, after her seventh month starts, and she can deliver there with the best medical facilities,' said Satya.

'No Baba,' replied Rhea, 'our child will be born in Shaktidham. I don't need anyone but you and Krish with me.'

'Rhea, you cannot be emotional about this decision,' he said.

'Yes Baba, it is a decision of faith.'

Satya put his hand on Rhea's head and smiled. She touched his feet.

Krishnam had work in London and then had to go on to New York. Rhea would accompany Krishnam to London and stay there, until his return.

Krishnam and Rhea both landed at Heathrow and drove to their London home in Leister Mews, a short distance from Hyde Park.

The next day, he waited in the car as Rhea rang the bell of Dr Vishnukant's house.

Raju opened the door and exclaimed in delight. 'Where is your bhaiya?' Rhea asked.

'Who is it, Raju kaka?' She heard Dr Vishnukant and walked in, as he was about to sit on the dining chair. He looked at her and stood still, then broke into a smile and walked towards her with open arms. Rhea walked into his arms and he held her for a bit. They said nothing. Later, Dr Vishnukant and Rhea went to drop Krishnam to the airport. Krishnam would take her back on his return, a fortnight later. Until then she would stay in London with Dr Vishnukant.

'Sam will drop me every day and you can keep the car to go anywhere you wish to,' said Dr Vishnukant to Rhea.

'Doc, I can call for the car and driver from Krishnam's office too. Please do not make it inconvenient for yourself.'

Dr Vishnukant looked at her with a look that said, 'I know you have every facility in London, but be quiet.'

Rhea promptly replied, 'Yes, it will be good if you can send Sam.'

'I will return early every day and we can go out wherever you want, madam,' said the driver, smiling.

Vishnu accompanied Rhea for a routine check-up with Dr Larkey.

'All is well. You are about to complete your fourth month. When will we get to meet your husband?' asked Dr Larkey. 'It was all so sudden and it was a shock to know that you had left.'

'Yes, it was sudden, as my father decided the wedding date and I had no choice but to return immediately,' she said softly. Dr Vishnukant was looking at Rhea.

'Krishnam is hosting a dinner on his return from New York and is looking forward to meeting all of you. He is an attorney and we have a place in London too, so we will be visiting London often. Actually, I have two homes—ours and Dr Vishnukant's—so no question of me staying alone in London.'

Dr Vishnukant smiled. 'Linda, Rhea can make a person feel good.'

'Or bad,' completed Dr Larkey, 'but nevertheless, I appreciate her straight dissection of the situation. It hurts at times though,' she said, winking at Rhea.

'But then who said that truth was always comforting?' said Rhea.

Both Dr Linda and Dr Vishnukant started laughing.

'This is Rhea for us,' said Dr Vishnukant.

It was Sunday the next day and Rhea decided to take Dr Vishnukant to her home. The house help opened the door and they walked in. Rhea showed her house to Dr Vishnukant and then they sat in the reception room.

As they were having tea, Rhea looked at Dr Vishnukant and said, 'Doc, will you forgive yourself and me? I cannot say that I never understood how you felt for me, but maybe I never wanted to address it, as I never could see beyond Krishnam. My biological parents died in a violent accident during my childhood. My family has been Baba and Krishnam.'

'You mean your Guru ji?'

'Yes, and Krishnam is his son.'

Dr Vishnukant was surprised.

'We grew up together, but he had to leave for reasons, which I don't want to bring up. We never really lived without each other in our minds. We always knew that it was a matter of time, before we would be together again. Everything I did, every step I took, was a step towards Krishnam, for us to be together. He was my strength and my goal. He left everything he had for me. He knew that with him around, I could never be where I was meant to be. It was also important that I moved out and interacted with the world in order to grow. Since my childhood I have led a very protected life at home, you could say like a princess. Whatever I said or I did was with the strength that Baba and Krishnam are there for me. Krishnam comes from a lineage of Tantra sadhaks and never required tools of rituals to be where he is. He is so rooted in his being and evolved to a point where I have still not been able to reach. He lives in this world but is beyond it. Baba loves me so much, that he let go of his only son. I know you were always confused about my unexplainable behaviour. Dr Vishnukant, that's who I am. Only Baba and Krishnam can understand my world. They have always placed me before themselves. Their love for me has been unconditional. Krishnam has possessed me without possessing me because he has loved me in a way no man can. I cannot love anyone the way I love Krishnam. At times, I feel he knows me better than I know myself. I am a sadhak, but he is the effortless saint,' said Rhea to Vishnukant.

After a long silence, Dr Vishnukant said, 'What I did is unpardonable.'

'I guess you did what you thought best to keep me with you.'

'I am sorry, Rhea. It was not really the best way to try and keep you. When I look back, I feel that I had almost turned into a demon; you must have been so fearful of me.'

'No, I was not fearful, but sad. I never wanted to be a source of pain to you, which I have become,' she said.

'No Rhea, you gave me a lot to smile about too and with time healing will come through. I will always cherish the memories of the time you spent with me.'

He got up and extended his hand towards Rhea, gave her a warm hug and said, 'I have realized that love is not about possessing someone. I know you love me too, else I would have been destroyed.'

Rhea looked at him, startled, and he smiled and said, 'I too understand a bit of your world. You would have never come back, had you not loved me. The day Krishnam took you away, he had said, "Rhea loves you too, Doc". Without saying anything else, in this one line Krishnam said everything about himself and about the two of you. He said who he was, who you were and what you were for each other. I knew if my understanding were in the right perspective, you would come back. Only a saint can forgive what I did.'

Krishnam hosted a party at one of the prominent London hotels. Neel had arrived a day before. That night, Neel, Dr Vishnukant, Krishnam and Rhea sat up late, talking and drinking at Krishnam and Rhea's house. All the guests called by Krishnam and Rhea were present at the party, the next day.

41

THE TIME FOR Rhea to deliver was nearing; Satya's anxiety was visible. He would get irritated at the slightest provocation. He would continuously sit in the sadhanasthal for his ritualistic puja.

Neel visited Rhea often. Rhea continued to oversee the working of Shaktidham. Krishnam was busy going through cases which needed his expertise. There seemed no complication and Rhea's pregnancy was progressing well.

It was the thirteenth day of the month, when she sat in the sadhanasthal meditating; the pain started at night.

She opened her eyes and said, 'Devima, I am in your hands and so is the child.'

The gaps between the pains were reducing as the night progressed. As she got up after offering the symbolic coconut, the water burst.

'I will not go anywhere. I will stay here and deliver my child,' she told Satya and Krishnam.

'Rhea, I refuse to let you be stupid,' said Satya.

'Baba, is faith ever reason-based?'

Dr Rageshwari reached in an hour carrying all that was required in the ambulance with two assistants. She saw Rhea lying on the floor of the sadhanasthal on a rug, with a pillow under her head. Krishnam held her hand. Satya and Meena were standing near the entrance of the sadhanasthal.

New life entered the world, and as it cried Rhea stopped breathing.

'No!' screamed Dr Rageshwari. 'This can't be happening.'

Rhea's Devima stood with open arms, shining, as blinding golden rays emitted from her. Rhea rushed into her arms. She whispered, 'Ma, Baba and Krish love me a lot. I have to go back.'

Dr Rageshwari was pumping her heart and injecting her with life-saving drugs. There was no visible sign of life in Rhea. Satya and Krishnam stood with folded hands in front of Goddess Kali. Rhea took a deep breath and opened her eyes.

It took almost two minutes to revive her. Dr Rageshwari finally heaved a sigh of relief.

God meets you at your level of expectations.

Faith is important for any victory.

The sun was shining bright in the sky.

The lineage went on.

Dr Rageshwari handed the newborn to Rhea.

'He looks like Krishnam,' she said smiling.

42

Eight years later...

SHIVA AND RHEA sat in the sadhanasthal chanting 'Om' in unison. After finishing, Shiva opened his eyes and said, 'Ma, I see this young man in the jungle and dark energy surrounds him.'

'Yes Shiva, but he still has the ability and the choice to

transform it into light. Whatever we give comes back to us.'

Satya was sitting with his eyes closed on the swing in the veranda. His hair was silver-grey and shining. Krishnam sat in the office engrossed in his work.

His secretary entered. 'Sir, we won the case and here is the order.'

One evening, Satya, Krishnam, Rhea and Shiva were having dinner together. 'Bade Baba, who is a saint, Baba or Ma?' asked Shiva.

'Not all questions have answers and not all questions can be answered until one is capable of understanding them,' replied Satya.

END

THE BOOK MAY be fiction; it may be reality, for everything that has been imagined exists. Maybe there is a Satya, maybe there is a Krishnam and maybe there is a Rhea. Maybe there is a lineage of Tantra sadhaks that still exists and lives amongst us. They live in the world like us but are beyond it. They are the sadhaks who live their lives on the principles of Tantra and follow the royal path in essence. The lineage goes on silently and discreetly in a world where Tantra is claimed to be a path of destruction and every act deplorable in a society is said to be a secret ritual of Tantra. The truth, however, will only be known by a handful of those who have lived it. As is said, 'The truth is for earnest seekers and cannot be known by people out of idle curiosity'.

ACKNOWLEDGEMENTS

Thank you Urvashi, Arjun, Mohit, Sanchit and Shalabh, for being a great support in innumerable ways.

Thank you, Vikas, for your immense contribution and Utsav, for reading the first draft, being a source of encouragement and believing in me always. Rohit, this book has been possible because of your help at every step where I needed you. Thank you!

Baba ji, words will always fall short when it comes to thanking a guru. This book is for my guru, without whom it would have never happened.

Thanks to the entire team at Rupa for the perfect understanding and handling of the project.